FINBAR'S
HOTEL

DERMOT BOLGER was born in Dublin in 1959 and is the author of six novels, including *The Journey Home*, *The Woman's Daughter*, *A Second Life* and, most recently, *Father's Music*, and of many plays, including *The Lament for Arthur Cleary* and *In High Germany* (published by Penguin as part of his *Dublin Quartet*), and *April Bright*. A poet and publisher, he is editor of *The Picador Book of Contemporary Irish Fiction*.

RODDY DOYLE was born in Dublin in 1958. The novels of his 'Barrytown Trilogy' (*The Commitments*, *The Snapper* and *The Van*) have all been made into successful films. His fourth novel, *Paddy Clarke, Ha Ha Ha*, won the Booker Prize in 1993. He also wrote the BBC series *Family*. His most recent novel, *The Woman Who Walked into Doors*, was published in 1996.

ANNE ENRIGHT was born in Dublin in 1962. A former television producer of the innovative RTE series *Night Hawks*, she has published one collection of short stories, *The Portable Virgin*, and a novel, *The Wig My Father Wore*.

HUGO HAMILTON was born in Dublin in 1953 of German and Irish parents. His first three novels, *Surrogate City*, *The Last Shot* and *The Love Test*, were set in Germany, while his most recent novel, *Headbanger*, takes place in Dublin. He is also the author of one collection of stories, *Dublin Where The Palm Trees Grow*.

JENNIFER JOHNSTON was born in Dublin in 1930 and has lived for many years in Derry. Her novels, many of which have been made into successful films, include *The Captains and the Kings*, *How Many Miles to Babylon*, *The Railway Station Man*, *The Old Jest*, *The Invisible Worm*, and, most recently, *The Illusionist*.

JOSEPH O'CONNOR was born in Dublin in 1963. He is the author of two novels, *Cowboys and Indians* and *Desperadoes*, and his third novel, *The Salesman*, is published in early 1998. He has published one collection of stories, *True Believers*, along with two best-selling volumes of comic writing, *The Secret World of the Irish Male* and *The Irish Male at Home and Abroad*; a travel book, *Sweet Liberty: Travels in Irish America*; and two stage plays, *Red Roses and Petrol* and *The Weeping of Angels* (premiered in October 1997 at the Gate Theatre, Dublin).

COLM TÓIBÍN was born in Enniscorthy, Co. Wexford in 1955 and has lived in Dublin for many years. A former editor of *Magill* and *In Dublin*, he is the author of three novels *The South*, *The Heather Blazing* and *The Story of the Night*, along with several non-fiction works, including *The Sign of the Cross: Travels in Catholic Europe* and *Homage to Barcelona*.

Dermot Bolger

Roddy Doyle

Anne Enright

Hugo Hamilton

Jennifer Johnston

Joseph O'Connor

Colm Tóibín

Each chapter in the book has
been written by a different author,
listed alphabetically and not in the order
they appear. We leave it to discerning
readers to identify them.

FINBAR'S HOTEL

Devised and edited by Dermot Bolger

PICADOR

NEW
ISLAND
BOOKS

First published 1997 by Picador

This edition published 1999 by Picador
an imprint of Macmillan Publishers Ltd
25 Eccleston Place, London SW1W 9NF
Basingstoke and Oxford
Associated companies throughout the world
www.macmillan.co.uk

And in Ireland by New Island Books
2 Brookside, Dundrum Road, Dublin 14

ISBN 0 330 37007 3 (Picador)
ISBN 1 902602 12 9 (New Island Books)

3 5 7 9 8 6 4

A CIP catalogue record for this book is available from
the British Library.

Typeset by SetSystems Ltd, Saffron Walden, Essex
Printed and bound in Great Britain by
Mackays of Chatham plc, Chatham, Kent

New Island Books receive financial support from
The Arts Council of Ireland (An Chomhairle Ealaíon), Dublin, Ireland.

For

Lar Cassidy, Imogen Parker and Dan Franklin

with thanks

FINBAR'S HOTEL

101

BENNY DOES DUBLIN

Ben Winters was looking for the minibar. He looked along the skirting board, followed it to the far corner. Minibars were a great invention; he'd seen them in dozens of films. He loved the size of the little bottles, the number and variety that you could pack into so neat a space. And crisps as well, if you wanted them. He'd always wanted to get down on his knees and have a good root around in one of them. But he'd been searching for ten minutes now and he couldn't find the fuckin' thing.

This was Ben's first time in a hotel room. He was happy enough. But the minibar's game of hide-and-seek was beginning to annoy him. It was one of the things he'd been looking forward to. He opened a drawer, the bottom one, the same one he kept his knickers and socks in at home, knowing full well that the minibar wasn't going to be in there. But he opened it anyway. And it wasn't.

Enough.

He went back over to the bed and sat on it. He bounced once. Not bad. And again. Good spring, no squeaks. It was a good bed for riding in. Not in, on. On top of the covers. And not just riding; making love. With the curtains open. And the minibar an arm's stretch away. It was in here somewhere. He could have phoned someone downstairs at the reception desk and asked: 'Where's the minibar?' But he'd have felt like an eejit; he'd have heard them grinning as they told him

3

to take two steps to the right and look behind the picture of the racehorse. He'd looked there already. Worse, they might have told him that there wasn't one. And where would that have left him? With his dreams in tatters, before he'd even brushed his teeth and put his shoes back on. No. It was in here. Somewhere obvious. Somewhere he hadn't thought of looking. Staring him in the face.

'I know you're in here,' he said out loud.

Then he listened. He was only three steps from the door and the corridor. Anyone going by would have heard him. So what, though? There was no one he knew out there. No one he'd ever see. He could do what he wanted. But so far what he'd done was: he'd sat on the bed and taken off his shoes, he'd gone hunting for the minibar and come back to the bed. He was having a wild time, all right.

But it was early days. The night was young. He'd shake himself in a minute, make decisions, put his shoes back on. In a minute. He liked the room. It wasn't bad at all. As good as home. He'd expected it to be a bit bigger, maybe, a bit more exotic – a bowl of fruit, maybe, or one of those white towel dressing gowns at the end of the bed or, better yet, two dressing gowns. But he was happy enough.

He'd never done anything like this before. And, God knew, it wasn't much. He'd only booked into a hotel for the night; that was all. But, all the same, he felt guilty. He felt like there was someone watching, waiting to catch him. He often felt that way. He'd lived chunks of his life in front of an imaginary camera. At home, he always put on a T-shirt going from the bedroom to the jacks in the middle of the night, in case there was a stranger on the landing, waiting there to stare at him. Or if he forgot about the T-shirt, or couldn't find one in the dark, he sucked in his gut and walked across the landing to the toilet door with a swagger that made his mickey hop, and he shoved the door open with his elbow and pissed loudly enough to entertain anyone who was still awake – and looking at him. When he was younger, he often carried his kids on his shoulders, even when they fought to stay on the ground, because he wanted to prove that he was a good father. And when he was younger than that he'd tried to get caught shoplifting – because no one would ever see him not being caught and it had seemed like a terrible waste of wildness. And now, at his age, he was still at it. Sitting on a hotel bed in a room all by himself because he was afraid to move in case he did something wrong.

His first night in a hotel room. He'd told his wife that he was going to stay the night in his brother's house, that they were both going to an old school chum's funeral in the morning. That was the excuse that had allowed him to walk out the door with his suit on. She'd even done his tie for him, and asked him if he was upset because someone he knew and his own age had died.

'Ah, a bit,' he'd said. 'I hadn't seen him in years, though.'

'Still,' Fran had said. 'It's terrible.'

'We sat beside each other for a while,' he'd said. 'In fifth class.'

She'd hugged him.

And now, here he was.

Aha.

He got up off the bed and went over to the chair beside the television. He looked behind it. No minibar. Just a pile of flexes climbing over each other to the socket. He turned on the television on his way back to the bed. The RTE news. Your man, their western correspondent, was interviewing some chap in a cap who was complaining about the noise his neighbour's ostriches made early in the morning. Ben looked for the remote control. He found it on the bedside locker – no minibar in there either. It was attached to the wall, with a length of curling plastic wire. A very short length of curling plastic wire. Ben had to lie back on the bed to point the remote at the telly. He lowered himself and felt the static tying him to the bed. The remote didn't work. He pressed the buttons that would have given him BBC 1 and Network 2 at home but nothing happened; an ostrich looked over a hedge at the mucker in the cap. He dropped the remote on the bed and started to get up again. Something slid away, across the bed. Ben skidded onto the floor. 'Christ, Jesus!' It was a fuckin' rat or something. He got his face well away from the edge of the bed and looked. It was the remote control; the plastic wire was claiming it back, dragging it towards the locker.

Ben wished he was at home. It was Thursday. He usually met his friends in the local on Thursday nights; he always enjoyed it. He was depriving himself. No one knew he was here. In a hotel room three miles from home. In his good suit, sitting on the floor, scared shitless by a crawling remote control. He didn't know why he was here. If Fran had walked in now, he couldn't have explained it, even if he'd wanted to be honest.

'What are you doing on the floor?'

'The remote control moved.'

'What are you doing in the hotel?'

That was a question and a half. He squirmed just thinking about having to answer it. He'd never been in a hotel room before. He wanted to see what staying in one was like. He was curious. All of these were right, honest answers. But why alone? Why so close to home? Why alone? Why alone, Ben? Why alone? Fran had never been in a hotel room either. As far as he knew. Why alone, Ben?

What would he have told her? He was unhappy. That was true too; he was unhappy. But how could he explain that? He had a job he was good at and liked; he had a wife he loved and who loved him back, who was in better nick than he was; he had three kids who had clear eyes in the mornings, who still kissed him goodnight if they went up to bed before he did; he wasn't as fat as most of his friends. All things to be grateful for – and he was. But he was still unhappy. If he'd been younger, he'd have said he was bored. 'Browned off' didn't capture it, or 'pissed off'. 'Suicidal' was too strong but sometimes, he felt, it wasn't too far off the mark. He was just unhappy.

He didn't know why.

He got up off the floor and went over to the telly. Walking to the telly; that was something he hadn't had to do in years. He turned it off. There might have been satellite channels he didn't have at home, the Playboy Channel or pornography from Poland and other places where they didn't have laws but he didn't care. He hadn't booked into the hotel to watch telly. That was one thing he was certain about.

The time had come for action. He'd put his shoes on. And, anyway, the telly would still be there when he came back.

Ben was forty-three. He could measure his life in decades. He'd been married for two decades. He'd been following Fulham for three and a half. He'd done his Leaving two and a half decades ago. He'd met his best friend and best man, Derek, thirty-one years ago. First Communion, thirty-five

7

years ago. First sex, twenty-four. He had a house that himself and Fran would own outright in ten years. He'd retire in twenty years. He'd die in thirty.

Fuckin' Fulham. That summed it up, really. That got close to explaining why he was here. Thirty-six years ago, when Ben and his friends were deciding which teams to support, making their own minds up or following in the steps of their brothers and fathers, Ben had chosen Fulham. The others had gone for United, Liverpool, Leeds, even Chelsea. But Ben had believed his brother, a United supporter. 'You can't have two people in the same house following the same team,' he'd told Ben. 'It's not allowed.' Ben remembered his eyes watering; he'd really, really wanted to follow Manchester United. He waited for his brother to grin and tell him that he was only codding him. 'You should follow Fulham,' said his brother. 'This is going to be their year.' And there followed three and a half decades of misery. Misery without end or pauses. These days, Ben's friends brought their kids to Anfield and Old Trafford. But Ben's youngest, Niall, had phoned Childline when Ben had suggested that they go to Craven Cottage. Niall – named after Ben's brother.

And it wasn't just the football. The football didn't matter. It was everything. He didn't mind his job, but he'd been putting new life into car engines for twenty-five years. He did it well – they called him Yuri Geller; they often handed him bent spoons in the canteen and asked him to straighten them – but he'd never done anything else. There were other things he could have done but it was too late; he'd never know. He loved Fran. He did. But that meant that there were dozens, hundreds, millions of women that he could never know and love. He knew that the thought was very unfair to Fran, that it was even ridiculous – the idea that the world's women had been deprived of him because he'd married her. But he loved looking at women and he wasn't a bad-looking chap and he had a good sense of humour and, Jesus, there were times when he could cry. (He remembered once, maybe ten years ago, he'd got talking to a woman on the bus. The bus had slowed and swerved around two cars that had smashed into each other in the middle of the road. 'God,' said Ben. 'Anyone hurt?' They'd both looked out as the bus passed. 'There's no one in the cars,' said the woman. 'That's good, anyway,' said Ben. 'The Mazda's only new. That's a pity.' 'Nice colour,' she said. And they'd talked on from there. She was nice looking; he couldn't remember details. She was older than him. There were wrinkles that suited her. They'd chatted away till the bus got to Marlborough Street and Ben remembered how sad he'd felt, how lost as he realized that he couldn't really talk to her. He couldn't allow himself. It wouldn't have been right; he was married. And she probably was too. That was how it went.) Promises hadn't been kept, chances had been missed. One job, one wife, one house, one country. All the world out there and he'd seen none of it. That wasn't quite true. He'd seen Tramore – seventeen times. They'd a mobile home down there, with the wheels taken off it. And his father had died a month ago. Sixty-seven years of age and his heart had exploded while he was shaving, and he was dead before the ambulance got there, before his mother phoned Ben.

Shoes.

The time had come. He sat on the edge of the bed and shoved his feet into his slip-ons. Ben had been wearing the same kind of shoes since he'd started buying his own. Because he wasn't very good at tying laces.

'Stop,' he said.

Just last week Ben had been dialling his parents' number, to tell his father the news that Raymond, his eldest, was being given a trial by Bohs, when he remembered that his father was dead. He had to remind himself every day, all the time. He was going to have to get used to missing him. He was going to have to stop crying every time he thought of something he wanted to tell his father.

He ran his tongue across his teeth and decided to brush them. He didn't want to send out the smell of his dinner every time he opened his mouth. Lamb chops on his breath and any woman would know immediately that he was married and out hunting. He'd brush the teeth till his fillings screamed for mercy.

He went into the bathroom. En suite. Right beside the bed. The lap of fuckin' luxury. He could nearly piss without having to get out of the bed. He switched on the light and the fan coughed awake.

He was disappearing. Just for one night. He wanted to see what happened. That was why he was here in Finbar's Hotel, to experience what he'd never had, to see what he'd been missing. Something would happen. That was what hotels were about – people left their real selves down at the reception desk and became whoever they wanted when they stepped out of the lift upstairs. The hotel would show Ben what life could have been like. Then, tomorrow, he'd go home. And live happily ever after.

He looked at himself in the mirror. Fran was right; he wasn't a bad-looking man. He looked well in the suit. Charcoal grey. Fran had pointed him towards it, said he'd look good in it. And he did. Although it was a bit tight under the arms and the waistband curled over when he sat down. She'd done a good job with the tie; the stripes slid perfectly into the knot. Fran had a thing about ties. She'd tied one around her waist, hiding her fanny, with the knot at her belly button. On their honeymoon. In a B&B in Galway. With the jacks miles down the hall, beside the landlady's bedroom. 'I heard the flush. Will you have your breakfast now?' At five in the morning. With Fran back in the room, waiting for him, standing on the bed with his tie on and nothing else. 'No, thanks,' said Ben to the darkness beyond the landlady's door. 'I was only having a piss.' And then he heard Fran. 'Hurry up, will yeh. I'm bloody freezing.' And he ran back down the hall, charging to get to the room before he started howling. They got under the covers and laughed till they'd no air left.

He wished he was at home.

He heard a cough. He thought he did. He turned off the cold tap and listened. A voice. Was it? He couldn't make out words or gaps. He stepped into the bath. Slowly, so his shoes didn't cause a clatter. He put his ear close to the wall. Another cough. Definitely. A woman's cough. Was she in the bathroom? Just behind this wall? Standing in the bath with her ear to it? He got out of the bath. He could hear two voices now. Two women in the room next door. Room 102. With a double bed like his? He listened. Still no words, but one of the voices had an English twang. Definitely. There was an English woman in there. With another woman. They were having a row.

Someone upstairs flushed a jacks. The pipes rattled behind the ceiling. He stopped at the bathroom door. Someone upstairs, maybe the same person straight off the jacks, was having a shower now; Ben knew that noise. A woman? Was she using the little bar of soap that you got with the room or did she have one of those yolks of shower gel that smelt like a mango's fart when you squeezed it? Or was it a couple? With shower gel?

Out.

It was time to go. He had a look out the window first. It wasn't raining, anyway. That was the Liffey down there. A room with a view, but he couldn't get worked up about it. It was only a river and too straight and narrow to get a gasp out of Ben. He looked for a way to open the window but there wasn't one. When he pressed his face to the glass he could see the corner of the train station, lit up. It looked good, a lot better than it did in daytime. Kingsbridge. Heuston Station. Named after one of the lads that was shot by the Brits in 1916. Ben would have liked that, to be executed for his country. 'Do you want a blindfold?' 'Shove it up your hole, Bonzo.' He let the curtain drop. He watched the dust diving around in the light and settling back onto the curtain. The place was actually dirty.

Enough.

Out.

He tapped his chest and felt his wallet.

He was off.

He shut the door behind him and checked that he couldn't open it again. He didn't need to check that the key was in his pocket because the big keyring with the room number carved into it was biting into his leg. He'd leave it in at the reception desk. Because, where it was now, if he crossed his legs too fast it would cut the bollix clean off him. And he didn't want to put it into a jacket pocket because that would leave it hanging lopsided on him. The sleeves, up at the shoulders, were digging into him. It hadn't been tight when he'd bought it, he was sure of that. He gave himself a good shake. Loosen the threads, disperse the fat.

The corridor. A row of closed doors. And a tray on the floor outside one of them. Someone didn't like their crusts. There was a whole, untouched triangle of toast on the plate. And, look it, a little pot of jam with the seal still on it. And not a sound anywhere. Ben looked under the napkin for a knife. Bingo. He had the lid off the pot and the knife in the jam when—

Oh fuck! One of the doors was opening. 102. The lezzers!

'After you, Cecil,' said one of them, the one that sounded English. He didn't hear the answer as he jumped away from the tray and tipped over onto the floor. He was back on his feet and staring at the carpet, looking for the cause of the accident, tapping it with the toe of his right foot, when the women walked past.

'Mind yourselves,' he said.

'Are you all right?' the smaller one asked, as the other one dashed past.

'I'm grand,' said Ben. 'The carpet's loose or something.'

He examined the floor again.

The women kept going. After you, Cecil. What had they been up to in there? Cecil wasn't one of those names that could be used for both men and women, like Fran or even Gerry. They were definitely lezzers. The one who'd spoken was a sour-looking specimen; she looked like she was carrying her loose change up her hole. And she was wearing those shoes, the black ones that his mother always called Protestant shoes. They didn't look like lesbians. The English one didn't, anyway. They stood at the lift doors. Ben heard the lift climbing. He wouldn't get into it with them; he'd wait. The Protestant one looked and caught Ben staring at them. And he was suddenly aware that he was still holding the toast. He dropped it into his pocket and turned. He pulled the door key from his trouser pocket. It dragged the lining with it. He heard the lift bringing the women downstairs as he got the door open. He'd wait a little while, then try again. He'd take the jacket off for a minute.

*

The public bar was big. Lots of wood and glass. There were a few couples at tables, one pair obviously in the middle of an argument; Ben could tell from the way she was stabbing the lemon slice in her glass with a blue cocktail sword. And a couple of loners, all male, up at the bar. There was some sort of a do going on in a far corner, lots of broken cheering and laughter, but it seemed like a long way away, way over there. Over a wide and empty carpet. Ben got out before he had time to be disappointed. He'd try again later.

'Anyway, what d'you mean you're sick of me sweating on you?' said the man to the woman with the sword, so loudly that, for a second, Ben thought that he was talking to him. 'I haven't been on or near you in fuckin' weeks.'

Ben kept going.

And the reception area wasn't exactly hopping. It was crowded all right, but most of the armchairs were full of old Americans in shiny clothes, most of them looking like they'd spent years in a freezer and were only now beginning to get back the use of their arms and mouths. They huddled around bowls of soup and cups of coffee. The good-looking girl with the Aideen badge on her waistcoat was still behind the reception desk, looking calm and busy. Above her, to the right of a painting of some pompous-looking gobshite, there was a clock and, under it, a bronze plate with DUBLIN on it. To remind the Yanks, Ben supposed.

He kept going. He'd seen a sign for the residents' lounge,

past the reception area. He liked the sound of it. Privacy, privilege, nice pints after closing time. He found it, past the restaurant and around a corner. It was quiet. If the two Yanks in the corner died, it would be empty. He nodded at them and went to the bar. The barman was stuffing a tea towel into a glass.

'I'm only staying the one night,' said Ben. 'Can I still come in?'

'Certainly, sir,' said the barman. 'What'll you have?'

Ben knew himself. If he had a pint here he'd stay put for the night and end up talking to the Yanks about violence and the weather.

'I was just checking,' he said. 'I'll be back later.'

He'd go back to the public bar.

He liked the look of the restaurant but he'd had his dinner before he left the house and he didn't feel like having another one. Anyway, he hated eating in public. That was the great thing about drinking: you didn't have to use a fork.

Shite!

The lezzers from 102 were coming!

He jumped into the restaurant. Too late. He was trapped now if they came in. He was blushing; he could feel it. He knew what he looked like – he was the world's worst blusher, a tomato with ears. He was burning. And he didn't know why. They were only women. Who liked each other.

They went past, down to the residents' lounge.

That was close.

'Would you like a table, sir?'

'Eh, no thanks.'

The house at home is full of tables. He'd have loved to have thrown that answer back over his shoulder, but he didn't. He just went back out, and made his way back to reception and through the thawing Yanks to the public bar. The rowing couple had made up. She was patting his cheeks and rubbing her nose over and back, across his forehead. And his hands were under her jacket. Ben could see his fingers crawling up her back. He was happy for them. The place was fuller now. There were fewer wide open spaces at the bar and a greater variety of people. The loners looked less alone and, over there, the office party, or whatever it was, was in full swing. Ben was suddenly sure that he was in the right place.

He ordered a pint and it was put in front of him before he'd his arse properly parked.

'Grand. How much is that?'

'Two twenty-five,' said the barman.

Ben was delighted. It was twenty-five pence dearer than it was in his local. He was living it up. He was in the company of people who didn't mind being robbed crooked. There were different rules here. Money didn't matter. And it wasn't a bad pint either. He looked over at the party. There was a chap swinging his jacket and singing 'Hey, Big Spender'. 'Sit down, yeh gobshite.' There was a woman with a flower in her mouth. Another woman stood up and roared, 'Public relations!' and fell back, laughing, into her seat. They all cheered. A man stood up, toppled and got back on his feet. 'Roads, streets and traffic!' They cheered again, laughed and lifted their glasses. He thought about going over. Bring his pint with him and just go over. But he couldn't. He didn't have the neck. He wouldn't have known how to get into the gang, how to be calm, the right thing to shout, the right time to laugh. If he concentrated hard enough, maybe one of the women would come over for drink or crisps and start talking to him while she was waiting. He just had to concentrate.

He stared at his pint till it swayed – come over, come over, come over, come over.

'Ken is the name. Ken Brogan.'

There was a man standing beside Ben, a man in some sort of a Temple Bar T-shirt, so close beside him that Ben nearly fell off his stool to put a few safe inches between them.

His hand was out. He wanted it shook.

'Ben,' said Ben.

And he felt his fingers being crushed, then released.

'Ken and Ben! That's a good one.'

Ben said nothing. It wasn't a good one at all. And he was still too close to Ben. He had that gel stuff in his hair. Ben could smell it. The bathroom at home was full of half-empty jars of it. It was like pink axle grease; Ben had put some on his chest hair once. And now, this guy was so close, Ben was afraid that it was going to drip on him.

'Come here, Ben,' he said. 'Do you think people in Ireland talk too much?'

'I suppose so,' said Ben, and he got his face away and tried to look as if he was searching for someone. Gel-head kept talking but Ben wasn't listening. But he had to turn back to him when gel-head started tapping his shoulder with, Ben saw, a phase tester.

'Do you ever listen to *Liveline*?' said gel-head. 'Marian Finucane?'

'What?' said Ben.

'It's some programme, that,' said gel-head. 'I can take any kind of junk, but not *Liveline*. I mean, I listen to it nearly every day. But she drives me crazy. All this "Oooh" and "Aaah" and "Oh my" and "Mind you . . ." It's all so fucking self-righteous. What do you think of her?'

'She's all right,' said Ben.

He'd have to get away. This bollix wasn't going to leave him alone. He should never have answered.

'D'you listen to her?' gel-head asked him.

'No,' said Ben.

He did, every day, and he thought Marian Finucane was great but he had to get away. He'd be stuck with this clown for the rest of the night if he didn't move. He might even have been a queer; he was much too old for the gel. Ben had nothing against queers but he had plenty against boring queers. He put down the rest of his pint.

'D'you know what I think?' said gel-head.

Ben was going.

'I've to meet somebody,' Ben said.

'She should keep her nose out of other people's business,' said gel-head.

Ben stood up. But gel-head was holding the back of the stool. Ben pushed back. Gel-head let go and the stool fell onto the floor behind him.

'Jesus!'

A woman skipped over it, through its legs, her hands holding up three full glasses. She was laughing and she managed not to spill anything. A good-looking woman in a black dress. Ben could have been talking to her instead of this prick. She'd have squeezed in beside Ben to get the barman's attention if bloody gel-head hadn't stuck himself there first. There she was now, back in the middle of the party. One of the other women stood up as Ben got to the door.

'Electricity and public lighting!

They cheered and clinked glasses. Something smashed.

*

He was outside now, walking. The fresh air was good. The suit didn't feel tight out here. He'd opened the jacket to let the air in around him. The tie was up over his shoulder. It wasn't that cold. As long as he kept moving.

'I think Marian Finucane's great. She's beautiful, intelligent and I hang on her every fuckin' word. Have you anything to say about that?'

He had gel-head's head dangling over the slops bucket behind the bar, over which he'd just flung him. The office party women were right behind him.

'Dunk him! Dunk him! Give him a dunk!'

The one in the black dress lifted her thumb from her fist and aimed it at the floor. She grinned and winked at Ben. Every bit of her was inside that dress. She licked her lips.

Ben stopped. He'd gone past Heuston Station. He was walking to Lucan and the motorway to the west. There was nothing out there. He was going the wrong way, away from the city.

'For fuck sake, Ben.'

It was fuckin' freezing.

*

The door wouldn't open; the knob wouldn't turn for him. It was the same key, on the same big keyring. He was positive it was. Aideen downstairs had given it to him a minute ago. 'I've to make a few phone calls,' he'd told her. It was definitely the right key.

This was all he needed now, to be locked out of his own room. There was a burly-looking chap down there, at the door of Room 107; he looked like a maintenance man or something. He didn't want to ask him, to have to admit that he couldn't manage the door, but it was better than going downstairs and confessing.

It slid in his hand. The knob. And clicked. The door was open. He was in.

Home.

That was what it felt like, after all that. He'd stay here for a few minutes and try again. Gel-head would be gone. The party would still be there. The nightclub in the basement would be open. He took his jacket off and brought it over to the radiator. The night was still young. He tried to get the jacket to stay on the rad but he couldn't. It wasn't that wet anyway. He took his shoes off, then opened both doors of the wardrobe. He opened them as wide as they'd go. Then he got his head out of the way of the light coming from the overhead bulb behind him, and looked into the wardrobe. He started in the bottom left corner, then over to the right, up, across and back down to the corner. No minibar. It was empty, except for the hangers. He got his jacket off the bed and hung it up. Do not turn on the telly. Do not turn on the telly. He sat on the bed. Was it too early to go down to the nightclub? Would gel-head be gone by now? The remote control was still lying there, up against the pillow. No no no. He put the pillow over the remote control.

'She should be the fuckin' president.'

He pushed the pillow into the bed.

He'd have a go at room service. And see what happened. A tray on wheels, with a flower in a thin white vase and a silver bucket full of ice. He picked up the phone. A card on the bedside locker told him to dial 505.

'Hello?'

He watched the remote control creeping out from under the pillow.

'Eh. Hello,' said Ben. 'Is that room service?'

'It can be, if you want.'

'What?'

'What would you like, sir?'

'Something to eat.'

'Fine. What?'

'Em. A few sandwiches.'

'Lovely. And some tea?'

'Yeah.'

'I'll send you up a big pot. Right so. It'll be a few minutes.'

'Thanks very—'

He put the phone down.

Gobshite.

He didn't want sandwiches. He didn't want tea. He didn't want anything like sandwiches and tea. He didn't even know what kind they were going to bring him. He hated cheese. He wasn't mad about ham. The colour of chicken made him sick if it wasn't white. He wasn't staying. He'd get out quick, before they got here.

He put his shoes back on.

At least he hadn't turned on the telly. That was something.

*

Jesus, it was dark. It was years since he'd been in a nightclub. He didn't remember them being this dark. He'd met Fran in a nightclub and he'd definitely been able to see her. He could see nothing here, though. He took a few more steps in, left the entrance behind him. It was like going into a cinema after the film had started. Worse. He'd have to wait till his eyes adjusted. It wasn't the darkness so much. It was the way the noise and the lights were coming at him, surrounding him; he could feel them on his skin. It was like walking through soup or something. He couldn't breathe. He put his hand to the wall. Was there someone in there behind the lights, looking at him? Someone with a snorkel and goggles? Gel-head? He took his hand down. He felt the bass tackling his knees as he was sucked into the centre of whatever was in front of him. He'd have to relax. The time had come to loosen the tie, maybe take it off altogether. He was in among the lights now. Part of the action. He could see things. The bar was over there. He'd go over. Could you drink Guinness in a nightclub? What would he do if someone offered him Ecstasy? He felt fine now; there was cool air coming from somewhere. There was no sign of a barman. He leaned back against the counter and looked around. He was used to it now. He was going to enjoy himself. He liked the music.

But he was the only one there. He could see now. The place was empty. Except for Ben and the lights.

He ran to the exit, back up to the hotel. There was a gang of six or seven coming down the steps. He'd have a wander around and try again in a few minutes.

Back down to the residents' lounge. There was no sign of the lezzers but the Yanks had taken over. Half of them were asleep. He went back to the public bar. The rowing couple were going around in the revolving doors, in front of reception, laughing and in love, wanting the world to see them. It was probably something they'd seen in a film. He stood at the door of the bar and searched the crowd for gel-head. There was no sign or sniff of him. He went in.

'Cleansing, waterworks, sewers!'

The office party had left Ben behind. There were a lot of rat-arsed people over in that corner. One chap, in particular, looked very pale around the gills. He'd be seeing his lunch sometime very soon, if Ben was any judge. He looked for the woman in black.

She was at the bar.

Perfect.

He shuffled between two groups of young fellas, all wearing T-shirts with 'Dave's Stag' printed on them, and came out at the bar. But she'd gone; she was back in the party. Ben watched her sit down. She just let herself fall back, between two men who quickly made room for her. Ben could almost feel her leg against his as he watched her landing between them. She leaned forward and grabbed her drink. She was pissed too, Ben could tell from the winding, slow route the glass took to her mouth. He gazed at the glass, tried to help it to her lips without spilling.

One of the stag lads bumped into him.

'Sorry, mate.'

He was English.

'You're all right,' said Ben.

He wanted a drink. He'd been out all night and he'd only had one pint, and he hadn't even finished it. He pushed gently to get near to a barman – he hated touching people he didn't know, he hated being rude – but then he stopped. There was nowhere for him here. No spare stools or counter to lean against. He'd have to stand still and hug his pint to his chest when he wasn't drinking it. All by himself. A spare prick and not even at a wedding. It was becoming the worst night of his life.

Back down to the nightclub.

He found it easier this time. He was fine. His eyes didn't take as long to adjust; he saw other people immediately. Some of them dancing, others watching the dancers or

standing around shouting over the music, none of them still
– the music was in their legs and shoulders. He liked this. He
moved towards the bar. One song became another; there
was no gap. Did men ask women up to dance any more?
How? In Ben's day, there were fast sets and slow sets, more
slow ones than fast towards the end of the night, and a
decent few seconds between each song so you could stand in
front of a young one and ask her up. What happened these
days? He'd get a drink first. Get that out of the way. He was
gasping for a pint; he usually had four on a Thursday. Again,
was it all right to drink Guinness? Would they laugh at him?
And what would he do with the pint if he did get dancing?

He walked into a woman.

She was suddenly there in front of him, out of nowhere.
And then he hit her and he saw her flying before he'd time
to know what had happened.

She was sitting on the floor.

'Are you all right?'

'There's no need to shout!'

'Sorry,' said Ben. 'It's the noise.'

Noise. He sounded like his father. No, he actually sounded
like himself. The last person he wanted to sound like tonight.

'Are you all right?' he tried again.

'It's these fuckin' shoes,' she said.

'They're very nice,' said Ben.

'They're fuckin' murder,' she said. 'Give us a hand.'

She was in her twenties, Ben guessed. On the home
stretch. Maybe even thirty. She was tallish, thinnish and
good-looking. And she was gone. She held onto his hand and
sleeve till she was upright and then, by the time he had the
jacket back on his shoulders, she wasn't there any more.

Maybe he'd just give up and go back up to the Yanks in the residents' lounge. They'd looked like a decent enough bunch, and he'd never had sex with a pensioner before. He'd be more at home up there.

No, though. He wasn't dead yet. He just needed a pint and time to calm down. He remembered the old days. Going up to a young one, on the edge of a shower of other young ones. Charging up to her before the next song started. Diving in before he had time to stop himself and slip back into the crowd. 'Do you want to dance?' 'No.' The number of times he'd been left high and dry, in the middle of the dance floor, with happy couples all around him, everyone in the building except Ben, dancing in tight, slow circles, sucking the fillings out of one another's teeth, madly, privately in love. While Ben stood there and waited for John Lennon to stop imagining or for Sylvia's mother to put the fuckin' phone down so he could get off the floor without pushing, could get his coat from off a chair and go home.

Before Fran rescued him.

He wished he was at home.

But he wasn't. And he wasn't going home. Until the morning. And he wasn't going back up to the Yanks or up to his room. He was here, so – he was here. He'd have a pint. He'd look around for a woman his own age or – the idea hit him so quickly he couldn't believe he'd thought of it himself – a woman ugly enough to want him. God, it was brilliant. Suddenly, life was easier. Just like that. He peered into the soup. He felt so happy. There was hope for him yet. If he could come up with more ideas like that one, if he could allow himself to have and maybe even use them and not let guilt smother them, there was some hope that he'd get through this. And then he'd go home. He'd been the owner of the idea for thirty seconds now and he still felt great about it. There was hope.

But that was the problem with nightclubs: they made everyone look gorgeous. He probably looked fantastic himself. He'd have to get closer to the women. He'd look around first, then get a drink. There was a bunch of girls over there. They looked bright and magnificent, all looking around and holding their heads back as they laughed. Hair like scribbled haloes. They looked great. But they couldn't all have been good-looking, not all of them – that never happened. Ben went a bit closer. There was a little fat one behind the others; no halo – Jesus, she was bald? Just out of hospital after chemotherapy? No, she was fine. There was another fat one beside her. Good, good. But why was he suddenly hunting fat women? Come on, come on. He'd have to do something very soon, act, ask one of them to dance, anyone – come on, come on. He was beginning to feel like a stalker or something—

Christ.

One of them would know him. He'd know one of them. Howyeh, Mr Winters. Jesus. One of his son's old girlfriends. A friend's daughter. One of the young ones from the local shops. Fran's sister. One of the girls from the office in work. What did you say? Did you ask me to dance? Jesus! Did you hear him, girls?

Gobshite.

Eejit.

Gobshite.

He left by the front door, past the bouncers.

'Night night now,' said one of them. Ben looked at him. He was black. And he'd an accent from Limerick or somewhere down near it.

'Goodnight,' said Ben. 'Thanks.'

'You're welcome,' said the other bouncer, the white one.

There was something horrible happening just up the steps, in front of the club. There was a man shouting at a woman. Right into her face.

'Get in!'

At an open taxi door. Right in front of the bouncers. Ben looked back down at them but they weren't interested. They were very deliberately looking elsewhere.

'Get in!'

'No!'

Ben knew them. It was the couple he'd last seen going around in the revolving doors.

'Come on!'

The man grabbed the woman's arm. She pulled back. He pulled her.

'Let go of me!'

Ben was furious. How could the bastard do that? Wreck their night, wreck the rest of their lives. Treat her like that. Just because she wouldn't do exactly what he wanted. Jesus, Ben knew so many fuckers like that.

'Let go of her.'

He'd gone over and grabbed the young man's arm. The taxi driver was staring straight ahead. There was a very brief nothing, not even a second, as Ben waited for the man to respond, to look at him, and then something crashed into his face, right onto his nose, and the ground was gone and he was falling backwards. Her elbow – he saw her bringing it back as he landed on the steps outside the club. She'd hit him an almighty smack. And his back, Christ; he'd driven it into one of the steps.

Ben heard the taxi door slam, then saw the driver struggle

back into his seat and drive away, the fat bastard, the back seat of the taxi still empty. Ben took his hand away from his face. There was blood on it. His nose was bleeding; he could feel it flowing over his mouth, taste it. And he saw the man and woman through the water that had already drenched his eyes and cheeks. He coughed. And he couldn't see them any more. Not a word from either of them. They were gone.

He could stand.

Another taxi arrived and another couple climbed out and skipped around Ben, down to the club, past the bouncers who let them pass and didn't look at Ben. His back was killing him but he could stand. He was on his feet again. The bleeding was bad. It was falling onto his shirt and jacket. He searched in his trouser pockets but couldn't find a tissue. The blood was roaring out of him; he could feel it pumping. He was a mess. He tried his jacket pockets. His finest hour. He'd tried to save a woman and got a broken nose for his troubles. From the woman. No tissues in his jacket either. But he found the toast. He'd forgotten he'd put it in there. Years ago, it seemed like.

His blood was hitting the ground. He watched it. He'd have to do something, get himself back in order. He put the toast to his nose. It was good for soaking up butter; it might do the same job with blood and, anyway, he'd nothing else and there was no one looking. And he didn't care. He pressed the toast to his nose – he didn't think it was broken now – and blew. He was afraid to look at the results. And the bouncers were looking at him now.

*

He managed the revolving doors quite well, considering. He felt the foyer carpet under his feet before he saw anything, and he jumped away from the doors. He felt them whacking past, just inches from his arse. He was safe. He stopped. His eyes were still watering, he couldn't stop blinking. He was holding his head up high, to slow down the blood. He hadn't had a nosebleed since he was a kid. The toast seemed to be doing the trick, though. He tried to remember where exactly the lift was, and where the low glass tables were. Over to the right, past the public bar. He looked. God, his head was hopping. That young one must have been on steroids. A swimmer or something. He'd have black eyes. How would he explain them when he went home tomorrow? He could feel the pain twisting, wringing the flesh around his nose and inside. But he could see the lift. It wasn't too far. There were no chairs or Americans in the way.

'God almighty, who did that to you?'

It was Aideen, from behind the reception desk.

'It's nothing,' said Ben.

He had to get to the lift.

'It is not nothing,' said Aideen. 'Come here with me. Simon! Bring some water for me.'

She took Ben's arm and led him. He didn't pull away or protest. He'd already been beaten up by one woman. She took him just a few paces and gently pushed him down into a deep chair.

'Let's see you now,' she said. 'Now, let me just—'

She'd found the toast.

Ben kept his eyes clamped. There was a horrible, short eternity when she said nothing and he could hear no movement, nothing at all, except his ears swallowing. Had she fainted? Or run away? God, he was an eejit. Then he felt warm water and a cloth that kissed his nose and continued all around his face. It was gone, and back, warmer again.

Over his face. He felt it take the years off him. He felt the nerve ends under his skin rising to touch it. He'd never felt so good.

'It's getting desperate,' she said. 'When you can't even go out for a walk.'

Tears crowded, pushed behind his lids. He let them out. He felt the cloth taking them away. Now it was over his eyes. He opened them. A blue and white J-cloth. It was nice and cool now. And so soothing. He wanted to hold it. To bring it up to bed with him. It moved away from his eyes and Ben saw Aideen looking down at him. Aideen and about twenty other people.

He closed his eyes again. He groaned.

'You poor thing.'

He could hear her rinsing the cloth. And felt it again, faster this time, crossing his face, turning, circling. He loved it, forgot about the people watching him. Completely. Fuck them. If only this could have gone on for ever. He knew: it was nearest he'd get to sex tonight. He hated himself for thinking it, wanted to hang himself but he loved it, savoured every last remaining second of it. He pushed his face into the cloth. His eyes were clear and fresh; his nose was no longer clogged. He could smell again. The cloth covered his face. He pressed his face to it. He could smell Jif.

Aideen took the cloth from his face when his coughing became frantic.

'You're grand now,' she said.

'Guess they thought you were a tourist,' said an American voice behind her.

*

30

The porter opened Ben's door for him. Ben had told him not to bother, he was all right, he could manage, but the porter had insisted. Simon. Aideen downstairs had called him that. A crumpy old mongrel. He hadn't said a word all the way up in the lift. And now he'd come into Ben's room. Ahead of Ben. He probably expected a tip but he'd get nothing from Ben.

Simon pointed at something on the bed. It was a tray with sandwiches and a teapot on it. There were two little blue swords stuck deep in the sandwiches' sides, holding them in a straight, peaked line on the plate.

'Did you order that food?' Simon asked.

'No,' said Ben.

'Well, someone did.'

'Well, it wasn't me.'

Simon picked up the tray off the bed. Ben was starving.

'You can leave them here, if you want,' he said.

'I thought you said you didn't order them,' said Simon.

'I didn't,' said Ben.

'Well then,' said Simon. 'Someone else might be waiting for them.'

He went to the door.

'What's in them, anyway?' said Ben.

'Chicken,' said Simon.

And he was gone. Ben sat on the bed. God, he was hollow, caving in; he hadn't eaten in years. And his face was sore again, killing him. And the skin around his nose was stinging; probably the Jif eating his face away. He brought his hand up to touch his nose.

He was still holding the toast. For a fragment of a second, before he threw it at the wall and stood up, Ben was going to eat it.

He stood up.

He wasn't going to stay here, in the same room as the telly and the toast. No way. He was going out. He wasn't even going to look at himself in the mirror. He buttoned his jacket. Its stains weren't as spectacular as those on his shirt.

Out.

He'd wash his hands first.

No, he wouldn't even do that. He knew that if he went into the bathroom he'd end up listening for noises from the women next door. He'd end up standing in the bath again with his ear to the wall. Taking up the floorboards, looking for the minibar.

Out.

He wasn't dead yet.

*

'It begins with a B,' she said. 'I'm nearly certain it does.'

The woman in the black dress was trying to remember her name.

By the time he'd got down to the public bar the party in the corner had exploded, just a few sleeping or legless bodies lying around. Including the woman in black who'd skipped over the falling stool earlier.

'Deirdre,' she said.

'That begins with D,' said Ben.

'Definitely Deirdre,' she said. 'I think.'

It was – had been – a party of corporation workers, from the civic offices down the quays. He'd found that out from a lounge boy who hadn't been there earlier. One of them was retiring or leaving. Or possibly dead, if it was the guy lying under the chair over there.

Ben had done something he never really thought he'd be

capable of doing. He'd gone straight over to the woman in black and had sat down beside her. Just like that. He hadn't even bothered getting a drink first. He hadn't needed it. He'd just gone straight over. Maybe it was the near-death experience he'd had outside; it had given him courage he'd never had or known about, or it had given him a different outlook on life; he didn't know. Something, anyway. He just sat down beside her and said hello.

She was rat-arsed. He could see that by the way her head was bobbing; her eyelids were going to sleep a few minutes before the rest of her. The little angel inside him told him that he was taking advantage of her but he told it to fuck off. And it did. Just like that.

The new Ben.

He was going to tell her his own name – no messing either; he was going to tell her his real name – but she spoke first.

'I'll tell you what,' she said.

She leaned, and nearly fell onto his shoulder. He felt his shoulder howling, waiting for her.

'You go over there,' she said, and pointed vaguely at the rest of the world. 'Go over there and wait a few minutes. Say, five. Then shout Deirdre and if I look up, then we'll definitely know it's my name.'

'OK,' said Ben.

He was out of his seat before his cop-on pulled him back.

'What happens if you don't look up?' he asked.

'Then just stay over there,' she said.

The old Ben.

'OK,' he said. 'No harm done.'

'No,' she said. 'It's just I prefer my men with their blood on the inside.'

As he left the bar there were two guards going in, and another one at the revolving doors. One of them, a young chap with spots having a riot on his neck and chin, looked at Ben's shirt, jacket, then his face. He looked at the other one, the sergeant, to see if he'd noticed Ben. But the sergeant had already walked into the bar, following a man in a suit who looked worried enough to be the manager. The manager lifted his hands into the air and brought them down as if gripping something. He was telling the barmen to close the bar; Ben knew that signal. The spotty garda followed his sergeant and Ben escaped. He headed for the residents' lounge. He looked at his watch. A present from Fran for his last birthday. ('Real hands on it, look. None of that digital rubbish for my man.') It was well after midnight. It would soon be time for breakfast.

*

At last.

He had a pint in front of him, settling. A good-looking pint. He'd drink it slowly, then go up and try to sleep. The night had been a disaster. This now, the pint, listening to the Yanks chatting here in the residents' lounge, was the high point. A complete and utter disaster. From start to finish.

One of the Americans spoke to him.

'How many of them jumped you, son?'

'I'm not sure,' said Ben. 'Three or four.'

'My oh my. Pretty courageous guys.'

'And they ripped your jacket too. For shame.'

Ben hadn't noticed that; he didn't bother looking. He tried the pint. Lovely. He could already feel it working at the pain behind his eyes. He was sitting very comfortably. For the first time in days, months, he wasn't restless, miserable, itching to get up. He'd go home tomorrow. He'd have an excuse for the nose and black eyes ready for Fran by then. He'd phone his brother and give him another story, a different version, one that would run into whatever story he made up for Fran.

A complete and utter fuckin' disaster. But he was the only person who knew about it. He knew: he'd get over it. He was already looking forward to next Thursday, the few pints with the lads, the crack. And he could forget about tonight.

He was surprised at the Yanks. Still up and chatting away, some of them lapping up the drink. They were talking about the weather, the rain, giving out quietly; they probably didn't want to hurt Irish feelings.

'And the drops. Big as mice.'

'I'll say.'

Ben listened. He wanted to hear something good, something really funny. Something he could bring home, to tell Fran. And the lads next Thursday.

They were a nice, gentle bunch. And they were obviously enjoying the holiday, even the rain. Anyway, Ben couldn't remember it raining that much over the last few days. He listened to the group at the next table.

'I guess I must have cousins there.'

'Although Cork's one of the big ones. From the map.'

'Yeah. The lady in the library said that. And Barry's one of the biggest names. She said that too.'

One of the women patted the speaker's hand.

'Poor Bill,' she said.

Poor Bill. A tall, lean man with more wrinkles on his face than Ben had ever seen. Except on the woman beside him who'd just patted his hand. Poor Bill. Ben felt sorry for him. A man that old, looking for his roots.

He could have some of Ben's. He could have them all, the whole fuckin' tree. And Ben could walk away. Free.

But no. He couldn't cope with freedom. He knew that. He couldn't use it. It had given him nothing, except a bloody nose and a headache that was fading now, leaving him. And the story of a disastrous night on the town that he could do nothing with, could never tell anyone.

'It would be easier if there'd been a patch of land in the family,' Bill was telling the others, 'the lady said. There'd be records. Maps.'

'Serves you right for being a peasant, boy.'

'I guess.'

'Excuse me.'

It was Ben.

'Sorry for interrupting yis.'

'No. Please,' said the woman who'd been kind to Bill. His wife, probably.

'I couldn't help hearing you,' said Ben. He was listening to himself, remembering, already telling it later on. 'About your roots and that.'

'Or lack of,' said Bill.

'Yeah,' said Ben. 'Exactly. But I was going to ask you for a bit of advice myself.'

Ben watched them all sitting up, every one of them, three tableloads. All dying to help him. He had no idea where the idea had come from, wasn't even fully aware of it when he'd interrupted them.

'You see,' he said. 'I was thinking of going over to look for my own roots.'

He could hear himself laughing, tomorrow morning, telling it to Fran.

'You see. My ancestors emigrated here,' Ben told them. 'From America.'

One voice spoke for them all.

'My oh my.'

'Yeah,' said Ben. 'It's a gas really. They came in 1847.'

'No!'

'Yeah. Honest to God. In the middle of the Famine.'

'Did you hear that, people?'

'We heard. They could have timed it better, huh.'

Ben looked at their eyes, from face to kind, concerned face. There wasn't one of them who didn't believe him. He was delighted. And it was harmless. He was making their night, as well as his own. And you'll never believe what happened to us in Dublin. Ben could hear them.

'Well, they'd no problem finding somewhere to live,' he told them. 'My grandmother told me. On her knee. Half the houses in the west were already empty.'

'Heh. That's interesting.'

'I never looked at it that way before. One man's hard luck.'

'Is another man's opportunity.'

'How fascinating.'

'What is your name, sir?'

'Ben Winters,' said Ben.

'Winters.'

They handed the name to each other, like a baby, from lap to lap.

'Chicago,' said Ben. 'My grandmother remembered the old ones talking about Chicago.'

'Heh, Al's from Chicago.'

'He's in bed.'

'Well, let's get him down here. He can't miss this.'

'I don't want to put you to any trouble,' said Ben.

He picked up his pint as the Americans elected a delega-
tion to go up and get Al out of the scratcher. They were
having a ball. And so was Ben. Happiness wriggled through
him. He couldn't wait to tell Fran. And his father. He could
see his father laughing, roaring, and it wasn't a shock. He
was fine. He couldn't wait. He had a story now, a classic,
with him in the middle of it, the inventor of it all. He
couldn't wait to get home.

102

WHITE LIES

Rose stood for a moment outside the door of Finbar's Hotel and watched the taxi drive away.

Bloody shark . . .

But she had been warned.

'Don't take a taxi from the airport if you value your money.'

Ivy had said that. Ivy was always right.

So, as usual, she had no one to blame but herself.

I won't tell Ivy, she thought.

I came in the bus to Bus Aras. Got a cab from there. If need be, that's what I will say.

White lies never hurt anyone. That's what her mother always told her, anyway. The problem was working out the difference between a white lie and a black lie. Rose reckoned she'd managed to get through her life so far on a series of greyish manipulations of the truth.

The same old smell rose from the river, dank and familiar under the street lights.

Not her favourite part of town.

Awful memories of Kingsbridge Station, as her mother had always insisted on calling it; the holidays over, school uniform, brave face, large leather suitcase in the guard's van.

Money would pass hands in Galway. 'Keep an eye on the child for me.' A nod, a wink, a reassuring smile and the coin passed hands.

So humiliating.

A half a crown!

She had always wanted to tackle her mother on that one.

'Am I only worth half a crown?' she had wanted to say, but never dared.

Her mother always came out best in those sort of conversations.

Like Ivy.

Rose sighed and pushed at the revolving door.

The door sighed as it shovelled her from the cold into the warmth of reception.

God, but I hate this sort of place. I bet the party faithful still gather here. Scratching each other's backs.

Bright lights and plastic flowers. Tastefully arranged plastic flowers. Almost worse than ostentatious vulgarity.

Why in the name of Jaysus had Ivy chosen this dump?

Keeping me in my place.

That's what.

Can't be lack of cash. Ivy and Joe are rolling.

Rohoholing!

Big, big, big mills near Tuam.

Catch of the year, everyone said.

Must have been a pretty poor year!

Those were still the days when mixed marriages were frowned upon. And for the daughter of a rural dean the choice was strictly limited.

Maybe, she thought, I have been saved a fate worse than . . . worse than what?

'Can I help you?'

The young woman behind the desk looked a bit tired round the eyes.

A hard day slaving over a hot computer . . . or just perhaps smiling at people.

'Thank you. Yes. There is a room booked for two. It will either be under FitzGibbon or Gately.'

The woman pressed some computer keys and stared at the screen. Reflected words flickered in her eyes.

'Room 102, first floor. Mrs Gately has already arrived. She collected the key about twenty minutes ago.'

'Thank you.'

'Mrs Gately says you will be paying by credit card . . . so . . .'

Bloody Ivy, thought Rose, putting her bag on the counter and fumbling in it.

'. . . if you wouldn't mind . . .'

Rose produced a leather wallet bursting with plastic cards. She chose one and put it on the counter.

So much for big, big, big mills near Tuam. Perhaps Joe keeps her short. Now that wouldn't be beyond the bounds of possibility.

'. . . Thank you, madam. Just one night, is that correct?'

It sure is.

'Yes. You seem busy.'

The woman smiled at her.

'Americans.' She mouthed rather than spoke the words and rolled her eyes. 'Will you be wanting breakfast in your room, Mrs . . . ah . . . ?'

'FitzGibbon. Capital G, two bs. And it's Miss. No, no thanks. We'll probably come down. My sister has to catch a train. I think breakfast downstairs will be the easiest.'

The woman handed Rose back her credit card.

'You can always ring down if you change your mind. I

hope everything will be to your satisfaction. The lift's just across the hall. First floor, turn to the left when you get out of the lift.'

The telephone on the desk buzzed and the woman picked it up.

'Reception. Can I help you?'

She raised a hand towards Rose.

'Room 102,' she mouthed.

An arrangement of ferns in a brass bucket faced Rose when she got out of the lift.

She walked over and felt one of the fronds.

It was real.

'Well, how about that?' She murmured the words aloud as she walked down the passage on the left.

She stopped outside room 102.

I could go home now. Taxi back to the airport. Last flight to London.

I could go to the Shelbourne, have a good meal, a few drinks and catch a plane in the morning.

She's never to know that I'm standing here deciding.

Not deciding.

Oh, fuck it. Oh, Ivy! What the hell am I doing here?

The door opened suddenly and Ivy stood looking at her.

'I heard the lift,' was all she said and stood aside to let Rose into the room.

'Oh, Ivy . . . oh, gosh . . . hello.' Rose stepped past her sister and threw her holdall onto the floor. 'You gave me a right turn.'

She turned to kiss her sister.

Ivy stood without moving, her back to the door, looking Rose up and down, then slowly she moved towards her and placed her soft cheek against Rose's soft cheek.

She smelt of lavender water.

'Lovely to see you, dear. You look tired.'

'Lovely to see you too. I am tired. I could murder a drink.'

Ivy shook her head. On the television set a woman with big hair also shook her head. She was talking silent news.

'No minibar,' said Ivy. 'I've searched every corner of this room.'

'Bathroom?' asked Rose.

'Don't be an ass.'

'What a dump. We'll just have to go down to the bar. I'm not going to last much longer without a drink.'

'Not the bar,' said Ivy. 'There seems to be a party of some sort in the bar.'

'We could also get out of here and go somewhere half civilized. We could take a taxi and go somewhere miles away.'

'There's nothing wrong with this hotel. It's warm, comfortable, clean. What more do you want?'

Rose took off her coat and threw it on the bed.

'A drink, but I also like a bit of style. However, you're the boss.' She picked up the phone. 'What'll you have?'

'What are you having?'

'Brandy and ginger. Large.'

Ivy thought for a moment, touching the skin beneath her right eye as if she were seeking some coded message through her fingers.

She nodded.

'That's fine,' she said.

Rose dialled room service.

'How's Joe?'

'He's fine. Work, work, work. You know the way he is.'

Rose shook her head slightly and frowned at the telephone.

'And the kids?'

'Fine. All fine, thank God.'

'We're all fine,' said Rose to the telephone, in her best Grace Kelly voice. 'Except for room service.'

'Have some patience.'

'Maybe they're all dead in room service. Bodies piled on the floor.'

She cut off the ringing tone with a finger and dialled reception.

'Give them time,' said Ivy, too late.

A voice squawked.

'Yes,' said Rose. 'I'm sorry to bother you. I couldn't raise room service . . . Yes. OK. That's OK. Could you . . . ? Oh thanks . . . Two brandies and ginger . . . Large, please. And ice. Yes, two large. Room 102. FitzGibbon. Large G. Sorry for bothering you.'

She put the receiver down.

'God!'

Before she could say another word, Ivy spoke.

'It's not grand enough for you. No need to deny it, Rose. It's written all over your face. Well it's quite good enough for me.' She muttered something underneath her breath that Rose couldn't quite catch, but it sounded like 'Paradise'.

Rose kicked off her shoes and walked across the room to her sister. Briefly she touched her shoulder.

'I'm sorry. Flying always makes me grumpy. I'm always shit scared up there and grumpy when I come down. Sit, for Heaven's sake, darling. Relax. You look as if you're going to run away.'

She laughed briefly inside herself; she, after all, had been the one who had thought of turning tail.

She pulled the curtain aside and stared out into the saffron-tinged darkness. On the bridge cars moved slowly and below them, the river, deep down between its walls, moved slowly also.

No glory there, she thought.

'Did you say Paradise?'

She pulled the curtains shut again, smoothing the shiny material with her fingers.

'Oh, Granny, what big ears you've got.'

'That sounds more like Ivy.'

Ivy was sitting upright in a high-backed chair. She smiled slightly at Rose's words.

She is not wearing well, thought Rose. Not wearing well at all. Forty-one next May and looks . . . well . . . looks like a middle-aged vicar's daughter. The story-book kind . . . spinster of this parish . . . Anyway, I'm mean, she looks like someone who no longer has any dreams. A state devoutly to be avoided.

Ivy was speaking to her.

'. . . It's just good to get a little break. Not that . . . just a few hours to yourself . . .'

'Next time I recommend the Shelbourne. Especially if I'm paying.'

Ivy blushed.

'Rose . . . I . . .'

'Don't worry. I shouldn't have said that. Cheap joke.'

'We were brought up to be frugal . . .'

Rose laughed.

'It's one of the teachings I'm glad I was able to throw away when I left home, along with chastity and godliness. The trouble with frugality is that it can also be called meanness.'

There was a knock on the door.

'Yes. In,' called Rose.

The door opened and an old man came in carrying a tray.

'I'm sorry you had a problem with room service.'

He walked across the room and put the tray down on a table by the window.

'We're at sixes and sevens this evening.' He wheezed slightly as he spoke. 'There's a big party below. Maybe you noticed when you came in. That could go on for the duration, and we've a bus load of Yanks came in this morning.'

'Thank you,' said Rose. 'I'm sorry to have bothered you.'

'No bother, ladies. It's all in the day's work.' He paused in his walk back towards the door and looked Rose up and down. His fragility disturbed her. She hoped that he would make it out of the room before falling to the ground. His fall, she thought, would make no sound.

'The restaurant is open for dinner or we could send you up sandwiches if you like. Anything at all don't hesitate to ask. Just dial five-oh-five.' He repeated the numbers as he moved on towards the door. 'Five-oh-five. Just ask for Simon.'

He bowed courteously and left them with their drinks. Rose handed Ivy a glass and twisted the top off the bottle of ginger ale.

'Say when?'

She held the bottle over Ivy's glass.

'Up to the top.'

Ivy's hand trembled as she held the glass out.

Rose threw some ice cubes into her glass and then a quick slash of ginger ale.

'No point in drowning it.'

She sat down facing her sister and held up her glass.

'Mud in your eye.'

Ivy nodded.

The two women drank in silence; Rose holding the liquid in her mouth for a moment, teasing herself by her postponement of pleasure.

Ivy drank like a child, two greedy gulps with eyes shut tight.

'Ivy.'

Ivy opened her eyes and looked at her sister.

She looked mildly surprised to see her, Rose thought.

'What's up? What's all this about? Why are we sitting in this dump drinking brandy?'

'I just thought it would be nice . . .'

'No need to be frugal with the truth. Is it Mother? Has something happened to Mother?'

Rose was surprised by the anxiety in her own voice. Anxiety about her mother was one of the last things she thought she would ever feel. Yet there was a little scratch of it at the side of her brain.

Ivy was shaking her head. It was as if the two gulps of brandy had loosened up the muscles in her neck.

'Mother's fine.' She paused. 'Yes. I mean at this moment, fine. Sometime, though . . . we'll have to . . . well, make decisions. You know what I mean.'

She took another gulp from her glass.

I should have ordered a bottle, Rose thought.

'I hate the thought of her out in that house all on her own. Some terrible things have happened, you know. Terrible violent things. Old people on their own are very vulnerable. I just thought I ought to alert you to . . .'

'Is she anxious?'

Ivy shook her head.

'Not a bit of her. You know the way she is.'

'She'd outface the devil.'

'It's not quite the same thing as chasing young men hell-bent on robbery with violence.'

'You exaggerate.'

'Have you ever known me to exaggerate?'

Rose giggled.

'Never, darling. If Mother doesn't have a problem, I don't think you should manufacture one. Leave her in peace.'

'Will you come back down with me and see her? See the situation for yourself? You've never even seen the house she bought after . . . It's so isolated . . . after Father . . .'

'I am not coming, Ivy. Get that into your head.'

'Ah, Rose, for Heaven's sake. She's your mother. You haven't seen her for years.'

Rose laughed.

'She wouldn't thank you if I walked in the door. She'd rather be confronted by a crazed teenager with a hammer.'

Ivy gulped down the last of her drink and stared into the empty glass.

'You're very unfair.'

'Whether I am or whether I'm not, no is the answer. You got through that in a jiffy anyway.'

Ivy put the glass down on the table.

'You're not just unfair to Mother, you're unfair to me. Why should I have to take on the responsibility for what happens to her? I have enough . . .' Her voice faded out. 'Sorry,' she said, after a long silence.

She picked her bag up from the floor and began to grope

inside it. She changed her mind and shut the bag with a snap. She stood up.

'Just . . .' She gestured towards the bathroom. 'Just . . . you know . . . loo.'

Ivy walked across the room with her bag tucked firmly under her arm. She shut the bathroom door and Rose heard her lock it behind her.

She heard the murmur of music from the next room.

She thought of her mother alone, locking doors against marauders . . . an ugly, but unlikely thought.

The last time she had seen her was at her father's funeral.

'I am the resurrection and the life,' the bishop had said, spreading his hands out towards the congregation, 'and whosoever liveth and believeth in me shall never die.'

Rose had cried.

She had cried because she didn't believe those words.

She had cried for her father, who had believed them and was now, to all intents and purposes, dead.

She had cried for her mother who had turned away her face when Rose had leant to kiss her after she had stepped out of the taxi from Galway.

Turned away her face.

Rose wondered if her father had seen that gesture, from wherever he had been hovering.

She hoped not.

She took another drink and swished it round in her mouth as if she were rinsing her teeth, then let it slowly slither down her throat.

Mother had remained composed, apparently, throughout the service and even at the graveside.

Man that is born of woman hath but a short time to live

and is full of misery. . . He cometh up and is cut down like a flower . . .

Mother had walked among the mourners, her eyes dry, her mouth speaking words. Well trained.

Rose had stood by the grave, someone's large floral offering in her arms, and broken the heads off the flowers and dropped them one by one into the open grave, while the men with the spades stood to one side and watched and presumably thought about overtime.

There's rosemary, that's for remembrance, and there is pansies . . .

Ivy had come and, putting an arm around her shoulders, had led her away.

I would give you some violets, but they withered all when my father died.

Ivy wasn't all that bad.

She had her moments.

Not many moments, but a few.

The bathroom door clicked open and Ivy came back into the room.

She had combed her hair and done something to her face.

She looked more composed.

She threw her bag onto the bed.

'Had your fix?' The words came unwanted from Rose's mouth.

Ivy looked at her, shocked.

'Rose . . .'

'I'm sorry. A rotten . . .'

'I've been rather nervous lately. The doctor . . . just mild tranquillizers. That's all. Nothing . . . you know . . . nothing.'

'Throw them away,' said Rose.

'I don't need your advice. I've a perfectly good doctor.'

'Pish.'

'And what does pish mean?'

'You know perfectly well. I thought you had more sense, Ivy. I thought I was the one in this family who couldn't be relied upon. Poor Rose, whisper her name, not to be relied upon. Poison. Don't be fooled by good, normal, responsible doctors. They also poison you. Throw the pills and potions away. The pain is preferable.'

'Thanks, Doctor.'

'Any time.'

Rose looked up at her sister and remembered how she had envied her on the day she had married Joe.

Tuam Cathedral had been filled with the sound of the organ and choir.

Praise to the holiest in the height and in the depths be praise.

A little wind had been blowing and women had clutched at their flower-laden hats. Skirts had flickered and billowed as they smiled for the photographers outside and people in the street had peered in through the gates to catch sight of the beautiful bride and the best catch in County Galway.

Radiant day.

Maybe, she had thought then, all those stories are true.

Maybe this is the happy door through which we all have to pass.

She smiled.

'What are you grinning about?'

'I just remembered those ghastly bridesmaids' dresses we had to wear at your wedding.'

Ivy thought back for a moment.

'They weren't all that bad.'

'Dresses from hell,' said Rose. 'Puce.'

'They were not puce.'

'Well, we all thought they were puce. Seriously unbecoming.'

Ivy laughed.

'It was meant to be my day. You were just extras.'

'No one explained that at the time.'

Rose got up and went over to her sister. She took Ivy's hand and held it for a moment against her cheek.

'Here we are,' she said.

They looked at each other.

After a moment Ivy's eyes fluttered and she looked away.

'I think we need another drink.'

'Good notion,' said Rose. 'Let's go down to the bar and get some sandwiches and a bottle of wine and bring them up. Save that poor old bugger the run up and down.'

'I . . .'

'I need to make sure that there's life outside this room.' Rose interrupted her sister. 'We could be in a capsule heading for Mars.'

'You say such silly things.'

'Always have. Come on. Quick sprint down the stairs. Let's live dangerously.'

Rose scooted across the room and opened the door with a flourish.

She bowed.

'After you, Cecil,' she called back to her sister.

Ivy laughed.

'No one's said that to me for years. No, after you, Claud.'

They went out into the corridor and let the door slam behind them.

Between them and the lift a man was picking himself up from the floor.

He looked as if he'd just fallen over a tray.

Or he'd been . . . a terrible bubble of laughter rose in Rose's throat.

The man tapped at the floor with a foot.

'Mind yourself,' he muttered, as they approached him.

Rose put her hand up to her mouth and hurried past.

Behind her she heard Ivy say something to the man.

She put her finger on the lift button as the explosion of laughter burst out of her.

Ivy came up behind her.

'What . . .'

Rose shook her head helplessly.

'That poor sod . . .'

'Oh, shhh, Rosie. He'll hear you.'

The lift purred.

'D–do you realize what he was up to?'

The lift doors wheezed open.

The two women moved in and the doors wheezed again.

Not long for this world, thought Rose, and began to laugh again.

'He tripped,' said Ivy.

'He was pinching jam from that tray. Caught in the act by Claud and Cecil. A bloody jam thief. Now that would never happen in the Shelbourne.'

A slight bump and the doors wheezed.

A hum of voices and laughter came at them from the bar and somewhere there was the distant throb of music.

'Have you actually stayed in this dump before?'

Ivy shook her head.

'Joe sometimes does, if he has to spend a night up here. It's so handy. There's a terrible crowd in the bar. I . . .'

Rose crossed to the reception desk.

The receptionist had the telephone receiver tucked under her chin.

She raised her eyebrows at Rose and smiled.

'Where is the residents' lounge, please?'

The woman nodded and pointed down the passage behind them.

'Thanks.'

The woman nodded again. She looked quite uninterested, but then why not? What was there to be interested in?

The residents' lounge was dark and had a faint smell of cigarette smoke and beer; the air, she thought, had probably been undisturbed for thirty years. Or more possibly, many, many more.

A tall man behind the bar was topping up a glass of Guinness. He nodded at her.

'Ladies?'

'Could we have two large brandy and ginger ales, please.'

He waved a hand towards a table in the corner.

'I'll be right with you.'

A pool of light shone on the wooden surface from a red-shaded lamp. They sat themselves side by side on a low banquette.

Their knees bumped against the table top. Their faces were in darkness.

Across the room other tables were focused by little pools of golden light.

Half a dozen people were scattered around, and the murmur of conversation was low.

'I told Mother you'd be coming down with me tomorrow,' Ivy said.

'That was pretty silly of you.'

'I left her airing the spare room.'

Anger rose up in Rose's throat and she clamped her mouth tight to prevent the words spilling out. She imagined those words scattering on the table, lying there in the pool of light, burning their way through the polish, through the table and onto the floor, lying in regretted heaps around their feet. So many words in the world that must never be said.

'There you are, ladies, two large brandies and two gingers. Will you sign for it?'

'No. I'll . . .' Ivy scrabbled in her bag as she spoke.

'It's OK, Ivy. It's my party.'

Ivy didn't argue.

'I'll sign.'

'Right you be.'

He put the docket down on the table next to her.

Ivy screwed the top off the ginger ale bottle and filled her glass to the brim again.

'And could we have a bottle of wine and some sandwiches to bring up to our room, please?'

'I'll have them sent up.'

'I thought . . . well . . . as you're so busy that we could . . .'

'No bother, madam. I'll see to it myself. What would you like in the way of sandwiches? We have cheese, ham, egg, beef, tomato, salad and very good home-made soup, if you'd like a bowl of soup? Mushroom, chicken . . . oh yes, we have chicken sandwiches too . . .'

'No thanks, no soup for . . .'

'I'd like soup,' said Ivy. ' I'd like mushroom soup.'

'One mushroom . . .' He was writing the words on his mind.

'Just sandwiches for me,' Rose said. ' Could we have a selection? Then we don't have to make decisions.'

He smiled slightly.

'And wine? Can I get you the wine list?'

'Don't bother. A bottle of house red will do fine.'

'House red. Selection of sandwiches and a bowl of mush-room soup.'

'Terrific. Thank you.'

'A pleasure, madam.'

He bowed and left them, heading for a table across the room where a man was waving at him.

'What's the betting he'll forget?' asked Rose. 'He didn't look as if he was concentrating.'

'Don't be so silly.'

'Why do you drown the brandy like that?'

'I hate the taste.' Ivy took a gulp. 'But it makes me feel better.'

'Look, Ivy, about Mother . . .'

'You will come, won't you? I know she'd love to see you. I know she's forgiven you . . . all that rotten stuff you said to her. She will let bygones be bygones.'

'Did she say that to you? Let bygones be bygones.' Rose's voice was incredulous.

Ivy shook her head. 'After all, she's old. If she can forgive, so can you.'

'What precisely do you think she's forgiving me for?'

There was a long silence.

Ivy examined the glass in her hand as if it were some rare object.

'I don't know the ins and outs of the whole thing.'

'Well, then, don't interfere. Don't make trouble.'

'Decisions are going to have to be made. I really would rather not have to take the full responsibility myself. Under those circumstances I think you should come down and see the situation for yourself. Speak to her.'

'Leave her alone. That's my advice to you. If she feels she needs your help she'll let you know soon enough. She's no fool.'

'She wants to see you.'

'She said that?'

'Well, not in so many words . . . but . . .'

'She was airing the spare room.'

Rose looked at her sister in silence for a moment.

'More like she was putting tarantulas in between the newly ironed sheets.'

Tears came into Ivy's eyes.

Rose leaned over the table and touched her hand.

'You never used to cry. I always admired that so much.'

Ivy shook her head and downed the last of her drink.

Swallow, swallow, swallow. Rose watched her neck bulge in and out as the liquid went down her throat.

'Even when Mother and I went to the station to see you off to school, you never cried.'

'I enjoyed school. I always missed my friends in the holidays. I don't mean that I wasn't happy at home, but I . . . well . . . I was always perfectly happy going back to school.'

She looked with a faint smile into the past.

'I loved the rules and just being together with all those people. I loved games. Having someone to whisper with in the dark after lights were out. All that company. I was never without company. We were like two only children really, weren't we? No common thoughts between us, no games we could play together. Seven years is such a big gap when you're a child. It doesn't mean anything now. But then . . . it was a lifetime. Didn't you think so?'

Rose nodded.

'To get back to Mother . . .'

'I thought we might be able to arrange for her to go into sheltered accommodation. There's a nice place in Galway . . . She could bring a lot of her own things with her. Furnish her own small apartment. We wouldn't have to worry about her safety there and we could all pop in and out to see her. The way things are at the moment she hardly ever sees the kids and I go out there only about once a . . .' Ivy paused, testing words in her mind. 'We used to have lunch on Sundays with her. It became a sort of tradition, but it interfered with his golf in the last year or so and we let it slip. Anyway she's too old to be cooking lunch for all of us.'

Rose held up her hand like a policeman.

'Stop.'

Ivy stopped.

For a moment she looked at Rose as if she couldn't remember who she was.

'Why? Why should I stop? I'm putting you in the picture. That's what they say, isn't it? Putting you in the picture. Welcome, sister, to the picture.'

Jesus Christ, thought Rose, she's spifflicated.

She was glad, at that moment, that they weren't in the Shelbourne.

Ivy groped for her glass and stared at its emptiness.

Rose stood up and held out a hand to her sister.

'Come on. I need my sandwiches. Let's go back to the room. This is a gloomy old place to have a conversation.'

Ivy took her hand and held it.

'I am not going to raise my voice,' she said.

'I know you're not, darling.'

'Joe never likes it when I raise my voice.'

'We can take off our shoes up there, stretch out on the beds. Relax. Eat our sandwiches. Come on.'

'You haven't finished your drink.'

'I'll bring it with me.'

She pulled Ivy up from the banquette, and gave her a little shove in the direction of the door.

She picked up her glass and turned to wave at the man who had returned to stand behind the bar. He nodded at her and pointed his finger upwards.

They walked down the passageway in silence. Ivy's feet carried her smoothly forward.

Perhaps she's not spifflicated at all, just a mite hysterical, menopausal, under the weather. Lists of descriptive words waltzed in Rose's head. Lonely. Perhaps, lonely. It must be quite a strain not being allowed to raise your voice.

'Will we walk up the stairs or take the lift?'

Ivy stopped by the lift and pressed the button.

The party in the bar seemed to be going from strength to strength.

She noticed the jam stealer standing by the doorway, his hands in his pockets, obviously wondering whether or not to join the fun.

She had the temptation to call across the hallway to him. Don't bother, she might call. You'd be better off going to the pictures.

My God, so would I. Ho. Ho. Perhaps we might even go together. She smiled at the ludicrous thought, and wondered what sort of films he might like.

'Rose.'

She heard Ivy's voice.

'Oh . . . ah . . . yes. Sorry.'

The lift had arrived and they stepped in.

'Do you ever dream about getting stuck in a lift?'

'How silly you can be.' Ivy's voice was back to sober normality.

'I gather it happens with remarkable frequency.'

Bump. Tick. Ping. The doors slid open.

'Not this time,' said Ivy, stepping out.

'No. Not this time.'

Rose took a sip of her drink and followed her sister along the passage.

The man had already set a tray on the round table by the window. White plates held sandwiches and a shining tureen with a lid stood neatly by a white soup plate. White napkins were folded and the wineglasses shone.

Music thudded from the next room.

Rose wriggled her feet out of her shoes and left them standing pigeon-toed by the door.

She began to undress; first her cream silk shirt which she threw onto a chair; then her very short black skirt.

'Phew, phew,' she muttered as she took off each garment.

She began to pull her tights down.

Ivy, ignoring her soup, poured herself a glass of wine and took a sandwich.

'What do you think you are doing?' she asked her sister.

'Making myself at home. I do it all the time. No restraints or constraints. It's one of the great advantages of living alone.'

'I wouldn't know. I've never tried it.'

Rose rolled her underclothes into a ball and threw them across the room. She rummaged in her holdall and pulled out a silk wrap. She put it on and then sat down on the bed.

'It's great. You can feel every bit of yourself relaxing. Pour me a glass of wine, there's a pet, and I'll have a couple of sangers.'

She arranged her pillows against the wall and leaned up against them.

'God, I hope that whoever is next door won't play that machine all night. Thanks.'

She took the wine from Ivy and sipped it.

'Now that stuff is truly grim.' She held the glass up towards Ivy. 'Here's to sisters just the same.'

Ivy smiled.

'Sisters.'

'Why don't you strip off too?'

'I'm all right.'

'You look bloody miserable.'

Ivy sat down and took another sandwich.

There was a crescendo of music from next door.

'Heavy metal.'

'What's that?' asked Ivy.

Rose rolled her eyes round and round.

'Oh, for God's sake, Ivy. Everyone knows what heavy metal is.'

She raised her hand above her head and rapped on the wall.

Nothing happened.

'Aren't you going to have your soup?'

'I changed my mind.'

'Look, darling, are you having problems? Not just worrying about Mother. Real problems.'

A dribble of mayonnaise escaped from the sandwich and smeared itself below Ivy's lower lip.

'What makes you think I'm having problems? Why should I have problems?'

'Most people do, at some stage in their lives. I mean it's quite normal for people to have problems.'

I'm not doing this very well, she thought.

The long silence was filled with heavy metal. It seemed as if the inhabitant of Room 103 was edging the volume up, little by little.

Some poor mad creature, Rose thought, drowning everything with impossible noise.

She rapped on the wall again.

Nothing happened.

I might kill someone, if this goes on much longer, she thought.

'Taking pills doesn't solve problems,' she said at last.

She reached out and picked up the telephone.

She dialled reception.

'It depends on the problems, Sister Cleverclogs,' said Ivy.

'Reception. Can I help you?'

'Would it be possible to ask whoever is in room number 103 to turn down the volume.'

'I beg your pardon?'

She held the receiver against the wall for a moment, then spoke into it again.

'Hear that? That's room 103 playing heavy metal. I have not paid for heavy metal. Either you ask whoever it is to stop or you find us another room. This is intolerable.'

'I'll do what I can, madam.'

Rose put the telephone down.

'See, she knows what heavy metal is. I can tell you something, this wouldn't happen in the Shelbourne.'

Rose laughed, then she took a drink.

Ivy slumped in her chair with mayonnaise on her chin.

The wine tasted of heavy metal. Rose remembered the taste from the days of her extreme youth; the bottles of Algerian plonk, liable to make you go blind or incapacitate you, and which always left you the next day with a clanging hangover that promised to stay with you for ever. It had in fact stayed with her for about three years.

She put the glass down and decided to drink no more of it.

She thought for a brief, uneasy moment of Joe and the puce dress and his hands pulling at her out in the garden as the dazzling bride danced to the beat of the local dance band, swirling her long white dress and smiling her happiness to all the friends and relations gathered for the happy occasion.

Catch of the year. Christ!

She cleared her throat.

'Is it Joe?' she asked, taking the bull by the horns.

Ivy shook her head.

'What do you mean, Joe? There's nothing the matter with Joe. Joe's fine. I'm fine. It's what I say, Rose. I want you to come home. I want you and Mother to be ... to be ... We were also brought up to be dutiful, and I don't believe that you are fulfilling your duty as a daughter ...'

'Just cut the crap. I have told you again and again that I'm not going down there. Mother slung me out seventeen years ago and I'm not going back. I'll go to her funeral, if that makes you happy.'

I will dance on her grave. A pavane, dignified and sorrowful. That should surprise them all, family, clergy, and the townspeople of Tuam.

And Joe.

She leant towards her sister and touched her knee gently.

'Why should we quarrel? We have no need to quarrel.'

The music stopped suddenly and they were both surprised by silence.

'Hallelujah,' said Rose. 'I don't suppose I have to explain that word to you, anyway.'

Ivy smiled bleakly and took another sandwich from the plate.

'Are the children all well? How are they doing at school?'

Uncontentious conversation seemed appropriate.

'Peter goes to college next autumn.'

'Is he that old? How time—'

She stopped herself in the nick of time.

'And Geraldine?'

'You'd like her. She's just like you at the same age.'

I hope not. I really hope not. I wouldn't wish that on anyone.

'A bit of a tearaway,' Ivy added.

'Is that what I was?'

'I think that's what they call it nowadays. She's not too keen on authority.'

'Ah, yes. You should send them over to stay in London sometime. I'd like that. We could have some fun together.'

'I thought of asking you last year if you'd have them for a week or two, but Joe . . . well, money was tight.'

'Money was tight? Come off it. Joe must make a fortune.'

'Hard-earned money is not meant to be thrown around. I manage well. He comments on that from time to time.'

'That's nice of him.'

'There is absolutely no need for you to be sarcastic.'

Ivy poured some more wine into her glass.

Rose watched her.

'That stuff is foul. I wouldn't drink any more of it if I were you.'

'And leave half a bottle?' Ivy looked incredulous.

'I'm paying. I can do what I like. After all, you're leaving your soup. You've got mayonnaise on your chin.'

Ivy rubbed at her chin with a finger.

Her hands were neat. Neat rings on the appropriate finger, nails neat and shining. A gold watch was clasped neatly round her wrist.

'It seems all right to me,' she said. 'I'm going to finish it, even if you won't help.'

'Suit yourself. You ought to take care, though, if you're on medication.'

'They're only pills for anxiety. I think it's the change, you know. My age. All that. Perfectly normal.'

There was a long silence between them.

Ivy sipped at her drink.

'I just wanted to see you,' she said eventually. 'Sometimes, I miss you.'

'That's nice. Thank you.'

'It's odd though, isn't it. We never had time to become friends. I thought that after Father's funeral you might come back from time to time.'

Rose shook her head.

'He came over to see me, you know. About once a year. Just fleeting visits.'

Ivy looked astonished.

'Father went over to London to see you? Did Mother know?'

'He never said. I shouldn't think so, though. White lies. She never thought that white lies mattered. Don't you remember that? He didn't come specially to see me of course. I just got incorporated into Anglican business from time to time. It was good. He used to come to dinner in my flat. We would drink wine and talk about a raft of things. Never home. Not a word about home passed our lips. That's why I came back for his funeral. I don't think I would have otherwise. He was a love. I loved him. I used to cry like mad after he left.'

She looked at her sister's face, and watched her considering this information.

'I really don't think you should tell Mother,' Rose said after a long silence. 'Just in case that's what's on your mind.'

'I haven't the faintest intention of telling Mother. I wouldn't want her upset.'

'Perish the thought. He was a love. He also believed in white lies.'

'I want you to tell me why you left, just disappeared like that. You upset them both so much. We were all so worried. It was a terribly cruel thing to do. Did you never give a thought to Mother and Father? How they felt? How desperate with anxiety they were?'

'Mother told you she was desperate with anxiety?'

'Of course.'

Rose leaned her head against the wall and laughed.

'I think the world is a better place when we don't know everything about each other. I believe in legitimate secrets.'

'Well, I need to know.' Ivy got unsteadily to her feet. 'I really think you owe it to me to tell me what happened between yourself and Mother.' She crossed the room and opened her case. 'It may have some relevance to the decisions I have to make with regards to what remains of her life.' She took her sponge bag out of the case and a pink satin nightdress. 'Decisions that you refuse to have any part in. I don't understand you at all, Rose, really I don't.' She went towards the bathroom. 'I am going to get ready for bed.'

She sounded like Miss Morphy. I am now leaving the room, Rose, and when I come back I want you to decline the future tense of the verb 'to think' for me. *Cogitare*. To think.

Ivy went into the bathroom and closed the door.

Rose pulled her pillows into a more comfortable position behind her neck and thought about white lies.

From somewhere a little tremor of air brushed her body. It ran from her bare ankles up, stirring her silk wrap and then touching her face, like a soft cool breath.

So Peter was just about to go to college, she thought.

The early summer breath had touched her back then, through the open window of her bedroom. That would have been just a few days after Peter was born. Doves had been murmuring under the eaves ... pigeons, they really were, but she used to like to lie in bed and think of them as doves as they crooed and chuckled. The mist lifting from the fields seemed also to veil her room. Nothing shone. The room faced west so she never experienced the morning sun tinting her possessions with colour.

I suppose I have to think this all again, she thought.

Mother was right, facts get forgotten, only the memory of hate remains.

I suppose I have to remember the truth in order to continue telling white lies. But maybe the time for lies was over now? Big, big question mark there.

Her bedroom had been high up at the back of the house, an attic, with dark corners and a high-pitched ceiling. Her clothes, she remembered, had hung round the walls like tapestries and the previous day's jeans and shirt were thrown over the back of her skewbald rocking horse.

She had heard the sound of a car crackling into the yard

three floors below, and, in the morning stillness, the scrape of the back door.

Joe.

What had he been up to?

She had presumed it was Joe.

Not visiting the hospital at this hour of the morning, that was for sure.

Night out with the lads? Celebrating the birth of his son?

Perhaps.

Perhaps not.

When the cat's away having kittens, the mice will play.

'We will mind Joe for you while you're in hospital, won't we, Rosie?'

Fait accompli.

Her mother had loved Joe.

Probably still did. No. Be fair. A certain distaste for him must have crept into her mind and never left.

She heard again in her head the creak of the back stairs that led uncarpeted up to her room and to the room next door which had been given over temporarily to Joe.

I wonder what happened to the rocking horse? she thought. It also used to creak as it galloped on the polished wooden floor.

I suppose Ivy took it for the children when they were small.

A slight noise had made her turn her head from the window.

Joe had been standing in her doorway.

'Waiting for me?' His voice was slurred.

She grabbed at the bedclothes and pulled them up tight over her.

'Pretty Rose.' He stepped carefully across the floor, needing silence. 'Kind Rose, waiting up for me.'

'Go to bed, Joe. It's almost morning.'

'All in good time,' he said.

He ripped the bedclothes out of her hands and stood for a moment looking down at her.

She tried to cover herself with her small hands.

'Pretty Rose,' was all he said and then he fell on her.

She beat at his face with her hands. She beat at his hot breath with her hands.

She tried to burst her way through the bottom of the bed. She tried to scream, but the scream that she had inside her wouldn't come out of her throat. It was stuck there like a boulder, hurting her as she tried to push it out into the open.

It took hardly any time.

The room was still washed with blue mist.

The pigeons still chuckled when he pushed himself up from the bed. He looked down at her and laughed.

'There you are, sister. That's what it's all about. I know all teenage girls are dying of curiosity. Now you know. For God's sake stop that snivelling and be your age. You should thank me. Yes, indeed you should.'

Unsteadily he headed for the door. He turned towards her as he opened it, pressing a finger against his lips.

'We wouldn't want to wake Mummy and Daddy. We wouldn't want to upset them. Think about Mummy and Daddy. Think about Ivy and the darling little baby.'

He was gone.

She had heard him moving in the next door room; the bed creaking as he threw his substantial weight onto it, his shoes dropping onto the wooden floor.

Ivy's voice called from the bathroom.

'Rose, I can hear a cat.'

'Don't be silly.'

The door opened and Ivy came out in her dressing gown, toothbrush in hand.

'I promise you. A cat miaouwed.'

She opened the wardrobe and peered in.

'It's all that wine,' Rose said.

'I tell you . . . shhh. Listen.' She held up the toothbrush. 'There it is again. I told you. A cat.'

'It must be out in the passage.'

'It sounded like it was in the bathroom with me.'

'Whatever happened to the rocking horse?'

Ivy went back into the bathroom and Rose could hear her rinsing out her mouth.

'Do you think I should ring reception?' Ivy called.

She came out of the bathroom shiny with scrubbing.

'What on earth for?'

'The cat. Maybe it's trapped somewhere. It sort of sounded trapped.'

'I wouldn't worry. It's probably the hotel cat, going about its legitimate business.'

Ivy pulled back the bedclothes and got into bed.

'The old rocking horse. I haven't thought about it for years. The kids used to love it when they were small. We sold it a couple of years ago.'

'You sold it! That was my rocking horse.'

'Mother gave it to the kids. It must have been after she and Father left the Rectory and went to the Deanery. Yes. Just after Geraldine was born. What use was a rocking horse to them?'

'It was mine.'

'It was ours, not just yours. You always had a tendency to say that things were yours. I remember that. We sold it . . . to some friend of Joe's in the furniture business. I think he gave us quite a lot of money for it. They're very hard to find these days, very desirable too. Especially those old ones. Anyway, what would you want with a rocking horse?'

'It just came into my mind. I used to keep my clothes on it.'

'Silly.'

She arranged herself comfortably, leaning on one elbow, facing Rose, as indeed she had done from time to time in younger, less complicated days.

In the bleak hotel light Rose could see the dark circles beneath her eyes and the tired skin stretched over her cheekbones.

Joe had a lot to answer for.

Ivy suddenly stretched out a hand across the gap between the beds.

'Tell me,' she said.

'What?'

'Tell me why you left home.'

Her fingers were cold on Rose's wrist.

Fuck, thought Rose. Oh, fuck.

That morning Rose had waited in her room until the house was silent. Father had gone to a diocesan meeting in Tuam; Joe had hurled himself out of bed and down the stairs, and finally driven himself off to work, shouting exuberant good-byes to her mother as he drove out of the yard.

Then she had moved. She had taken the sheets off her bed and folded them neatly and put them in the laundry basket out on the landing.

She had had a bath.

She had cried.

Finally she had washed away her tears and she had gone down the back stairs into the kitchen.

Mother had been making a sponge cake.

Bowls and beaters and the linen flour bag were spread on the kitchen table.

Once you start making a sponge cake you cannot stop. That's a well-known fact.

She had listened to what Rose was saying, her face without expression.

She hadn't stopped beating the egg whites. They stood up in the bowl like shining minarets.

When Rose finished speaking she watched in silence as her mother folded the whites into egg yolks and the flour. She took two cake tins from the press and filled them with the mixture. Then she walked across the kitchen and put them in the oven of the old black range. She stood looking down at the floor for a moment and then wiped her hands on her apron. She walked slowly back to the table, as if she didn't really want to get there. Rose thought that as she watched her.

'Is this true?' she had asked, at last.

Tears began to bubble again out of Rose's eyes.

'Of course it's true.'

Her mother sighed and sat down.

'I only ask because sometimes children invent these stories for reasons of their own.'

'I have invented nothing and I'm not a child. I'm seventeen. This man has . . .'

Her mother had put a hand across the table and taken hold of Rose's hand.

'He is your sister's husband. I am trying to think very clearly. Please believe that. We have to tread very carefully here.'

'He didn't tread carefully. Why the hell should I?'

'Language,' said her mother.

Rose put her head down on the kitchen table and began to cry.

Her mother touched her hair for a moment.

'You're going to have to pull yourself together, dear. Your father mustn't get to hear of this . . . or indeed Ivy. She's just had a baby, after all. We don't want her to be upset. I think . . . He is, after all, her husband.' She looked down at the long scrubbed table as she thought.

'Do you know how I feel? Don't you care how I feel?'

Rose had spoken the words very softly and she didn't know whether her mother heard them or not. She certainly gave no signs of having heard them.

'I think it has to be a secret, just between you and me and . . .'

'Bloody Joe.'

'Language.'

The word had been spoken automatically.

'We will have to put it away into the back of our minds. Forget, in fact, if to do such a thing is possible. Yes, yes, of course it is possible to forget. We must think about your father. Sometime soon, he hopes to be made a dean. I don't think this . . .' She didn't think it was necessary to finish the sentence.

She pushed back her chair and stood up.

'I'm going to telephone to Aunt Molly in London. I really do not want your father to know about this. I will have to

. . . to . . . White lies. Rose, white lies are sometimes the only solution. You must go at once and pack. The sooner we get you out of here, the better.'

'Do you mean to say that you are throwing me out of the house? I have done nothing wrong, Mother. I have done nothing wrong,' Rose had screamed at her mother across the bleached table. 'You can't send me to London. I won't go.'

'You will go. You cannot stay here with . . .'

'Bloody Joe. Why don't you throw him out? Why don't you send him packing? Why don't you . . . ?'

'Go and pack. We'll have to catch the lunchtime train.'

'Mother . . .'

'You know you like Molly. I will have to tell her and then she and I will arrange everything. It will be all right. You will see the sense of all this in time. I promise you that. In time.'

'I will never come back. If you do this to me, I will never come back. I promise you that.'

Her mother had left the room.

'I will never come back.' She had shouted the words then, all those years ago, just a couple of days after Peter had been born.

'I will never go back,' she said now in quite a matter-of-fact voice to Ivy.

She took Ivy's cold fingers into her warm hand as she spoke.

'You haven't told me why? Why not?'

'Mother and I just had a row about . . . well, some boy I fancied. She didn't approve. So . . .'

'That's not a good enough reason for you to stay away all this time.'

'She said a lot of wicked things.'

'I don't believe you, Rose. She's not a wicked woman. She

probably didn't say any more than you deserved. Family rows are only storms in teacups.'

'We have to agree to differ.'

'We've always differed. Haven't we?'

'I suppose so. We haven't much in common really. You were right when you said that.' Rose laughed suddenly. 'I know one thing we do have in common.'

'What's that?'

Rose drew herself up until her back was flat against the wall. She threw her head back and began to sing.

'"O be joyful in the Lord, all ye lands; serve the Lord with gladness and come before his presence with a song.

'"Be ye sure that the Lord he is God: it is He that has made us and not we ourselves; we are His people and the sheep of His pasture."'

Her voice was sweet.

She hadn't given a thought to those words for years and now they filled her head.

In the next room someone had turned on the music again. Rose felt the vibration of it all the way up her back.

She smiled at Ivy.

'Remember that?'

'Of course I remember. I still sing in the choir. Geraldine does too. She has a nice voice. Like you. You always sang better than I did. I remember that too. That used to annoy me. I bet you didn't know that. How annoyed I was. I think of that sometimes when I hear Geraldine sing.'

'Promise me you'll mind her well.'

'Of course I will. What a strange thing to say.'

Rose held her sister's hand tight.

The music thudded louder from next door.

'I will not come back, Ivy. I can't do that. Mother

understands, you know, even if you think she doesn't. I'll write to her, though. I'll write her a long, long letter. Chatty. And enquiring. I'll enquire about her. I will show a dutiful interest in her. If that will make you happy. Will that make you happy?'

Before Ivy could answer, Rose pulled her sister over onto her bed.

'Let's sing. Fortissimo. Let's show Mr Heavy Metal a thing or two.'

She threw her head back.

'"O go your way into His gates with thanksgiving, and into His courts with praise". '

To her surprise, Ivy joined in, fortissimo, as demanded.

Both their voices were strong and clear.

'"Be thankful unto him, and speak good of His Name."'

Ivy wriggled up the bed and they sat side by side, their backs against the wall, the heavy metal thudding through their bones.

Father had always said, sing loud, so that your voices may be heard, and she had always laughed at him. Sing loud now. We can never understand, but we can sing loud.

'"For the Lord is gracious, His mercy is everlasting: and His truth endureth from generation to generation.

'"Glory be to the Father and to the Son and to the Holy Ghost; as it was in the beginning, is now and ever shall be, world without end. Amen."'

103

NO PETS PLEASE

Ken Brogan stood at the reception desk with his suitcase and his ghetto blaster on the floor beside him, looking at the sign saying: NO PETS. He smiled right at it, then turned his back to the desk while the receptionist was still dealing with another guest. A woman was being offered a room with a king-sized double bed. Brogan winked. The idea of a double bed sounded so inviting, the first time he'd heard the actual words in ages.

He looked the woman up and down. She was a little older, perhaps in her forties, but still in good nick, he noticed, as she walked away towards the lift.

Brogan was cool and patient, but also a little anxious to get settled in. When the receptionist finally slid his credit card through the machine and gave him the key to his room there was a distinct sound of a cat. The receptionist looked across the counter at his luggage. 'I'm afraid we don't allow any pets,' was written all over her eyes, though she was reluctant to make any direct accusations. He didn't look like the type of man who had a cat. And to avoid any further suspicion, he just picked up his ghetto blaster, as if to indicate that a portable CD player was the only kind of pet he could live with.

He was just in time to get into the lift with the older woman. He stuck his foot into the doors at the last minute. 'You can't escape that easily, missus,' he seemed to say, and the woman inside instinctively reached out her hand as though she was hitting a panic button, trying to keep the doors open, or closed, who knows? Like she would prefer to go up in the lift alone. It was a moment of high tension, where she appeared to have made a clean getaway, only to be caught at the last moment. Brogan's Adidas sneaker was wedged into the gap. The doors struggled with the obstacle; that moment of electromechanical indecision before they were prised open again and the man with the ghetto blaster stood grinning at her.

'Nearly lost my leg there,' he said to her as he stepped inside. She smiled nervously but said nothing.

He placed the suitcase and the ghetto blaster on the floor of the lift and took out his phase tester. Just to put the woman at ease, he tapped it against the control panel, then listened to it like a tuning fork. Brogan had made certain discoveries like this over the years: it relaxed people when they realized he was an electrician. A man to be trusted. The cheerful type. People liked the sincerity of simple things like a pencil stub lodged on a carpenter's ear; a measuring tape in a trouser pocket; peat moss on a gardener's hands. And Brogan liked to demonstrate the humble icons of his own trade. That genuine, handsome look of an honest spark, humming and tapping a screwdriver on the door of the lift.

The woman turned her back on him and looked at herself in the mirror. What did I tell you? Brogan thought to himself. It was clear that she fancied him. Though in a kind of demure way. There was something deeply closeted about her, like she had just been to a funeral or something. It wasn't helped by the fact that the faint mewling of the cat came back again at that very moment. Made Brogan look like one of those workmen who did lewd cat sounds into a woman's ear.

When the lift door opened, he picked up his gear and shot out, whistling as he walked along the corridor, looking for his room. He took one look back as he opened the door, just to get a vague idea what room the woman in the lift had taken.

Brogan locked the door of his room behind him, set up his ghetto blaster and tuned into a radio station. Then he opened the suitcase and let the cat out. So what if the woman in the lift had heard. The creature was now *in situ*, as they say; it leaped straight onto the window ledge and took up its position there, staring out at the river and the constant traffic along the quays.

'You're dead, mate,' Brogan said out loud to the cat. Then he looked around at the shabby room. There was a halo of grey fingerprints around the light switches. An essential B&B painting of cattle by the lakeside over the bed. Lime-green bedside lampshades. The decor in general was like a cross-breed between classic theatrical grandeur and sixties James Bond modernity.

Brogan took a shower. Sang along with the radio. He never sang an entire song, only a chorus line here and there which he remembered in advance but seldom timed right. Always came in early, or too late. *I'm gonna hold you till I die, till we both break down and cry.* As an electrician, he spent most of his day howling along like this. Occasionally making an impromptu Stratocaster out of a piece of cable casing, whenever the song demanded it. It didn't matter that he hadn't got a note in his head. As he got dressed and gelled his hair up into a little frozen surf at the top of his forehead he even did a little shuffle in front of the mirror, while the cat looked back from the window with the usual feline disdain. Brogan's dancing wasn't much better than his singing.

Wearing his Temple Bar T-shirt and his lucky leather jacket, collar turned up, Brogan was a man with a purpose. The inevitable phase tester in the inside pocket was a vital boost to his personality which would never be complete or fully prepared for action without it. He was ready to deal with any woman's fuseboard, so to speak. And he himself was fully wired to specification, according to Electricity Board guidelines.

But he would first have to deal with the cat. So he went downstairs again and walked back into the lobby with a confident swagger, still whistling, smiling to himself as though he recalled some filthy joke. The hotel porter, an elderly man with a straight, ironing-board walk which was beginning to bend into a stoop with age, was coming through from the bar carrying a tray with coffee and whiskey.

'I'll take that for you, Simon,' the manager of the hotel said, taking the tray off him. The porter was left standing there in the lobby, a little stunned.

'Fire away so.'

Brogan spoke to the receptionist. She rang the kitchen and they turned out to be a bit awkward about his special gastronomic requirements. He wanted a plain meal of fish sent up to the room. None of that hollandaise sauce rubbish. She said there was no fish on the menu. So Brogan took out a fiver and discreetly approached the porter who said he would look into it. Mission Impossible. Big undercover operation in the kitchen while Brogan went to make a phone call. He stood at the public phone with his legs crossed into a leisurely X, elbow against the wall, looking straight at the revolving doors of the hotel. A woman answered the phone and he allowed a moment of silence to elapse before he spoke.

'Moggi, Moggi, Moggi,' he said. The woman on the other end of the line went into hysterics. Screaming and bellowing, while Brogan smiled at the passing guests with great satisfaction. Then he put down the receiver.

The porter came back and spoke in a whisper, proud to pass on the good news. He had been able to twist the chef's arm. Why all the shaggin' subterfuge? Brogan wondered. What was the big deal? But Brogan understood the tortured politics of the Irish kitchen and quietly asked him if he could also bring up a jug of milk, and a bowl. Again there was that look of suspicion, as though the porter was about to make some recorded announcement about pets. Brogan had obviously tipped him well enough, because there was nothing said about it. The meal would arrive in about twenty minutes.

Time enough to have a quick drink. Brogan marched right into the bar and stood beside a man contemplating his pint. He ordered a tequila and smiled at the man beside him. Brogan was not the type to start talking about the weather or build up gradually into a conversation. He took it for granted that this man was on for a chat and stuck out his hand.

'Ken is the name,' he said. 'Ken Brogan.'

'Ben,' the other man said reluctantly, shaking hands. He seemed to be a little introverted. Lost for company maybe. Perhaps he was the solitary type who needed to be taken out of himself.

'Ken and Ben! That's a good one,' Brogan said, generating

a strained camaraderie. He was being extra-cheerful. After all, Brogan was the communicative type. Ken and Ben. It looked like they could have a bit of fun together.

'Come 'ere, Ben. Do you think people in Ireland talk too much?' Brogan asked. It was a serious question, because he wanted to know this man's opinion. Brogan was being friendly, like.

'I suppose so,' the man agreed politely. He was acting as a kind of spokesman for himself. Well done, Ben. You can talk. Jesus, if you said any more, they'd say you were definitely bordering on the verbose.

Brogan went on to explain that he listened to the radio all day. He was an electrician. Pulled out his phase tester to prove it. Tapped Ben on his shoulder and said he was a 'radio freak' actually. Never watched TV. Never read a newspaper in his life. Only radio.

'Do you ever listen to *Liveline*?' he asked. 'Marian Finucane?'

'What?'

The other man shifted around on his bar stool. Brogan was certain that Ben was in the same frame of mind. He didn't look like the type who would waste his time listening to Marian Finucane gabbing on about nothing all day.

'It's some programme, that,' Brogan continued. 'I can take any kind of junk, but not *Liveline*. I mean, I listen to it nearly every day. But she drives me crazy. All this "Oooh" and "Aaah" and "Oh my" and "Mind you . . ." It's all so fucking self-righteous.' He looked Ben over. 'What do you think of her?'

'She's all right,' Ben spluttered.

Brogan was taken aback a little. Was Ben going to start to

arguing with him? As far as he was concerned it was a cut and dried issue.

'D'you listen to her?' he asked.

'No,' Ben replied.

'Do you know what I think?'

'I've got to meet somebody,' Ben said, becoming increasingly agitated. But Brogan ignored this last remark and just went on to deliver his message as directly and succinctly as possible; the way a man liked it.

'She should keep her nose out of other people's business,' he said. It was important to be honest about things like that. Straight up. If Ken and Ben were going to rip into a few pints together, then they had to get that Marian Finucane business cleared up to begin with.

There was a puzzled look on Ben's face at this point. He was suddenly acting like he was sitting beside a psychopath. He started looking around for the bar staff, coughing for help. You'd think Brogan had uttered the most unspeakable blasphemy. Whereas, he was merely giving this man the benefit of his honest opinion, that was all. There was no need to look so terrified. Had he misjudged this man? There wasn't going to be a Ken and Ben drinking partnership after all. Because, after first encouraging him, Ben was now basically telling him to fuck off, in as gentle as possible a manner. I happen to admire the arse off Marian Finucane, he was saying. To me, she's as hip as a box of KVI marshmallows. So piss off, you ignorant little electrician. Who asked for your opinion anyway?

Brogan was holding on to Ben's bar stool. It was a sign of camaraderie which was now going badly wrong and had already become an invasion of privacy.

Ben almost fell off his chair. You'd think he'd just been shot in the back, the way his leg went into spasm and his arse buckled out to one side. There was that stunned look on his face. His mouth looked like an exit wound, and his eyes bore a victim's look of disbelief, as though he was telling himself he was immortal and couldn't possibly die.

He pushed back his bar stool. Brogan let go and it began to topple over, in slow motion, hitting the floor with a thud that made people look up and think these two men at the bar were having a speechless contest over a chair. For a moment, they both looked down as though it was a special chair, over which they were ready to fight to the death. Ben's bar stool, like the name of a big movie. Then Ben walked away.

'Jesus,' a woman said as she skipped over it. She was carrying a round of drinks and laughing as though she'd cleared the last fence in a steeplechase.

Fair enough. Brogan knows when he's not wanted. He drank down his tequila and orange juice and left to go back upstairs. He wasn't going to waste any more time drinking in the company of a closet *Liveline* fan with a styrofoam brain.

On the way up, Brogan made another phone call. 'Moggi, Moggi, Moggi.' Once again, he listened to the hysterical woman on the other end of the phone. Again the smug smile of a deviant radiating through the lobby.

Back in his room, with the cat safely put away in the wardrobe, Brogan opened the door and allowed the porter to place the tray down on the table. He locked the door after him and let the cat out again for a hangman's meal of fish, mashed potato and peas. Real College of Catering stuff. With sputum-coloured custard trifle congealing in a glass bowl. Mogs seemed more than happy with it.

Brogan turned up the ghetto blaster and started dancing again. While the cat was lapping up the dried-out plaice, he took a hammer from the suitcase and did a jig with it, holding it up in the air like a dancing warrior. He then kneeled down and put it up to the cat's head, just to see how easy it would be to brain this animal. Splat! Break his lowry arse with a quick clatter, while he was sniffing around the custard. How to execute a cat, by Ken Brogan. Hammer horror. But Moggi, the cute hoor, jumped away. As though it knew there was something odd about a hammer in a hotel bedroom. You're not fooling me, dancing around like some kind of DIY shaman. You think you can soften me up with a piece of leathery old sole on the bone and then sneak up on me with that Iron Age weapon.

Suspicious fucker. It would never work. Brogan would end up having to chase the cat all around the bed. After the hammer episode the cat lost its appetite and wouldn't eat any more, unless Brogan was at least three yards away on the far side of the room. So the idea of sneaking up with a black refuse bag wasn't going to work either. There are many ways to kill a cat, Brogan contemplated. But he didn't really want the mess. On the other hand, the cat had it coming, and he might get pleasure out of cutting Moggi up into four hundred and fifty-two pieces with his phase tester. Hang all the bits out to dry around the room, with some of the peas and mashed potato mixed in to enhance the aesthetics. The name 'Moggi' daubed on the wall in custard. A proper Ballymalloe murder mystery. A real Hannibal Lecter job, with cat blood smeared around his mouth to pretend he did it all with his own teeth. Some of the cat's vital organs missing. And not flushed down the toilet either, if you get the drift.

Oh my goodness! Oh dear! How about that now, Marian?

How would you like that for a phone call on *Liveline*? Listener on line one. Brogan the cat killer. That would give you something to talk about and express revulsion at. You could have a moral Mardi Gras on that one, with all the cat lovers in the country weeping kitten tears on the radio.

Celine Dion started shaking her tonsils out like a dust rag over the ghetto blaster. Singing like she was at the doctor's and told to say: 'Aaagh.' It sounded like a really bad case of laryngitis, Brogan thought, as he looked out across the city, at the river and the railway station. The lights of cars flashed at him as they came across the bridge. He could not see water, but he knew the river was flowing by silently. The big coronary artery of the city.

Of course, why not? The river was Brogan's friend. That was the obvious solution. Why had he not thought of it before? So he put the hammer back into the suitcase. Looked around for some other heavy object and found a massive marble ashtray, the size of a toilet seat almost, on a coffee table. The weight of it! He placed it into the suitcase and stood back with a grin. Perfect. Everything could be done without any of the mess.

There was a knock on the door. It took a moment or two before Brogan could restore a sense of trust in the cat; he stroked it a half-dozen times and then put it away in the wardrobe again. He opened the door and found the porter outside telling him they had a complaint about the music. Some of the guests at the hotel were sensitive to high frequencies. Celine Dion gave them altitude sickness.

'Oh, right, boss. No problem,' Brogan agreed with a nod. Then he looked back and waved at the ghetto blaster as though he was telling it to hush. He was more than eager to show regard for other guests. In fact, he was all 'regard' and went over to switch the lofty larynx right down.

'Will I take the tray?' the porter asked.

'Oh right. Why not?'

'Was that OK for you?'

'Dead on. Thanks, boss. I love a bit of fish. My compliments to the chef and all that.'

But there was something odd about the fact that the cutlery was still neatly wrapped up in the serviette. Neither the mash nor the peas had been touched. In fact the mash had developed a protective outer skin or shell-like covering. The peas were hard and gaunt as gallstones. And the silicone membrane of custard had only been partially removed from the trifle. The porter took away the tray without a word. Nobody was forcing anyone to eat their peas here. And it had nothing to do with him if people were savages. If a guest wanted to eat fish with his bare hands and lick the custard while listening to Celine Dion or Mary Black getting sick on the radio, that was his prerogative. As long as he kept it down and didn't freak out the other guests.

When the porter had his back turned, and Brogan was about to close the door, there was another cry of help from inside the wardrobe. The porter looked back. It could have been a crucial junction in the cat's destiny. A small humanitarian initiative on the part of the porter might have put a swift end to this delicate hostage saga. But he ignored the desperate plea and walked away, leaving the cat to his own fate. In any case, although there was no smell of alcohol, Brogan got the impression that the porter had been drinking.

Brogan let cat out again, placed it on his lap and started stroking it, building up a doomed intimacy with this animal on death row. Then he made another phone call and the hysterical woman answered once more.

'Listen,' Brogan growled down the phone. The woman went silent. He placed the receiver up to the cat and allowed the purring sound to travel down the line. This time it was the woman on the other end of the line who said: 'Moggi, Moggi, Moggi,' in a high-pitched whine, before a man's voice suddenly broke in and started shouting. The cat gave Brogan a look of deep mistrust, as though it suspected Brogan of planning something really slick with the telephone wire. Like wrap the curly cable around its lowry neck. But Brogan hadn't thought of that one and he just put the cat back in the wardrobe. He listened to the male voice barking on the phone for a while, alternating occasionally with the hysterical female voice, the cat answering back plaintively from inside the wardrobe, until he finally hung up and went downstairs again.

The porter was hovering around the reception. The bar looked more populated, but Brogan didn't feel like another one-way conversation about *Liveline*. He didn't see any women with flush-mounted sockets either. So he decided to go over and talk to the porter.

'Come 'ere, when does the nightclub open up?'

The porter looked at his watch and said it should be starting up any minute.

'Sounds OK to me,' Brogan said. 'Nothing else to do with myself, so I might as well.'

The hint of resignation seemed to hit a chord with the porter. He didn't look too busy himself either, standing with his hands behind his back in a kind of 'talk to me' stance. He looked a little troubled, as though he had been dealt a bad deal. As though he was sceptical about the whole world, but still keeping an open mind on the concept of happiness. Nothing was going to change dramatically in the porter's life at this stage. Perhaps he had taken a wrong turn somewhere, because he seemed to be ready to withdraw from life altogether and scuttle back into his little hatch behind the reception if it wasn't for the possibility a conversation might put his own biography in the shade and reassure him that other people had flawed lives too. If you've recently been cheated, then I'm happy to have a chat with you, he seemed to be saying. As long as you don't talk about soccer or snooker. He had NO SPORT stamped on his weathered forehead.

'Do I look like I would talk about fucking football?' Brogan wanted to say. 'Do I look like some total prick who would start spouting off all that masculine shite about Alan Shearer not being able to score goals because he forgot to remove the condom?' Because Brogan was on a different board game altogether. He was the sensitive type: aware; in touch with the feminine side of his nature. Ready to go directly to the heart of the matter and talk about feelings, relationships, mucous membranes and multiple orgasms.

'I'm in between places,' Brogan ventured. 'Might have to stay a few nights before I can sort myself out. Got turned out of my flat, like.'

'That's a bit of a bummer,' the porter agreed.

'Yeah. She threw me out,' Brogan said and then laughed, holding out his hands in supplication. 'Took in a new boy and threw me out. What can you do?'

It was Brogan's way of connecting with people. Laugh at yourself. Offer them the worst possible news about yourself as a show of submission and humble friendship. The loss-leader approach. Stands to reason in a small country like

Ireland that if you tell somebody you're doing well, and that you're happy and well-adjusted and on the way up in the world, they'll fucking hate you. Success is a big turn-off. Brogan's tactical strategy was to wear the smile of the meek and announce that he was a happy loser. Not a whiner, mind you, but a bearer of precious intimate gifts in order to demonstrate that he was no threat to anyone. The self-deprecating protocol.

Of course, Brogan was ready to walk away if the porter didn't want to hear any more. But the porter could not ignore such an honest signal of fellow male distress.

'There's no justice in love and war,' he responded with total allegiance. The hotel porter of perpetual succour.

It was a perfectly neutral thing to say. It showed the porter's concern without taking sides. It was a dodgy matter, entering into domestic disputes of any kind as a third party. No point in stepping into the untamed world of other people's personal squabbles without marking off the escape routes first. For Brogan, however, it was exactly the right answer. There was no justice in love and war.

'You're dead right, man,' Brogan agreed, looking at the porter like he was a prophet.

'Come 'ere. What's your poison?' he enquired. 'I'm just going up to the bar to get a drink. What'll you have?'

The porter looked around furtively.

'A drop of vodka. No ice, thanks!' he whispered and then nodded towards his hatch. 'I've plenty of tonic in there.'

Brogan went to the bar and ordered a double vodka, and another double tequila and orange for himself. There was a nice crowd in the bar now. Ben, the garrulous geek he had spoken to earlier, was still wandering around like a lost soul, probably waiting for the disco to open. Back out in the lobby,

Brogan gave the porter his drink and introduced himself. The porter's name was Simon. And in no time at all, they were talking about their lives, feeling, relationships, the whole shaggin' lot.

'Come 'ere,' Brogan said. 'What do you think of cats?'

That was a sudden question. A very tricky one at that. How could you come up with a committed answer that would suit the cat lover and the cat killer at the same time? Because there were only two types of people in the world: cat lovers and cat killers. As a porter you had to be careful to spot which was which, or steer a nebulous course along a middle line. Ireland hadn't held on to its neutrality for nothing. And the porter knew that the most neutral response was another question.

'What do I think about cats?'

'Cold creatures.' Brogan jumped in to the rescue. 'They give you nothing. You show them loads of affection. Best of food. Total devotion. And what do you get in return? Nothing.'

The porter still wasn't sure if these could be the sentiments of a disenchanted cat lover. He decided to cover himself and just said that a cat was her own boss, generally.

'If you don't mind me saying so,' Brogan continued bluntly, 'a cat doesn't give a fuck about you. A cat will use you and then turn around and walk away. A dog is different. A dog will lay down his life for you. Whereas a cat will take everything from you and then throw you out on your ear. Where's the loyalty in that?'

It was a sad state of affairs. No cat was to be trusted. By now, Brogan and the porter had reached a pinnacle of agreement on that one. And sooner or later, because Brogan had freely offered his most personal and deeply felt opinions, the porter knew he had to give something back in return. The gift of intimacy had to be reciprocated. In fact, the porter was going to do more than reciprocate, he was going to outdo Brogan in the happy doom stakes. So inevitably, he revealed that his job at the hotel was finished, because the hotel was being pulled down. It was only a matter of time now. Not that it made much difference in the long run, because it turned out that Simon had run into a bit of very bad luck lately. He had been struck down by the big C.

'I'm marked for demolition myself,' he said.

'Jesus! I'm sorry to hear that. The big C. Fucking hell, man. I thought I had problems.'

Brogan listened as the porter quietly spoke about his condition. He was composed and almost nonchalant about it. There was not much hope. What could you do except have a drink. The porter was sorry to talk about such morbid matters and urged Brogan to go ahead to the nightclub. Go and enjoy himself. Make the most of his life while he had the chance, and all that. But Brogan wouldn't go. He wasn't going to desert a dying confederate like this.

'Are you on the treatment?'

'Forget it. They more or less said there was no point. Sure, look at me.'

'That's outrageous. I'd get something done about it, Simon. Don't let them get away with it. Pressure them.'

'They're after giving me six months. A year, maybe at the most,' the porter said.

'Jesus. That's not fair, Simon.'

They approached the delicate subject of pain. And Brogan admitted he was a total coward when it came to the least mortification of the flesh. He was afraid of suffering, to be perfectly honest. He couldn't even endure a simple pain in the arse.

'Who cares about the pain,' the porter said stoically. Pain was all in the head. There was no point in worrying about it. That was the porter's outlook on life. No matter how long you had before the demolition team arrived, it was essential to make the most of life. An old man like Simon could pack more into a year than a lot of these young pups.

'I'm thinking of doing a degree,' he said.

'Fair play to you, Simon.'

But Brogan couldn't begin to fathom this level of humility and self-inflicted purgatory in the face of death. What was the point in enlightenment on your deathbed. Getting educated for the grave? Brogan would be demanding straightforward pleasure at that point. It would be all cream doughnuts. No more vegetables. A private bed in the hospice with gourmet junk food and the best of porn movies. Booze on tap and a steady stream of gorgeous nurses monitoring his temperature. Not to mention direct access to slow-releasing morphine. A degree in something like Irish history. Fucking hell. That was no joke.

'Go and live a hundred per cent while you can,' the porter advised.

Again he tried to urge Brogan to head on down to the nightclub. It even sounded for a moment like he was on a commission from the dungeon downstairs. Brogan was so moved by the porter's story that he could not head on to the nightclub without buying another round of drinks. More double vodkas and double tequilas. He stood his ground with the dying porter. Admired his courage. Hung around at the reception until he looked like he belonged to the doomed hotel staff himself. They were both getting drunk and were about to start singing in solidarity, any minute. If it wasn't for some of the older residents of the hotel passing by occasionally, they would have burst into 'Boulavogue'.

Brogan was touched by this meeting. When he finally moved on to Upstarts below, he was in a buoyant mood, ready to live life to the point of exhaustion. The nightclub was a bit of a kip, really, but it would do. Initially, he felt like telling the patrons how stupid they looked, dancing around. They were totally unaware of the porter upstairs and his private suffering. If only they could see themselves.

Some of them looked like they had been stung by a bee or bitten by a spider whose venom had given them a kind of accelerated dementia. Formula One category of dancing. They were not even looking at anyone, just buzzing away on some exotic fuel. Brogan wondered if there were any toxic substances around. He saw some shady individuals at the door. One of them wearing sunglasses in the darkness; it was a wonder he could see anything at all, if he wasn't totally blind.

Brogan found himself a place to roost at the bar, where he could place his glass and survey the club. It allowed him to make an assessment of the talent. He thought of going for a half tab of E. Not for himself, but for the cat upstairs. Brogan found alcohol perfectly adequate for his own needs. But it would be great crack to see how the cat would react to a designer drug like E or Special K. Maybe it would start romping out of control, chasing imaginary mice around the room all night, like Tom and Jerry cartoons till five in the morning – getting clobbered, flattened, electrocuted, blown up, scorched and dismembered, but rising up intact each time and asking for more, while the invisible mouse was leaning with his elbow against the skirting board, grinning and checking his fingernails.

Brogan spotted some other dancers who were more in the saloon car bracket. Three soft-tops who all looked like the Olympic swimmer Michelle Smith. For a moment, he thought he had overdone the tequila and was seeing everything in triplicate. The three Michelles were doing some kind of synchronized swimming to a rave beat. In separate lanes. No bathing caps. They all had frizzy, high-voltage blonde hair, and were joined by another young woman who had straight bronze hair and looked totally out of place. Brogan swaggered over and tried to join them, but got the instant rejection slip. Buzz off. Go and try the paddling pool. He didn't let that put him off, however, and performed an adventurous underwater shuffle in front of them. Splashing up a lot of bubbles and foam in the effort, to make it look like he had a medal or two himself. But they gazed at him with great concern. 'What in the name of Jesus are you trying to do to yourself?' they seemed to be asking. 'You'll only give yourself a groin injury that way.'

The three Michelles turned their backs. But that only encouraged Brogan even more, until they eventually had enough and just walked off the floor. It looked like they had gone back to pick up their towels and start drying each other's hair, muttering back at him from the poolside seats. 'You fucking loser, Brogan,' they appeared to say. 'You never won anything in your life. You couldn't even win a free car wash.' Everybody was staring at him as though his Bermudas were hanging off him and exposing his hairy bottom-line bum cleavage. Brogan persisted in the hope that the brunette would stay with him at least. 'Look, I've got the backside of an ostrich,' he was saying to her. 'My buttocks are made of

Sheffield steel.' And she was wearing a particularly nice leopardskin one-piece swimsuit – high leg and low back. But she soon deserted him as well, just when he was about to break the current record in treading water.

Brogan went back to the bar to refuel. How was he supposed to keep up with the E generation if he couldn't even impress the alco-pop girls? He was willing to give it another go. But why exert himself like that? Maybe he had picked the wrong style. Maybe he should have worn the leather jacket half off his shoulders and just kept walking forward and back, pointing enigmatically at the floor all the time as if he was trying to tell them something important. Cool. Less willing to smile. More inclined to remain mute and to utter only the essential statement. 'I've seen you guys before, but I can't tell you apart no more, . . . uh, uh . . . and how dare you call me a bore, because you're dancin' on my floor . . . uh, uh!'

What was the point?

Brogan decided to have another tequila. He sat down and thought about the porter upstairs, drinking neat vodka on his own in his little hatch behind the reception. Brogan was beginning to feel sorry for himself too, when a young woman came over to sit close to him at the bar. She seemed to be alone. Maybe she had appreciated his dancing, because she smiled right at him. And he soon found himself buying her a Remy Martin. No need to go through all that spontaneous training on the floor. In any case, it was companionship he wanted, not some great heart-and-lung romance, born out of heat and sweat.

She introduced herself as Collette. She was vague on what she did for a living. But she was sympathetic from the start and willing to listen to Brogan as he stirred his tequila with his screwdriver and talked about himself. He was fed up wiring sockets every day. But he didn't have enough guts to go back and do a degree or anything like that. And besides, his girlfriend had thrown him out and taken in another man. Some total clown with big pectorals and prime buttocks.

'You're not so bad yourself,' Collette reassured him, and he was grateful for that. She was willing to see him as a person in his own right. She had indicated that she fancied him for his mind, and not just his body. The horsepower of his buttocks didn't concern her. And what was more, she agreed with his opinions. Somehow, they were on the same wavelength, right from the start. Because he had asked her what she thought about *Liveline*, and she immediately said she never listened to it. She was rarely even up at that hour of the day. And all that moral outrage was a bit hard to take so early in the day. Oh my goodness! Oh dear!

They were a perfect match. She was even wearing a leather jacket, just like Brogan's. She said she would love to discuss the subject in greater depth, upstairs, if that suited him. The fact that she never listened to *Liveline* suddenly made it very tempting. She wasn't carrying any excess baggage.

It didn't bother him either when he discovered that he would have to pay Collette for her time. He could write it off as a donation or a once-off consultancy fee. He was willing to pay her twice as much, as long as she would agree with everything he said. And not argue or demand anything from him in return. Not sigh or threaten to leave him if he happened to say something that wasn't altogether politically correct. There was an immense purity in such a transaction. OK, money was power and all that, but this was an honest-to-God piece of late capitalism. It eliminated any notion of contest and allowed them to establish a set of preconditions. He didn't want any of this gold-medal honesty. It was such a relief not to have to hear the truth, for one night at least.

As Brogan walked back through the reception with Collette, he noticed the receptionist wiping blood from a man's nose. Who was it – only Ben, the man with the stryrofoam intellect. Somebody must have finally had no alternative but to give this asshole a decent smack in the nose.

Now he was bleeding his shaggin' DNA all over the hotel.

When they got to the room upstairs, Collette sat down on the bed. She took off her shoes and discreetly opened a button or two on her blouse, to show that she had a ring in her belly button. She was wearing a short black skirt and Brogan caught a glimpse of her red knickers as she lay back. He gave her all the pillows and made sure she was comfortable, ready to listen to him, with her legs straight out along the bed and her arms cradling her breasts. She was wearing an Affinity bra. She was full of affinity, in fact, and twiddled her red toenails in acknowledgement to every word as he walked up and down, talking. It was as though he was reading her a fairy tale.

'She went and phoned the radio,' Brogan finally revealed. 'Told them all about me.'

'Who?'

'My partner. My ex-partner. I know it was her. I'd know my own partner's voice on the radio. Don't you think? I swear. She told them everything.'

'Like what?'

'She said I was always trying to get her cat drunk. Whenever she was out of the house, I was meant to be trying everything in my power to turn the cat into an alcoholic, feeding it trifle and catfood marinated in stale Beck's.'

'And did you?'

'Collette, I ask you? Do I look like a man who would do such a thing?'

'No way! How could she even think that?'

'She also said I had no feelings. She had never met a man with less feelings than I had. She said I was a dirty dog and that I urinated on the cat. I swear. She accused me of pissing on her Moggi.'

'That's not right, calling anyone a dog,' Collette said. 'That's prejudice.'

'She said I had no feelings and no regard. Jesus, Collette, I've got regard coming out of my back pockets. I'm haemorrhaging regard.'

'Regard for what?' she asked.

Outside, they heard people going home. People from Upstarts arguing and laughing. Taxis left their motors running. Car doors banging. The night was over and the city was beginning to close down. The three Michelles and the brunette were going home. Nobody was going to see any medals tonight. And all the E generation were still buzzing to the point of collapse in the back of the taxis, twitching to keep their blood pressure down.

Collette looked at Brogan with great sympathy. She patted the duvet and told him to sit beside her, so she could stroke his arm and encourage him. What kind of ghoulish female had he been consorting with? He was better off without a woman like that. She was no good for him. He had done the right thing, running away. And now Collette was here to protect him. She was ready to give Miss Cat-Piss a stiletto in the forehead. Mud wrestling, lady boxing, you name it; she was ready to get into hand-to-hand combat on a perilous precipice to defend Brogan's honour. And suddenly, he felt elated at the thought of her going off to do battle on his behalf.

'What else did she say?'

'Jesus, there was a lot more. All kinds of things like me not cleaning up after shaving. Leaving stubble in the sink and stuff like that. It was she who left the stubble in the sink after shaving her cactus legs with my razor blades. I swear. And then she has the nerve to accuse me of leaving the sink looking like George Michael's face. With his plughole full of foam.'

'The wagon!'

'It was very hurtful.'

'Why did she have to phone the radio, though? That's what I can't understand. I mean, you didn't do anything to her?'

'I told her she looked sexy when she was angry. That's all. I was trying to be nice to her. She was in the bedroom, with the cat in her lap, and I told her she looked great. I told her I'd love to be her cat. And she told me to piss off. She was still raging about the sink argument and the more I said I wanted her, the more angry she got.'

'What happened then?'

'She blew her top. Ape-shit. Total hair-loss. Went into a great sulk and next day, she phoned up Marian Finucane on *Liveline*.'

'The bitch!'

'I know. It's outrageous. And I don't care what she said any more. I know I'm a loser. I'd be the first to admit it. What bothers me is that all the lads at work heard it. They were all listening. The whole country heard it. It was all real personal stuff. And she had no right to divulge any of it.'

Brogan started pacing up and down again when the cat

suddenly piped up inside the wardrobe. He had no option but to let it out. It leaped up onto the window ledge and looked out at the river. After such a long spell in solitary confinement, the view of the bridge and the station lit up under yellow lights was like a movie. Everybody was gone home now. The last taxi had departed, and there was no sign of the crack-troop rescue team.

'Come here, Kitty,' Collette said.

'Her name is Moggi,' Brogan corrected.

The cat wasn't sure at first. But after some reflection, it took a chance and thought it best to go over and start purring for sympathy, tail up in the air like one of those dodgem cars. Collette began to stroke her, allowing Moggi to make a total fool of her, letting the cat push its head against her body. It brushed off her breasts and nestled right in under the Affinity bra for protection. Collette's red knickers were flashing and flickering, like one of those eternal Sacred Heart lamps on the landing. Her toes curling up.

'You took her cat,' Collette said.

'You're dead right I did.'

'To get your own back?'

'She'll never see that cat alive again. That's for sure.' And Brogan gave the cat a really filthy look back. As much as to say, he was still considering the whole Hannibal Lecter, Ballymaloe denouement. He had just run out of 'regard' that minute. So the cat could snuggle up all it liked. The time for retribution was approaching fast.

He looked out the window at the river, listening to the purring sound for a while, until he noticed that Collette pushed the cat away and beckoned to him. She winked at him and asked him to lie beside her. Opened the buttons of his shirt and started stroking his welcome mat. The cat decided to sit this one out by the window instead, looking out lustfully at the seagulls coming up the river, while Brogan now lay there on the bed in its place and snuggled up to Collette with his eyes closed, purring.

Downstairs, the porter had dozed off. He was alone in the lobby now. All the yobs from the nightclub had finally gone home and it had given him a chance to wind down. All the fights and the hassles outside the club had come to an end. An intermission of pure peace had fallen across Finbar's Hotel, when there was a sudden, irritating knock on the glass door with a key or a coin. There is nothing worse than the profane sound of metal on glass. The porter squinted and tried to see who it was, hoping they would go away. Come back in the morning, for Jesus' sake. But the tapping continued and he was forced to go and see, in case it was something to do with that dangerous bastard from Room 107. Instead it was some irate woman and her partner in a sheepskin coat. As soon as the porter opened the door, she was inside and dragging her male friend in after her, shouting her head off and swearing that she was going to break up the place.

'You've got a Mr Brogan here in this hotel, haven't you?' she demanded.

'Now hold on a minute,' the porter said in a daze.

'Hold on nothing,' she said, striding over towards the reception. 'I want to know what room he's in, because he's got my cat.'

'Look, madam. We don't allow any pets in this hotel.'

She stared at the porter with a great look of disgust and revulsion. You'd think she had just stood on a used condom in the street. And the squishy sensation had only now registered on her face. Like she was afraid to look down and

acknowledge the sordid presence of somebody else's squalid
sex life underfoot.

'You're in big trouble if you don't tell me where he is,'
she said. 'Right now. This minute!'

'She's serious,' echoed her partner in the sheepskin coat,
offering a bit of man-to-man advice. There was a painful look
on his face, as though he was trying to tell the porter
something important about female determination. 'Look, I
understand women,' he seemed to say. 'This is heavy stuff.
This could get nasty.'

The porter studied them both and weighed up his options.
He knew Brogan had been holding a cat hostage upstairs. All
that business about the fish didn't fool him. But he didn't
like the idea of some extended shouting match in the upstairs
corridor at this hour of the night. Besides, it was a question
of loyalty. He and Brogan had become great comrades earlier
on in the evening over a few drinks. An unassailable male
bond had been forged between them.

Who cared whose pussy it was at this point in time? And
what's more, this hysterical woman had just woken the
porter out of a pleasant, vodka-soaked reverie. She had
brought him back to reality and reminded him that he was
dying of cancer: an unforgivable error.

If only Brogan had been there at that moment. He would
have simply told Miss Cactus Legs to fuck off. Take your
lowry friend with the butane buttocks along with you. And
mind you don't slip on that condom outside.

'I'm afraid you'll have to leave,' the porter said. 'You've
no business here.'

But she would not give up. She started ranting and trying
to get in behind the reception, asking for the manager. The
man in the sheepskin coat was attempting to calm her down,

pulling her back out again before she did any damage, while the porter threatened to call the guards. And when she found no registration book, she said she would go and wake up the entire hotel, knock on every room until she found the bastard who had her cat.

'I'm calling the guards,' the porter said at last, lifting up the phone.

'Let them come,' she responded viciously. 'You're harbouring a cat killer.'

'Patricia, please.' The man with the horse buttocks tried to plead with her. He was pulling her away towards the door again, dragging her with all his might, whispering to her and encouraging her to leave. They could find other ways of avenging her cat in due course.

'I'm going to phone *Liveline* about this,' she shouted from the door. 'I'm going to ruin this hotel. I'll have this place closed down.'

There was a look of laconic endurance on the porter's face. Like he was about to laugh.

Brogan would have been so pleased to see this. 'Oooh . . . ,' he would have said. 'We're all terrified and quaking in our underpants now. We're all shitting shrapnel. Please, anything but the radio.' Listen here, Miss Ireland, this hotel was finished long ago. Let Simon tell you about it. There's nothing you or any half-arsed radio programme can do to make anything worse for him. Do you think Simon gives a shaman's shite what Marian Finucane is going to say about Finbar's Hotel?

'I'm going to wait outside until I get satisfaction,' was the last word from her.

The porter managed to shut the door behind them. He stared out through the glass and watched them walking away

to a parked car. They got in and waited there. If they had
bothered to look up at the building, they would have seen
the cat sitting in the window right above them, desperately
trying to make eye contact. But the hysterical woman kept
her frenzied eyes trained on the door of the hotel, waiting
for Brogan to emerge.

An hour or two later, Brogan woke up and got dressed.
He left Collette asleep in the bed. Left lots of money on the
bedside table and wrote a brief note on Finbar's Hotel
notepaper. He stepped out into the corridor with his ghetto
blaster and his suitcase. When he reached the lobby, the
porter came out to warn him. Simon seemed a little excited.

'She's outside in the car, waiting,' he explained. 'With her
heavy new boyfriend.'

But Brogan didn't seem very worried any more. He smiled
and wanted to know what pub the porter drank in. He asked
when Simon was normally off duty, because he was going to
have a drink with him one of these days. They would meet
at the Wind Jammer next Tuesday night. The porter was to
mind his health in the meantime. Get all the treatment he
could. And the best of luck with his degree.

'Take care of that cat,' the porter said, pointing down at
Brogan's suitcase.

'I intend to,' Brogan smiled.

The porter let him out and Brogan walked away towards
the river. He watched him swagger away, straight past the
red car outside. The occupants must have been asleep,
because nobody got out of the car. In fact there was another
car too with a man quietly watching all of this, but not
moving. Brogan even had time to turn around and look back
at the hotel windows upstairs. Seagulls had begun to descend
on the deserted streets, looking for scraps, scavenging for

discarded chips, fragments of ketchup-stained burger buns, anything but the used condom. Brogan looked up at the room he had occupied and then resumed his single-minded march towards the quays.

It was only then that Miss Cactus Legs woke up and saw him. She jumped out of the car, then back in again, waking up her partner. What kind of surveillance operation was this, falling asleep and letting Brogan slip away at a crucial moment; letting the most notorious cat killer of all time elude the net? She then started shouting at Brogan to come back. Ordering her boyfriend to sprint and catch up with him, running across the silent streets, leaving the car doors open behind them.

By now, Brogan had reached the river. He never bothered to quicken his step, and hardly even considered looking behind him again until he got to the wall of the river and looked down at the orange-brown water. On the far side, there was steam rising from the brewery. Some early morning trucks were making their way along the quays. It was only then that he looked back and saw the couple running towards him. He waited for an instant and then threw the suitcase into the river. He watched it floating at first before it began to sink. Seagulls were circling overhead. One of them tried to land on the handle of the suitcase, then flew away and wheeled around again.

Brogan walked on, heading into the city, sauntering with his ghetto blaster in his hand.

Miss Cactus Legs stopped at the spot where the suitcase was still partially visible above the surface of the river. She shouted some foul language in the direction of Brogan. Something obscene about his phase tester. But there were more urgent things to be considered. She began punching her buttock boyfriend and commanding him to go down and rescue the cat, urging him down a steel ladder along the quay towards the murky water below. When he got as far as the surface of the flowing river, he tried to reach out towards the handle of the suitcase.

'Go on, get it,' she shouted.

'I can't,' he pleaded, because the suitcase was just out of reach, drifting away and sinking fast.

'Oh, for Heaven's sake. What kind of a man are you?'

'Look, Patricia. I'm trying.' But the suitcase was almost submerged by now. Bubbles were anxiously escaping out through the sides.

'You're bloody useless.'

He looked up and saw her glaring down at him with an expression of cold fury. From his point of view, it was hard to tell which was worse, the filthy look on her face or the filthy look of the slimy green river below.

'Go on,' she screamed. 'Don't come up this ladder without it.'

At the door of the hotel, the porter stood watching. He had his hands behind his back, breathing in the fresh morning air. It was dawn, almost. The sky was beginning to pale, and he thought of having a quick cup of tea before everything started up again. He wasn't going off duty until eleven because of staff shortages. He stepped back inside and heard the lift doors opening.

A taxi pulled up outside the hotel at that moment, just as Collette came walking through the lobby with the cat on her arm. She spoke briefly to the porter on her way out.

'Good night, Simon,' she said as she stopped to let him see her new cat.

The purring was so loud it could be heard throughout the

deserted lobby, like an echo of the taxi's diesel engine purring outside. There was such a grin of contentment on Moggi's face as it stretched and gripped Collette's leather jacket with its claws. Collette smiled as the porter held the door open for her. She walked out and got into the back seat, spoke to the driver and stroked the cat all the time as the taxi pulled away.

1✿4

THE NIGHT MANAGER

There was something wrong about the ponytailed man booking in for the night. Decades of experience, long before he ever dreamt that he'd become manager of Finbar's Hotel, had taught Johnny Farrell that. It had also trained to stay back, watching as Aideen, the receptionist, gave him a card to fill in. She reached behind her for the key to 104 and put it on the counter beside the man's leather-jacketed arm. He seemed to be alone, with just one item of well-travelled hand luggage.

He leaned forward and spoke, but Johnny knew from Aideen's smile that whatever joke he'd tried on her wasn't funny. Since starting work in the hotel Aideen had always been her own woman, not easily impressed by anyone. He wondered if perhaps a younger girl, fresh from school, might have hung on to this guest's every word. Because, even from this distance, he seemed to possess a carefully cultivated charm and a vaguely familiar aura which Johnny found disturbing, although he still couldn't be certain why.

This was shaping up to be an odd evening. Some nights were like that, when you sensed trouble like a miasma in the air. Johnny knew that the man who'd earlier booked into 101, like a schoolboy on the mitch, had no real reason to be here. It was possible his wife had kicked him out, but he didn't have that hangdog look which Johnny could easily spot by now. Neither had he the furtive eyes of somebody

waiting for an illicit rendezvous later on. In all probability he
was harmless, but Johnny made a note to maintain a discreet
eye on him, just in case. Often this was what a hotel
manager's work consisted of, positioning yourself in the right
place like a good goalkeeper, so that the job looked effortless.

Of more potential concern was the guest whom Simon
had referred to in a dark mutter as 'the cowboy from 103'.
Johnny's instincts also told him there was something which
didn't gel about the two Dutch journalists booked into Room
205. Yet this was merely the minor flotsam of any busy night
in Finbar's and Johnny would have happily gone home by
now, leaving Simon to cast a cynical eye over affairs, had it
not been for the stocky Dubliner who had booked himself
into his favourite room, 107, at the end of the first-floor
corridor. Years ago as a child it had been through watching
the hotel's first owner, old Finbar FitzSimons (after whom it
was named), at work that Johnny had learnt the importance
of remaining on the premises for as long as the risk of serious
trouble existed. He was amazed how nobody on the staff
seemed to know who the Dubliner was, except for Simon,
of course, and the night porter and himself understood never
to acknowledge or discuss such matters.

Back at the counter, the ponytailed man had picked up
the key to 104. Johnny noticed how he never looked around,
although he had stared up for some time at the faded portrait
of Finbar FitzSimons' only son, Finbar Og, which still hung
behind the desk. It was one of the few pathetic details which
Finbar Og had insisted on when the consortium of senior
staff bought the hotel off the FitzSimons family over twenty
years ago: that his portrait remain above the desk and his
father's name stay over the door of the hotel. Simon emerged
at the coffee alcove beside Aideen's desk and briefly glanced

at the ponytailed man as he picked his bag up. Johnny caught a glimpse of the side of his face, which looked far older than his sleek black ponytail suggested. His hair had to be dyed, because the man would never see forty again. He strolled over to the lift and stood for a moment as the doors opened and several Americans emerged to join the remnants of the coach party seated in the lobby. The thought crossed Johnny's mind that perhaps the man could sense himself being watched. Johnny looked away for a moment, as if afraid of being caught, when the man stepped inside the lift and the doors closed. The lift rose and all Johnny was left with were vague impressions: a glimpse of nose, the hunch of his shoulders, his way of walking, and an irrational, almost paralysing sense of unease.

Simon emerged with coffee and biscuits for one of the tables of elderly Americans. He stooped slightly under the weight of the tray in a way which would never have showed a year ago. Yet there was nothing in the old porter's face to hint at whatever pain he might be in. This was another reason why Johnny Farrell was glad Finbar's Hotel was closing after Christmas, with all the staff being laid off while the new owners rebuilt from scratch. Otherwise Simon would refuse to stop working until his cancer grew so bad that he physically collapsed on the premises, and, although Johnny wasn't afraid of harsh decisions, he knew that Simon was the one person there whom he could never bring himself to sack.

Johnny walked over to the wooden alcove which was Simon's private kingdom. Other porters worked from this hatch as well, but they knew which shelves were Simon's and had to be left untouched. As Johnny stared up at the coffee pots and cheap biscuits waiting to be transferred into expensive tins, he could remember himself and Finbar Og's daughter, Roisin FitzSimons, hiding in here with Simon when they were both six years of age. Roisin had christened Simon 'Albert', after the faithful butler in *Batman and Robin*, and Simon was the only person there who had never scoffed when Roisin played Batman and Johnny was Robin.

That was over thirty years ago when everything still glistened in Finbar Og's white elephant of a new hotel, after a fire had destroyed the original building. Even the brightly coloured Navan carpets had the FitzSimons logo and the owner's initials of 'FF' woven into them in Celtic script like a ruling motif. Huge bouquets of artificial flowers had stood on the reception desk and Johnny could remember his father and grandfather, who both worked there, smiling again, happy to be employed once more by the FitzSimons after the eighteen months it had taken for the insurance company to pay up and the new hotel to be completed.

Looking back, those two weeks before it reopened were the happiest of his life. Roisin FitzSimons had regarded the new building as her private kingdom. There were four floors of freshly painted rooms to explore, twin beds to jump on and cartoon villains like The Joker and Two Face to chase in and out of the lifts. Chambermaids scolded them and work-men cursed, but old Finbar FitzSimons had been their protector. Because if Finbar Og only ever had time for his son, Alfie – Roisin's big brother, whom Finbar Og was grooming to take over the business one day – then old Finbar's special delight had been in his granddaughter, Roisin, and nobody dared cross old Finbar, even if Finbar Og's name had by then been officially on the deeds of the new hotel.

Simon returned to the alcove with the empty tray and spotted Johnny hovering there. 'Mean shites of Yanks,' he muttered sourly, dropping a coin into his box of tips. 'I'll never work my way through college on this.' It was Simon's long-standing joke, picked up from American soaps, that he was really doing a degree in Irish history. He took a sip from the glass in front of him. Johnny had lost track of how long it was since Simon had started the pretence that the clear liquid in the glass perpetually in front of him was water. At first Simon was so discreet about pilfering vodka that only Johnny's instincts had told him what was going on. Now, over the last year, it had become so blatant that even the barmen complained about him. Yet vodka seemed as good a painkiller as any and so Johnny continued to play his part in the deception.

He found it hard not to feel guilty about Simon, although back in the 1970s the other staff had offered him the chance to join in their buy-out of Finbar Og FitzSimons. 'All I want from here is a wage and no shite,' Simon had told Johnny's father, who coordinated the takeover. For most of the time since this had seemed a wise choice. Maybe with just one owner Finbar's Hotel might have reinvented itself as a vibrant concern, but even the elderly consortium had recognized that their style of joint management was too unwieldy to compete. Wages had been paid but what was once a famous hotel only limped along on weekend specials and the proceeds from Upstarts nightclub in the basement. Nobody could have foreseen the advent of the Dublin hotel boom and that – when Finbar's was sold at auction to a Dutch rock singer and his Irish wife – four of the original five consortium members, plus Johnny as inheritor of his father's stake, were each about to retire with a virtual fortune from their share of the property.

Simon would just receive his statutory redundancy,

although the old porter never mentioned this to Johnny. Perhaps, as realistically he only had months to live and nobody to leave the money to, this was immaterial to him, but Johnny had long suspected a resentment deep within him. Nobody could tell what was buried inside Simon, but Johnny knew that every tip was logged in his mind and every guest judged accordingly. The porter took another deliberate sip of vodka, staring at Johnny as though defying him to comment.

'Ponytails,' Johnny murmured, trying to lure a response from Simon. 'Never liked them, even on ponies.'

Simon stood up again, ignoring Johnny as he leaned forward to listen to an elderly American lady who had come up to the alcove with a request. Johnny slipped out past him and paused beside the reception desk. He indicated for Aideen to show him the last card which had been filled in: Edward McCann, with an address in outer London. 0181 territory.

'A steady Eddie,' Aideen mocked, watching Johnny read the name. 'He looked like the oldest swinger in town.'

'What did you make of him?'

'He'll frighten some poor girl in Upstarts later on. She'll think it's the night of the living dead when his dentures show up in the strobe lights. Is he trouble? Do you know him?'

'No. Just curious.' Johnny was anxious to change the subject. 'You know I've a reference inside for you whenever you want.'

Aideen smiled. 'It's time enough, Mr Farrell. I've a sister in London, I'll join her there after Christmas and see what happens.'

'It's no problem for me to put a word in with the new

owners,' Johnny said. 'They'll be a few months reopening but you're good at your job.'

'It's time to spread my tiny wings and fly away,' Aideen replied, in a mock sing-song voice. 'I mean, who the hell wants to work in the one job all their life?'

Johnny nodded, handing her back the card. She hadn't even noticed her insult, although he couldn't honestly say he had worked in the one job all his life. Just in the one hotel. Nobody could ever have guessed that he would be manager here one day, though the fates of the FitzSimons and Farrell families had been connected since 1924 when old Finbar first opened his hotel in a terrace on Victoria Quay, opposite what was then called Kingsbridge Railway Station.

There were still photographs of Finbar and his wife that first year, staring out at a starving city, shattered from the Civil War which had torn Ireland asunder. It was a bad time to start any business and the hotel might have quickly gone under had it not been for its proximity to the railway station, plus the reputation for discretion built up by old Finbar and by Johnny's own grandfather, James 'The Count' Farrell, who worked as head porter. Instead it quickly became a haven for rural curates on annual drinking batters in Dublin. The public rarely saw into the residents' lounge and the elderly male staff, handpicked to work there, never spoke about what occurred in that inner sanctum.

In his old age, the Count often told Johnny how clerical collars were discreetly slipped off on arrival in Dublin, during the short walk from the station. They were replaced just as discreetly, by Finbar himself after he ensured that the bill was paid and the curate reasonably sobered up with black coffee. The Count would always remain on the platform to ensure no unforeseen hint of scandal happened as each guest was safely dispatched back to the country for another year. It was the first disappointment in Johnny's life, discovering his grandfather's papal knighthood was simply a nickname 'earned for services bestowed on Mother Church', as the old man used to say, cackling at a joke young Johnny never understood.

Johnny wondered what the Count would make of Finbar's Hotel now, as he stared through the open doors into the public bar, where an office party was heating up. Pete Spencer, the younger barman there, was bitter at losing his job in January. Johnny sensed he wouldn't be above fiddling people's change if he could get away with it later in the night. Gerry, the older barman from Cork, still harboured hopes of regaining his job after the hotel reopened. He'd mentioned it to Johnny on several occasions, but this wasn't the time to make the man aware that he hadn't a chance. No new owner wanted bar staff who knew more about the takings than he did. The buyer might be a rock star, but he was still a Dutchman when it came to money. Aideen would stand a good chance, if Johnny put a word in for her. But Aideen's future wasn't his problem, so why had he offered to take responsibility for it?

He turned and saw her trying to catch his eye. The desk was quiet and he went back across to her.

'That was a silly thing for me to say,' she told him. 'About people working in the one place. I didn't mean any offence, you're obviously cut out for hotels. It's just that I want something different.'

'You're right to try all kinds of things,' Johnny replied. 'I often wish I had.'

The receptionist laughed good-naturedly as though he was humouring her.

'Get away out of that,' she said. 'This hotel fits you like a glove. I couldn't see you ever doing anything else.' Aideen looked at him, in the open way staff do when they realize that soon you won't be their boss any more. Johnny was surprised to see a hint of genuine affection there.

'You'll miss Finbar's terribly when it goes.'

'No,' he replied.

'Don't be codding me. All your life spent here. You must have so many memories.'

'I remember very little really, just faces coming and going.'

'They say all the big-shot politicians used to drink here when they were younger.'

'There's none of them big-shot politicians any more.' Johnny played down the past. 'They were more innocent days.'

Old Finbar had never approved of his son weaving his initials 'FF' into the carpet, knowing it was a flattery which the ruling Fianna Fáil party neither needed nor welcomed. It wasn't party allegiances which drew Brian Lenihan, Donagh O'Malley, Charles Haughey and the other Young Turks of Fianna Fáil to drink in the back lounge of the original hotel in the 1960s. It was the discretion which old Finbar and the Count were famous for, the kind that was always beyond Finbar Og and which only Johnny and Simon really understood now.

'Simon always says it hadn't a three-star rating back then, but a three-P one,' Aideen said, unsure of what the joke meant. It was the Count who had coined that phrase. By the 1950s Finbar's had became popular as a late-night drinking spot for senior policemen and – after the death of old Finbar's mother – for respectable women of the night.

'Finbar's never gained a PP rating,' Johnny explained to her. 'As being suitable for Parish Priests. We were PPP. Priests, Policemen and Prostitutes.'

Aideen laughed. He saw that she didn't know whether to believe him. But, back then, with the residents' lounge gaining a reputation for flexible licensing hours, it was only natural that two further Ps were soon added to Finbar's rating: a suitability for Promising Politicians.

'Is that old story about Brian Lenihan really true?' Aideen asked. 'About the young policeman, raiding here for after-hours drinking, being asked if he wanted a pint or a transfer to the Aran Islands?'

Sometimes when the Count told that story the government minister involved was Lenihan and other times it was Donagh O'Malley. But the Count had only told it in private. It was Finbar Og who had repeated the escapade so often and so loudly that the Young Turks grew annoyed and would have walked out with one final snap of their coloured braces if old Finbar hadn't intervened to close his son's mouth.

'That's just a legend,' Johnny told her now. 'I'm sure it never happened.'

There had been such a crowd in Finbar's that night that afterwards nobody really knew who had threatened the young policeman or if he had simply taken one look around the room and fled. Finbar's warning to his son had been effective for a while, until the insurance money from the fire (which had fortuitously occurred at the time Finbar Og was encountering opposition to his plans to demolish the original hotel) went to his head. But during the period it had taken the hotel to be rebuilt, drink took such a hold on Finbar Og that soon it was impossible to shut his mouth or stem the haemorrhage of money from his wallet.

Johnny glanced up at Finbar Og's portrait behind the counter. There was something about those shoulders he had always feared. Not that Finbar Og ever threatened him or had really paid any attention to Johnny's existence around the hotel as a boy. It was the same with Finbar Og's son, Alfie, who – although only two years older than Johnny – had always treated him with the same disdain of an adult for an inconsequential child. Aideen turned to stare at the portrait as well.

'That gouger gives me the creeps some nights,' she said. 'Wasn't he was the owner's son or something?'

Johnny could sense the hotel's imminent closure making the staff start to feel nostalgic. But tonight of all nights Finbar Og wasn't someone he wished to talk about. He looked away from those shoulders and put the clues back together again about the guest who had just booked in: the ponytail, that half glimpse of his face, the way he had walked to the lift. He was glad when two American women engaged Aideen's attention, searching for Ray Dempsey, their tour guide. Johnny had noticed the tour guide slipping away into the restaurant a short while before, but he said nothing. When not smiling in public Dempsey had a long-suffering look. Let him at least enjoy his meal in peace.

Johnny walked away towards the residents' lounge. There was no sign of the stocky Dubliner from 107. Johnny wanted him to slip down, like he often did, and silently leave his key on the desk. 107 never booked out. He always paid in advance and you simply knew when he left his key down that he wasn't coming back. Johnny felt suddenly jaded. He didn't just want to be gone from the hotel for the night, he wanted the whole building closed, those stupid carpets ripped up and dust everywhere, with floorboards and walls torn apart by the builders like an exorcism. He wanted this sense of responsibility finally ended. Finbar's had just never felt like it fully belonged to him. Maybe the whole consortium had felt the same. That was why even when they got Sean Blake, one of Dublin's best photographers, to do a group portrait they never got around to putting it up on the wall beside Katherine Proctor's painting of Finbar Og.

Yet this was Johnny's hotel, for a few more weeks at least. He could kick anyone he wanted out. He could march up to Room 104 this very moment and say there had been a mistake, a double-booking. There was nothing to stop him, the past had no bearing on it. So what made him so afraid to do so?

The residents' lounge was almost deserted, with just a few more of the Americans quietly trying to make their drinks last. He nodded to Eddie the barman to take his break and stared at the assorted brandy bottles. It wasn't like him to want a drink this early. He resisted the urge. You should never show that you were rattled. Two guests came in, women who looked like they had nothing in common. The well-dressed and confident younger one did all the talking, the older one looked nervy and out of place. A Protestant, West of Ireland type, too tired to keep appearances up any longer. Before he had married Prudence he would never have noticed these things. He brought them over brandies and took an order for room service. He should have passed it on to Simon but he waited till the barman came back, then went down to the kitchens himself.

It was ridiculous, but he felt that he needed an excuse to go upstairs. He waited until the tray was ready, then carried the soup, sandwiches and wine up to the door of Room 102. He walked on, not wanting to venture too close to 107. Music came from 103. He stopped outside 104. He felt uncomfortable, as though the occupant was staring at him through the spyhole. Though this is how the ponytailed man would expect to find Johnny, servile, carrying a tray, waiting for permission to enter.

Johnny stood for a moment, paralysed by his inability to know how much, if anything, Roisin FitzSimons had ever told her brother about them, then walked quietly back to 102 and used his skeleton key to get in. He put the tray down and neatly folded the white napkins beside the wine-glasses. His hands were shaking. Roisin. It felt like mentioning a ghost. This was how he thought of her, as being dead. No, that wasn't true. He had simply trained his mind never to think of her, among so many other things. He knew that he should leave the room before the women came back, but he sat on one of the beds unable to prevent those memories from returning.

He had been eight years old that summer when Old Finbar brought Roisin and himself on his boneshaker bicycle up to Aras an Uachtaráin in the Phoenix Park when de Valera was President. Roisin had sat on Finbar's folded jacket on the crossbar, singing 'My Boy Lollipop', with Johnny perched like an afterthought on the back carrier. Finbar had been almost eighty but strong as a bull. When Johnny dared to crane his neck he could see Roisin's red hair blown back as the bike plummeted through the Furry Glen.

Back then, the death of Finbar's wife had awakened an interest in God in the old man, although this didn't prevent him presiding over infamous all-night poker sessions with the Taoiseach, Sean Lemass, and other businessmen in a suite in the hotel. But every fortnight he cycled to sit in the Aras kitchen with de Valera who liked nothing better than to cook them massive fry-ups as they chatted in Irish into the night. The fact that de Valera's wife had taught Finbar Irish dancing, and Finbar and Sean O'Casey were both once rivals for her hand, only made the men closer in their old age.

Johnny remembered being terrified on that journey. It was like being brought to meet God, as the old man sang along with his granddaughter, both of them oblivious to Johnny's presence on the carrier. Yet, when they reached the Aras, de Valera wasn't even in – 'too busy shovelling earth on some poor fecker's coffin' – and the afternoon was spent with Roisin and himself being taught to ride the boneshaker around the president's private lake.

That was what being with the FitzSimons had been like, having casual access to places the public could never dream of. Roisin had been bored by the excursion, whereas Johnny was terrified, waiting to be thrown out. His brother Charles, four years older than Alfie FitzSimons, never seemed to feel the same apprehension when mixing with the FitzSimons. He might be a porter's son, but everyone knew he was marked for better things. Already old Finbar had arranged for him to serve his time in a major London hotel. It felt like there was a star above Charles' head. Even Alfie FitzSimons followed him like a dog. Charles would have impressed de Valera so much that the President would have enquired about him for years afterwards, whereas Johnny had crouched in the lakeside bracken every time a car approached the Aras gates.

A noise in the corridor made Johnny look around. A woman in her forties passed by the open door, heading for the lift. The two women would be up soon. There was no sound from Room 104. It could be mistaken identity. Maybe the closure of Finbar's was rattling him more than he thought. Johnny closed the door over softly and walked back downstairs to the residents' lounge, fingering the estate agents' brochure in his inside suit pocket. The private sale was agreed two months ago, yet Johnny still carried the brochure around with him without ever having shown anyone in Finbar's that picture of a Palladian villa nestling among woodland in the hills near Enniscorthy.

Prudence and himself would have eight en suite guest bedrooms when renovations on the villa were complete, and seating for eighteen gourmet diners in the library overlooking the small pond when it was dug out. Eighteen was the correct number. Anything above that and the illusion of intimacy was ruined. There was no problem filling bed nights in Ireland any more. It was a case of targeting discerning guests. Europeans were more willing to pay for the ambience of an Irish country villa. Americans were generally so rich they wanted trans-American comforts in the Shelbourne or else they were like the few sad members of the coach party nursing their coffees in the residents' lounge as Johnny nodded to the two women from 102 and pointed with his finger to tell them that their order was waiting upstairs.

The regular barman came back and Johnny wandered out into the lobby. The European visitors understood good wine and cognac better, he thought, once you kept prices sufficiently high to weed out the sandal brigade. Prudence had been surprised when he insisted that the villa trade under her name when it opens. 'Let's call it Mount Farrell,' she'd protested. 'God knows, you've slaved long enough under somebody else's name.' But that was the point, Farrell's seemed like an echo of Finbar's for him. Let it be called

Cuffe's, a Protestant name with class and no baggage. Johnny didn't want to bring any goodwill or contacts with him to Enniscorthy or to write blurbs about the Farrell family enjoying three-quarters of a century of experience in welcoming visitors. He wanted a full stop on the past and then to start again somewhere new. He wanted anonymous guests who stayed up late beside log fires, quietly discussing business in a babble of foreign tongues while a floodlit fountain gurgled soothingly outside. He'd had a lifetime of sad people who paid in cash. He wanted American Express Gold cards. He wanted twelve-and-a-half per cent service charge with no Simon waiting to cadge a tip. He wanted gold embossed menus printed on watermarked conquer board and diners who studied the fish dishes first and not the prices.

Johnny winced, recalling the misprint he'd spotted on tonight's restaurant menu. Such mistakes hurt his pride. He had to remind himself that the kitchen staff knew their jobs were going and he had no intention of sacking them between now and Christmas. Just another six weeks and it was over. So it didn't matter if the entire remnants of the FitzSimons family were just after booking into Room 104. The important thing he had learnt was to focus on the job in hand. Old Finbar's advice from thirty years ago had always stood him in good stead. Johnny walked to the restaurant door and looked in. It was quiet, with staff preparing to set out the breakfast cutlery. A salesman was talking away at one table, more loudly than was necessary. There was always a danger in approaching any man who found his own stories funnier than anyone else. It would take Johnny seven or eight minutes to escape from a courtesy halt there.

He settled instead for Dempsey, the American coach party guide, who seemed to have found himself company, the middle-aged woman he had glimpsed passing the door of 102. Johnny walked down to them, smiling and yet gravely solicitous.

'How is your meal?' he asked. 'Are you being well looked after?'

They both nodded, seeming a little awkward at being caught together. The woman's glass hadn't been washed properly but she didn't seem to notice. Johnny smiled and moved on. It was something which guests at Cuffe's Villa would automatically expect, the host to come to their table and answer questions about the age of the house, local golf and fishing, to advise on wine selection and immediately offer to take back any dish which proved disappointing. It would be a far cry from the days when Finbar used to fawn his way back to the kitchens with a rejected steak from some old-time Fine Gael Blue-shirt with instructions to the chef to, 'Give that a quick rub around your balls for more flavour and wait five minutes before sending it back out to the fecker at table six.'

Johnny and his wife had planned their move carefully, waiting for the right property to come on the market. His wife spoke French and German fluently and Johnny had been trained to bypass the problems of language. Recently Prudence had wanted to come into the kitchens in Finbar's and practice her menus, but Johnny told her that she would quickly unlearn every good usage there she had been taught during the advanced cookery courses in Ballymaloe House. He checked his watch again. His shift was long over. He could just walk out of the hotel. What did it matter if there was some sort of incident later on? The place had been sold. He owed no duty to anyone any more. Yet Johnny knew that it wasn't in his nature to leave. He closed his eyes and once again puzzled over the details of the ponytailed man. Might Edward McCann be his real name? Any similarity in features could be coincidental. But the chill inside him told Johnny that his instincts were correct.

Yet if he knew who the man was, then he didn't know why he was here. What was the sense in returning now? Johnny left the restaurant, but found that he couldn't stay still. Simon was speaking on the telephone, filling in one of the pale blue dockets for room service orders. Johnny moved into the public bar. A blonde girl at the counter had ordered a huge round for the office party she was with. Pete Spencer, the younger barman, had just finished serving her.

'Always check your change, miss,' Johnny warned quietly behind her. 'And check your handbag regularly throughout the evening. I'm afraid we get pickpockets in every hotel coming up towards the weekend.'

The girl nodded and began to ferry the drinks down. Pete loaded up a tray for her, sneaking a quick glance at Johnny. He'd said just enough to plant suspicion in the barman's head that he was being watched, but not enough for the words to be construed as an accusation. Johnny knew that Spencer wasn't sure if his employers were aware that his cousin had been shot in a robbery in Malahide last year, half in and half out of a stolen car he couldn't even drive. It was a habit the Count had taught Johnny years ago: ignore the headlines, they don't concern real people. Always read the small reports in newspapers instead. Make the connection between names but never let anyone know how much you know. Johnny needed Spencer to remain on until the 1st of January, although he suspected that it might be wise to sack him quietly a week before they closed. He checked the ashtrays, then followed Simon, who was carrying a room service order, back out into the foyer. The cowboy in the Temple Bar T-shirt had come down to reception as Johnny caught up with Simon and glanced at the docket on the tray. Coffee and a double whiskey for Room 104.

'I'll take that up for you, Simon.'

The porter looked at him quizzically, as though considering whether this was a slur on his health.

'Fire away so,' the porter said.

Johnny picked up the tray and crossed to the lift, aware of being closely watched by both Simon and the Temple Bar geek. He had no plan formulated about how to handle the situation if his suspicions were correct. Raised and drunken voices came from behind the door of 102. There was a story there. He walked on to knock at Room 104 and waited until the ponytailed man opened the door. Seeing him straight on, Johnny knew at once that his instincts were right, although the man had aged in the twenty years since he had last seen him. Yet even as a child his hair had never been so dark. Johnny found something pathetic about the manner in which he was dressed, in a desperate attempt to remain young looking and hip. Yet the bags under his eyes belonged to a far older man, his clothes were the type you saw in second-hand charity shops, where rich students browsed, attempting to dress down. Johnny carried the tray across to the window table and politely held the docket out to be signed. He had taken everything in without making direct eye-contact. Let the past lie. He decided that he didn't want to know why the man was back here. His signature was a plausible enough scrawl. Johnny had retreated out into the corridor when the man called him back by name. His voice hadn't altered, still mildly condescending beneath a spuriously gregarious tone.

'You've never bloody changed, have you, Johnny Farrell? You were born an old man. As fucking inscrutable as ever.'

Johnny turned around to stare at Alfie FitzSimons, puzzled as to what in his own demeanour had made FitzSimons realize Johnny knew who he was.

'Alfie FitzSimons, is it? Well, well, my goodness, I'd never have recognized you.'

'You'd be hard to mistake. Jaysus, I thought we buried the old Count in that suit.'

'My grandfather never wore grey.' He cursed himself for the unintentional defensiveness which had crept into his voice. The corridor was empty. Johnny wanted to get away to his own office, to any place where he could bolt the door and think. Once he stepped back into Room 104 he knew he was in the paying guest's territory. But he sensed that Alfie wouldn't be lured down into the public bar. Alfie smiled.

'I'm only joking,' he said. 'Don't look so serious. I mean you look really great, you've done so well for yourself. It's amazing seeing you again. I spent all of last night talking about you.'

Even by Alfie's standards this last lie was laying it on thick. Years ago, if Alfie had been stuck with nobody to play with or had needed a message run, then maybe he might have addressed Johnny. Otherwise he had moved through any room Johnny was in as though the younger boy was invisible. Johnny wondered what he wanted from him now.

'Come in and join me for a drink,' Alfie was saying. 'I didn't really want this coffee anyway. You take it, or the whiskey if you prefer. It's just amazing to see you. You look so good, man.'

Johnny walked in and closed the door. The bed was disturbed where Alfie had been lying down. The television was on, MTV videos with the volume off. Alfie's unopened bag was thrown in the corner and his leather jacket hanging up. A free night's accommodation in another hotel plus fifty quid – no, a hundred – was the maximum Johnny was willing to pay to be rid of him.

'Well, here we are, old pals together again, eh?' Alfie poured the coffee and held it out for him. Johnny took the saucer and watched Alfie cross the room. He paused in front of the television to eye the dancers. 'God, the arses on these young ones today,' he said. 'You'd need to be dug out of them with a knife and fork.' The seductive images faded and a Sinead O'Connor video began. Alfie switched the set off with a snort. 'A right virago, eh?' Sitting on the edge of the bed, he took a sip of whiskey and looked around.

'You gave me Rosie Lynch's room,' he said and Johnny joined cagily in Alfie's laughter. Rosie Lynch had been a novice call-girl in 1968 when an elderly priest from Leitrim suffered a heart attack while being entertained by her in Room 104. It had taken all of old Finbar's experience, plus the connections of the young Turks, to ensure that his death had remained a rumour only, laughed at by those in the know in Dublin society. 'Frighten me,' the priest was reported to have urged the young girl after she bound his wrists to the bedposts. 'Frighten me even more,' he was said to have insisted until she leaned her breasts down into his face and whispered three words: 'John Charles McQuaid.'

Alfie repeated the name of Dublin's former autocratic archbishop with a chortle. 'John Charles McQuaid. That was the ultimate triple bypass, by Jaysus, eh? There were some great times in this old place, all the same.' He stopped and looked at Johnny, apologetically. 'I hope you don't mind if I didn't use my real name booking in. I wanted to be anonymous – not that the staff would know of me anyway – but, you know yourself, there's so many memories. I see you kept the Da's portrait up in the lobby.'

'It was agreed in the contract.'

Alfie laughed again. 'Ah come 'ere now, take it easy. I'm not checking up on you. I mean the Da is long dead, there's nobody left who cares if you set fire to that painting years ago.'

'Guests like it,' Johnny said. 'They often ask about him.'

'What do you tell them?'

There was no malice in the question but Johnny was uneasy, cautious in the way that you had to be when dealing with a drunk standing on his dignity in the public bar. God knows, Finbar Og had stood on his dignity there often enough after having to sell the hotel, like a young King Lear, unrecognizable from Proctor's portrait, as his former staff kept a weather eye out that he didn't bother the punters too much and the punters didn't bother him. Johnny's father had always ensured that he was coaxed into a taxi paid for by the hotel every night. Former owners should die or else vanish as far away as possible.

'We tell the guests it's a portrait of the original owner's son, the man responsible for rebuilding the hotel after it was burnt down,' Johnny said.

'Those shagging firemen,' Alfie said. 'Remember that fecker from Drimnagh up on the ladder wanting to be a hero. The bastard almost saved the shagging dump.'

'Your father would have got permission to knock it down anyway,' Johnny said. 'It was just a few Trinity College eggheads going on about architectural heritage in the papers.'

'What are you saying?' Alfie said suddenly.

'I wasn't saying anything.'

'That fire started accidentally. But if it happened it happened. What was the point in trying to save half the place?'

'He rebuilt it well,' Johnny said carefully.

'He did. Here's to the Da.' Alfie raised his glass in a silent toast before taking another slug of whiskey. 'He was unlucky. This place could have worked. Your father and the others showed that.'

Johnny said nothing, undecided about whether Alfie was angling to pick an argument. Finbar Og was unlucky all right, in that the reopening of his new hotel was delayed by a builder's strike, while the Young Turks were forced to find other drinking quarters. No expense had been spared by Finbar Og and the hotel's labyrinthical lay-out was designed to assist clandestine tête-à-têtes or other late night political activities. But the problem was that the Young Turks never really came back. They had settled into new watering holes and higher public profiles. Then the North erupted and the Arms Trial came. The Young Turks were divided and scattered. The new Taoiseach's sole vice of pipe-smoking hardly encouraged a culture of debauchery, while the Cosgrave government which followed (in Finbar Og's words) 'wouldn't spend the steam off their piss'.

Vatican II didn't help business either, with curates starting to play guitars and be seen in local pubs. Finbar Og was also unlucky in that soon after old Finbar died the hotel started being raided for late-night drinking. When this happened a third time the Young Turks didn't even bother intervening so that Finbar Og almost lost his licence before Justice Eamon Redmond. It was then that Johnny's father and the others stepped in, so that if after-hours drinking didn't stop, it was confined to Finbar Og himself. That was the year he had his portrait done by Proctor, insisting she base it on a photo ten years out of date. But he was ageing so quickly that he was unrecognizable from the portrait, even before it was done.

Johnny could see traces of Finbar Og's features in Alfie now, as the man finished his whiskey. The fingers shook slightly although there were none of the tell-tale signs of an alcoholic. This wasn't how life was meant to work out. It should be Alfie in this suit, owning this hotel, with Roisin married into an important Dublin family. But there again, nothing in life had worked out.

'I heard about Charles,' Alfie said. 'I always looked up to him. I was sorry.'

Johnny nodded, unsure if this was Alfie's way of nudging him into mentioning Roisin in return. It was Charles Farrell whom the consortium had always hoped might return as their saviour. Maybe if their father had died sooner, Charles would have returned to claim his inheritance and buy the others out. Johnny would never know. His brother was a stranger to him always. The five years between them was too big a gap to be bridged until later life, by which time Charles had gone to Canada, leaving only his shadow behind. Assistant manager in the Lord Nelson in Halifax, Nova Scotia, then manager of the Montreal Hilton. Brothers don't write, especially with nothing in common. On his rare visits home Johnny had treated Charles with circumspection, like you would a future boss. When their mother died, Johnny's father cried for days. Yet he had taken the telephone call informing them of Charles' death quite differently, retreating into a terrible silence from which he never fully emerged. Johnny had watched, knowing his own death would never have affected his father so. Johnny had married and given him grandchildren, but still he was overlooked.

'At least Simon is going strong,' Alfie said, anxious to break the silence Johnny seemed lost within. 'I caught a glimpse of him earlier on.'

'Sure that fellow will last for ever,' Johnny replied. 'One of the unkillable children of the poor.'

The people who die are always those whom you least expect to. Johnny had given little thought to Charles during his life, knowing he would always suffer by comparison. When he flew to Canada to sort out his brother's belongings he had been going to a stranger's apartment. Whatever secrets were part of Charles' bachelor life had been carefully destroyed before his arrival, although many of the books and paintings there had left clues enough. But Johnny hadn't found one letter or diary, though his colleagues in the Hilton seemed to have known about his illness long before his family did. All that had remained of his brother were the volumes on those crowded shelves and, gradually, in bundles here and there, Johnny had started to recognize obscure book titles with a numb sense of shock, for having them himself at home. He had thought that he alone had inherited the Count's fascination with travel within Ireland and by Irishmen abroad, but here, thumb-marked and underlined, was a first edition of Denis Johnston's *Nine Rivers from Jordan*, which Johnny had chased a book dealer in London to find. Books like Conroy's *History of Railways in Ireland* published in 1928 in London, Calcutta, Bombay and Madras might have come from the Count's own collection, others like Patterson's *The Lough Swilly Railway* could have been purchased before Charles left for Canada. But Johnny had been stunned by the lengths Charles must have gone to acquire recent titles like Ruth Delaney's *Ireland's Royal Canal*, published in Dublin, or the one-off printing of

Frank Forde's study of Irish ships during the war, *The Long Watch*.

As dusk had fallen over Montreal he had fingered Patrick Myler's *The Fighting Irish* and biographies of Stephen Roche, Barry McGuigan and almost every other modern Irish sporting champion. There had been so much they might have talked about in excited phone calls on nights when Ireland won medals or if only Johnny had allowed himself to take a holiday. Even their record collections had seemed almost identical. Johnny had sat in Charles' apartment, crying like he hadn't allowed himself to cry since childhood, for the loss of a soulmate he'd never known.

Johnny looked up. He didn't know how long Alfie had been watching him. Alfie looked away now, fingering the ice in his glass. 'Fuck it,' he said to Johnny. 'Let's order a bottle of whiskey up, for old times' sake. We'll call Simon on room service. My treat.'

'I'd love to,' Johnny lied. 'But I'm snowed under tonight. End of the month returns coming up. Let's have one drink down in the bar instead. Honestly, that's all I've time for.'

'You shouldn't work so hard,' Alfie said, concerned. 'I mean you look harassed. Relax, sit back and have a drink. It's just one night, for God's sake, pal.'

'Any other night but this . . .' Johnny began, but Alfie cut across him.

'Listen, you're here now. Forget about your fucking hotel for five minutes. Will you just sit down, right!' Alfie was agitated. He couldn't keep still. 'That's the way with old friends. It doesn't matter whether you like them or not, they're still your old friends.'

Here it comes, Johnny thought, the sting. Everything he'd inherited was by fluke. He'd simply been last in line, the dull workhorse trudging away when fortune fell into his lap. For years here he'd waited for someone to dredge up the undeniable fact that he deserved none of it. Not just his share of the hotel but the three hundred thousand Canadian dollars left intestate in Charles' estate. In Montreal there were rumours of a will, but the businessman who nursed Charles to his death before phoning Dublin had allegedly torn it up, wanting nothing. Johnny didn't know how many people he'd have to buy off before feeling comfortable with this wealth that had been meant for someone else. Reluctantly he sat back on his chair. The coffee was cold but he sipped it anyway.

'I know you're a busy man,' Alfie was saying. 'It's amazing how you've turned this hotel around, but could you not find time for even just one visit to Roisin? I mean, Johnny, you're all the woman ever talks about.'

This was an approach Johnny hadn't expected. It threw him as he tried to figure out how it would lead back to what Alfie actually wanted.

'Roisin wouldn't know me,' Johnny replied. 'It's nineteen years since I last saw her.'

'Time doesn't matter,' Alfie said. 'Nineteen years or ninety, it's all the same to her. Her life stopped at the age of seventeen, do you not understand? There's been nothing since then. I wanted to bring her over to London a few times, but the doctors . . . well, it's like there's this chemical cocktail holding her together. She needs medical back-up for her own sake. But she's out of the hospital now, did you know that?'

'No.' Johnny shook his head. He decided that he'd pay two hundred and fifty quid just to be rid of him.

'It's a sort of halfway house,' Alfie said, 'but it's as far as she'll ever get. There's eight of them in sheltered care, with a nurse on duty full time. From the outside you'd swear it was just an ordinary house. They're really good to her there, but I'm the only one who visits.'

'You live in London,' Johnny protested.

'There's airlines,' Alfie replied, almost fiercely. 'Apex tickets. She's my only sister, for God's sake. Six times a year, every year, I come home for her. The first of every month she writes. I think the nurses got her started writing as a therapy. I've letters here if you want to see them.'

'No,' Johnny said as Alfie seemed about to reach for his bag. 'They're private. Family matters.'

'If you're not family, then who the fuck is,' Alfie replied, looking down at his empty glass again. It would be impossible to ask Simon to bring up just one round of drinks. But a bottle meant being trapped here all night. Back in the '70s, Alfie had started flitting back and forth to London, doing lights and even claiming to manage young Irish bands nobody ever heard of again. He would call into the hotel, talking loudly about deals he was always on the verge of setting up. The last time he'd been seen was at the afters for Finbar Og's funeral, when he booked the main suite for the FitzSimons family gathering and ran up a vindictively excessive bill for his relations, while the consortium gathered to shake his hand, knowing his cheque was certain to bounce. It was a bad debt they didn't mind, knowing it would finally rid them of the FitzSimons. Anything Johnny had heard about him in the years since was mostly hearsay, being seen selling encyclopedias in London or working in fast-food restaurants. He had always feared Alfie's grasping personality, yet it was only now, face to face, that Johnny allowed himself to admit just how much he had come to look down on him. But, for all that, he was convinced that Alfie was telling the truth about returning to visit Roisin over the years.

Now, even if Johnny could stop Alfie opening Roisin's letters, he couldn't prevent him from describing them.

'There's nothing from the last twenty years she ever mentions, do you understand?' he was saying. 'Even after she moved into the sheltered housing she never mentioned her room or the other residents. Unless something happened before her seventeenth birthday it just didn't exist for her. All she does is talk about the pair of yous. I don't even get a look in. Do you know what I'm trying to say to you, man?'

Johnny didn't know or couldn't be sure. He let Alfie ramble on, finding his conversation unnerving. Half the things Alfie claimed that Roisin talked about them doing were memories which were so distant they might not have existed for him. Casual, unimportant events he had no reason to remember. Yet he found it shocking to be perfectly preserved, as a boy, in Roisin's imagination, so that she seemed to own his past more than he did. It was like seeing a child's embalmed body being dug from a bog. He had no way of knowing just how much Roisin had told Alfie. The FitzSimons had always trusted Johnny, to the point of overlooking his presence when he was present, as if invisible, during blazing rows between Roisin's parents.

Even as a small boy he'd had that same serious, responsible look, content to be allowed to help out in the kitchens or clean the toilets if they were short-staffed. His devotion to Roisin was taken for granted, yet it had been implicitly understood that Johnny knew his place. From the age of five they might have been inseparable, living out their childhood fantasies, but socially their parents were miles apart. Not even the advent of puberty had caused the FitzSimons to worry about Roisin and Johnny when they went away on hostelling weekends. He was seen more as chaperon than suitor, a dull counterweight to Roisin's natural wildness, ensuring she would still be untainted when the time came for the FitzSimons to marry her into Dublin's social elite.

'Remember that day the pair of you got lost on a bog in Wicklow?' Alfie was saying. 'She talks about it all the time. You'd swear it was yesterday.'

Johnny tried to calm the dull knot of fear inside him. A memory came back, from centuries ago, of car headlights taking an eternity to reach them, bobbing in and out of sight along the bends of a mountainy road, and the pair of them in the back seat as they were driven to the hostel, cold and mute after hours shivering in the dark.

He tried to recollect some sense of himself as that young boy frozen in her imagination as Alfie spoke, but it was only Roisin who was still vivid, aged fourteen on that flat expanse of twilit bog. There seemed no detail of her body he couldn't suddenly remember, in the moment when he emerged from behind a rick of cut sods to find she had stripped off her jumper and blouse. The evening had turned to dusk, making the turf chocolate-brown and her skin darker than he could ever have imagined it to be. Even her small nipples were brown in the light as she taunted him to follow suit, starting to unzip her jeans. There was no lovemaking, they had not even kissed. He hadn't yet discovered masturbation and didn't know to ask her to take him in her mouth. Instead they had laughed insanely and kicked their legs in the freedom of the twilit air, their bodies never actually touching as they danced and spun until it was so dark they could hardly find their clothes again.

'I don't remember it at all,' Johnny replied. 'I'm sorry, but it was years ago.'

Alfie was looking at him closely, as if almost commanding him to continue talking.

'Maybe I was too close to her to notice things,' Johnny said. 'All I remember about being in Wicklow was overhearing some girls in one of the hostels complaining that Roisin kept them awake in the dormitory, talking and laughing in her sleep.'

'There were signs we all missed,' Alfie agreed. 'None of us wanted to see them.'

Listening to the girls in that hostel, Johnny had been so terrified Roisin had given their secret away in her sleep that he hadn't had time to think of anything else. People claimed that it was Finbar Og having to sell the hotel which caused Rosin's nervous breakdown, but in fact she was mentally disturbed before then, without her family being able to face the shame of her needing help. Even before that twilight on the bog Johnny had begun to feel uncomfortable with her. Things had been different between them ever since she entered secondary school in the Loreto Convent in Stephen's Green and started boasting about her new, affluent friends. Some afternoons these classmates would visit the hotel, when Johnny was helping his father out after school, a boisterous cluster of legs and uniforms crowding into the lift to be treated like royalty in the FitzSimons' suite. Roisin ignored him on those occasions and he kept his head down.

But the visits stopped once whispers started in Loreto about Finbar Og. Roisin would come home alone, troubled looking and desperate to escape into their fantasy world which Johnny had shared in so willing a year before but now knew they should have both outgrown. As the FitzSimons' empire collapsed he would shake his head when people asked if he noticed anything odd about her, but it seemed like a decade of friendship had been eclipsed by one hour dancing naked on a Wicklow bog. He had known that his father would lose his job if Roisin uttered a single word.

'It took that obsession about staying out of the sun before people copped on,' Johnny said. 'She had started talking so much that I only really half listened, but she went on and on about the sun boiling her blood.'

'Daddy was just . . .' Alfie stopped. He looked in genuine pain. Johnny wished suddenly that he had the same ability to show it. 'Daddy was like a king to me,' Alfie said. 'Do you know what it was like to see a king who's broken? He used to come into my room at three or four in the morning. He was the loneliest poor fucker. I was just a kid, but I'd get up, we'd sit, talking. The plans he had. You know, if you can find anyone to listen to your plans long enough you'll wind up still believing in them yourself. I don't know if he was talking to me or just himself, but I was like a knight at his side. The last faithful knight of a king in fantasy land.'

Even when his mother died, and then Charles, Johnny never remembered his father really talking to him. There simply had never been time. Only the Count and old Finbar ever had long conversations and, looking back, he knew that was only because they were lonely in old age. Between them they had made an old man of him.

'All that time,' Alfie was saying, 'my father was a sinking ship. Maybe I could have saved Roisin. It has fucking haunted me for years, Johnny, I was so caught up in his lousy fucking battles. I didn't want to bring any more grief down on him. But it was obvious she had acute psychosis, she was deluded, for God's sake, hallucinating, and all they cared about was making sure there was no scandal or talk of hospitals, as if anyone in their right mind was coming to come along and marry the daughter of a bankrupt drunk.'

Alfie lowered his head into his hands and was silent for a moment. Johnny stared at his bent head, fighting the urge to pity him. Alfie FitzSimons. Johnny could remember his mother scrubbing him, fretting nervously over his hair before he was forced to attend Alfie's birthday parties, the way Alfie would casually tear the expensive wrapping paper his mother had bought, barely bothering to glance at the present before running off to play with his friends. The pity was gone. An echo of the same fear from two decades ago returned as he wondered just how much Roisin had told Alfie. Her naked childlike dance had been repeated a dozen times over the following year when they were left alone in the FitzSimons' suite. Once Alfie returned and Johnny had to hide behind Roisin's bed while she pretended she was taking a shower. Their games should have been sexual but somehow they weren't for her. He quickly realized that Roisin wouldn't have resisted if he had tried to have intercourse with her. But she had clung to him more like a frightened child, knowing she was losing everything around her and trying to hold back time. Roisin always insisted on them both being naked, yet never paid any attention to his teenage erection. Every time he had to struggle against himself, knowing what a nightmare it would be if she became pregnant. In the end it was fear which made him block out his feelings and avoid her. It was never desertion. It was survival for his father and for his brother Charles, already making a name in London hotels due to the FitzSimons connection.

Alfie had started talking again, like he couldn't stop.

Johnny cursed him for turning up now, just when he was finally about to close down this hotel which he realized he had always hated. He needed a drink badly himself.

'I've to get back to work soon, Alfie,' he said, interrupting the flow of words. 'Let's go down to the bar and have that last drink together.'

'We'll have it up here, like I said,' Alfie replied. 'I'm ordering a bottle off Simon. I'll pay myself. I have money. I'm not looking for no favours, you know.'

'I don't owe you no favours,' Johnny replied, sharper than he meant to. 'None of us do. My father's consortium paid a fair price for this hotel.'

'They could easily afford to,' Alfie snapped back, 'seeing as all of you were robbing my father blind for years before that.'

Johnny stood up, angry now, and Alfie rose from the bed, his hands out stretched in apology.

'Listen, I'm sorry, all right,' he said hastily, looking like his father had, a dozen times on the verge of being barred. 'I was just joking, I shouldn't have said that. I know you owe me nothing, but what about Roisin, eh?'

'I told you, I don't even know your sister any more.'

'Come off it,' Alfie snorted. 'You were like peas in a pod. Didn't I catch you at it one afternoon upstairs. You'd the hots for her for years, go on, man, admit it.'

'I don't remember that.'

'You seem to bloody well remember what you like.'

'I remember you and the Count,' Johnny said.

'What?' Alfie looked puzzled.

'The day after he retired he went back into the kitchens to say hello to people. He'd worked here since 1924, for

God's sake. You passed by and said to him, "This area is for current staff only. You should wait out in the public bar."'

'Jesus, I was just a kid at the time.'

'Your father wouldn't have said it to him, or your grand-father. Almost fifty years in the place and he was still just another worker to you.'

'This has nothing to do with Roisin,' Alfie protested. 'You're just using this stuff against me.'

'Roisin was well out of my league and your family made sure I knew it.'

'Out of your league?' Alfie laughed with open bitterness. 'Look at the cut of you. You only went off and married some rich South Dublin Fine Gael Horse Prod. The very sort of real jewels, fake orgasms bitches who always looked down their noses at us.'

'You don't know my wife,' Johnny almost shouted, physically restraining himself. 'Or what she's like. You know nothing about who I am now. What I did with my life is none of your concern.'

'You're still the same man,' Alfie taunted as if trying to get under his skin.

'And so are you, FitzSimons.' Johnny reined in his temper to a whisper. 'Alfie with an E.' The very quietude of his voice was enough to unsettle Alfie.

'What do you mean by that?' he asked.

'I mean that this room is double-booked,' Johnny looked down at his suit, the expensive shoes he had carefully shone. They reminded himself of who he was and that the rule in these situations was to never let the argument get personal. 'There's been a mistake,' he said. 'Aideen at reception should never have given it to you.'

'I don't see anyone else booked in here.'

'The fault is entirely ours. We'll ensure that you're taken by taxi to an alternative hotel to spend the night as our guest.'

'Taxis were the same trick you used to get rid of my da at night after you'd all fleeced him,' Alfie said. 'Well, it so happens that I like it just fine here. Me and Rosie Lynch's ghost, eh.'

'Why have you really come here tonight?' Johnny asked.

'I wanted to talk to you, Farrell, just once, man to man about Roisin. Can't you see there's nobody else left to look out for her? Could you not make even one visit for old times' sake?'

'How come, if you came here looking for me, you used an assumed name?' Johnny said.

'Because I didn't know if I'd get in the fucking door,' Alfie retorted. 'I've not forgotten there's bad debts here since my father's funeral. I know they're twenty years old, but you were always such a fastidious little fuck that I knew there was no fear you'd have forgotten either. Can you not blame me wanting to take one look around the old place first before it's all torn down in a few weeks' time? Or have you forgotten that one day all this was supposed to be mine?'

'Finbar's a different hotel now,' Johnny replied. 'Only the name's the same.'

'It looks the same to me.'

'There's been big changes. Upstarts nightclub in the basement, for example.'

'What about it?' Alfie said.

'Maybe you were thinking of paying a little visit there later on?'

'Maybe I was. Don't you know that young girls these days

go for more experienced men.' Alfie winked conspiratorially, but Johnny sensed that childhood mockery behind his tone. 'Or maybe you still haven't figured out what to do with your dick yet?'

'I want you out of here now.' Johnny tried not to read too much into the comment. Take deep breaths, old Finbar had always advised, never let the punters see that you're rattled.

'You're getting too big for your boots, Farrell,' Alfie retorted. 'Or is it your brother's boots you're wearing now?'

'Leave our families out of this,' Johnny told him. 'This has nothing to do with Charles, or Roisin for that matter. I don't even know if you ever see the girl.'

'I just told you, didn't I?' Alfie said. 'Now what the fuck are you on about? I always said that it was hanging around with an old grandfather like you which drove Roisin crazy.'

Johnny stepped quickly across the room to grab Alfie's unpacked bag. He opened the door and stepped outside, putting the bag down in the corridor beside him.

'There's a taxi rank outside,' he said. 'This is your last chance. We'll put you up for free in another hotel but I want you out of here now.'

'My father built this hotel, Farrell,' Alfie shouted, 'and my money's as good as anyone else's.'

'Your father burnt this hotel,' Johnny retorted, 'when it was a proper hotel. One that your grandfather and my grandfather built up between them. He never built nothing in its place but a house of cards and it was only the likes of my father who kept it from tumbling down.'

'Why don't you just fuck off back to the kitchens where you belong,' Alfie said, his voice little more than a whisper now, his face white with rage. 'Tell Simon on your way that I want that bottle of whiskey brought up here now.'

'You've been barred from Finbar's Hotel since your father's funeral,' Johnny informed him. 'And I'm barring you from Upstarts as of now.'

'You? Bar me?' Alfie mocked. 'You and whose army?'

'Me and the police.'

'What are you going to charge me with? Peeping into my sister's bedroom while the kitchen boy took advantage of her?'

'The same thing you were charged with last year in that nightclub in Luton.'

Alfie stopped, the mockery gone from his features. What replaced it didn't so much seem like hatred as anguish. Anything that's important to real people is always buried in the small paragraphs, the Count had always said. Few readers might have noticed the tiny report in the *Evening Herald* that an Irishman had been charged with trying to sell Ecstasy tablets in a shabby nightclub in Luton. Simon would have spotted the name too, during his microscopic perusal of the evening paper in his cubby hole each night, but Simon rarely mentioned anything.

'You bastard,' Alfie said softly. 'Anyone can make a mistake once. But that's nothing to do with wanting to spend one final night here.'

'I don't want to know what's in your bag,' Johnny said, touching it with his feet. 'I don't want to have to open it up and find that my suspicions are right.'

'There's letters all about you in that bag if you'd only bother to read them.'

'Are there?' Johnny looked down. 'Will I open it up so?'

Alfie glared at him and Johnny stared back, trying to keep his gaze steady in this game of bluff. He didn't know which he was most afraid of finding if forced to open that bag.

'There's personal items in there as well,' Alfie said. 'All I have left. I'm moving home to Dublin. This is my first night here. Now give me back that bag.'

'Come out here and get it,' Johnny told him. It was always easier to control these situations in a corridor. Johnny found his hands were sweating. He had the absurd notion that there were photos of Roisin in the bag at his feet, her fourteen-year-old nipples brown on a twilit bog, her face captured at a quizzical, bewildered angle. Aborigines once believed their souls could be stolen by a photograph. Now Johnny felt that his soul, or at least the person whom he had once been, had been snatched from him. That child lived on only in those letters, if they really existed, every memory he had carefully put away, every childhood humiliation. His hands trembled as he knelt as if to undo the zip. The movement provoked Alfie out into the corridor like Johnny knew it would. He pushed Johnny back and picked the bag up.

'This bag is private,' he said, almost hugging it. 'Only I get to open it.'

'Stay away from my nightclub,' Johnny told him. 'We close down Finbar's Hotel in a few weeks' time with a twenty-year clean licence. We've seen off enough two-bit hustlers trying to sell their wares down there.'

'If I made one mistake then I did my time for it,' Alfie said bitterly. 'My past is none of your concern. I'm coming home. My grandfather started with nothing and you just watch me do the same. I've plans you wouldn't know about. You were always just the spastic brother, never cut out to be anything more that a kitchen skivvy.'

A bedroom door opened at the far end of the corridor and Alfie's head turned. Johnny caught a look of recognition and then genuine terror in Alfie's eyes. He was the first person inside the hotel to recognize who the guest in Room 107 was. The two Dutch journalists emerged behind the stocky Dublin man. Alfie hugged the bag closer to him. His door was wide open, his leather jacket still hanging there but Alfie started walking. There was nothing in the stocky Dubliner's face to say if he had recognized Alfie, but there again, that face never betrayed anything. Johnny followed Alfie, sensing that he was trying not to run. He reached the lift but turned for the stairs instead, as though afraid of being forced to share the elevator with him.

Johnny kept four or five paces behind. They emerged into the foyer, which was filled with the excited bustle from a party going on in the public bar. Alfie stopped and Johnny watched him.

'Just go and see Roisin for me once, eh?' Alfie muttered, defeated.

'The offer of a room somewhere else for the night still stands.'

'Fuck your charity.' Alfie glanced across at the portrait of his father. 'There's none of us ever needed handouts from the likes of you.'

The doors of the lift began to open. Alfie didn't wait to find out who was there. He walked quickly towards the exit. Johnny watched him, knowing he would recognize the slouch of those shoulders anywhere. That slouch belonged to Finbar Og on all those nights when Johnny's father coaxed him towards a paid taxi home to the shabby flat at Island-bridge where he was found dead after hotel staff hadn't seen him come in looking for his cure for several mornings. The Dubliner from 107 stepped out from the lift. This time he didn't leave his key, but walked towards the revolving door, with the Dutch journalists following a short distance behind as though they were not with him.

Johnny found that he was shaking now. He retreated into Simon's cubby hole to pour himself a large brandy from the emergency bottle kept there. Aideen came in for something and looked at the drink in surprise. Johnny downed it, no longer caring how out of character he was behaving. He poured himself another brandy. Pete Spencer could fiddle the entire clientele in the bar for all he cared now. Simon could drink his way through the hotel's stock of vodka. That stupid carpet with its FFs, which had just refused to wear out, could go on fire. The walls of this hotel could tumble down and still Johnny knew it wouldn't rid him of this sense of guilt. Simon returned and put his empty tray down. Only someone who knew the porter well would have noticed how drunk he was now. He looked at the glass in Johnny's hand.

'He's gone,' he said and Johnny nodded. Simon glanced out at reception. 'I always hated the smug little bollix,' he added quietly.

Johnny stared at the back of the old man's head, knowing that, in his heart, Simon would say the same about him.

'Are you OK? Are you sure you're able to work until eleven in the morning?' he asked, realizing that Simon was the only person he would miss from Finbar's Hotel.

'Me?' Simon replied. 'Right as rain. Sure, haven't I got a cat's life.' The porter meowed softly as if at some private joke, then moved off. Johnny finished the brandy and pulled himself together, blocking Alfie's visit from his mind. The guest from 107 hadn't left his key. That meant he was coming back. The police had started to come checking these nights just after closing time. A careful balance to be struck between profit and caution in deciding when to stop serving.

Two more American ladies approached the counter, looking for Simon. Johnny stared at the brandy bottle, then slipped it out of sight. Decades of training took over as he leaned towards the ladies and smiled, as smoothly as old Finbar himself would have done, with his mind focused purely on this hotel which still had to be run.

105

THE TEST

Although it had been on her list for many months, Maureen Connolly had never tried Finbar's Hotel before. She had noticed it one hot numb afternoon around the time that the bad news about the test had come, and had thought even in her bewilderment and shock that it might be a suitable place for her purposes. Looking at it now, she was not quite so sure. The façade was not at all impressive in this light, she thought, as she crossed quickly from the station through the damp cold air of a Dublin October evening; the place had seen better days and showed severe signs of wear and tear. The whole building appeared a little weary. In fact, to be absolutely honest, it looked as though it was about to fall down into the street. But fair is fair, she told herself; after all, perhaps these things could be said with some justification about herself. She had mixed feelings, there was no denying it. But at least she had those. Mixed feelings were better than none at all.

Yet as soon as she stepped through the heavy revolving door she knew that she had been absolutely right to come. Finbar's Hotel belonged on her list, she could tell. Yes, even here, in the small, sad, crumbling lobby so redolent of mould and decay and lost expectations, she experienced a surge of the blissful thrill to which she had looked forward all week long. It gripped her heart. It curled itself around her spine like a hot hand. There was very little doubt about it. Finbar's Hotel was a good idea.

Queuing at the counter and asking for a room had made her feel illicit and somehow furtive, especially when the receptionist had informed her that there was only a king-sized double left. Her face had grown suddenly and terrifically hot, she had half turned away from the counter towards the breeze from the revolving door, only to find a grinning young man behind her with crazy hair and an ugly Temple Bar T-shirt. He had winked at her, she was sure of it. Or was he winking at the *receptionist* for some reason? But perhaps he was winking because there was something wrong with him; he had looked as though there might well be. For a moment she had the idea that he was some kind of lunatic recently released on one of those care in the community schemes. People nowadays had all sorts of modern ideas about lunatics and what to do with them. Especially in Dublin. Here in Dublin, just about anything was possible. In any case, she was quite sure that she had been blushing even more deeply as she turned back towards the counter and told the girl that the king-sized double would be just fine.

'Grand,' said the receptionist, in a chirpy voice. 'Room 105. First floor. Lift over there.'

The strange grinning man followed her to the lift and got in. His mad, gelled hair looked like a plate of cold tagliatelle. Almost immediately he clicked his tongue in a vaguely melodramatic way, plonked his suitcase and ghetto blaster on the floor, pulled a phase tester from his pocket and began tapping rhythmically on the doors and the control panel, humming to himself as he did so. She thought she recognized the tune. He tapped harder and impressively snorted a few times. He was clearly looking for attention. She turned away and pretended to ignore him. In the mirror she gazed at her reflection and thought herself – she had to admit it – still attractive. Maybe her husband was not just being polite and salving his conscience when he told her this. His guilt for what he was secretly doing would be appalling, she knew that much. He was not a bad man at heart, not nearly so bad as he wished to be. He was the kind of Irishman who finds his own innate decency an embarrassment. She went closer to the mirror, licked her finger and smoothed her right eyebrow. From behind, she heard a soft, faint mewling sound coming from the lunatic. The poor boy was clearly astray in the head.

The lift stopped at the first floor. To her dismay her companion got out. She was in two minds about whether or not to follow, but after a moment she did. He did not look as though he would do her any harm. The fact that he was whistling she found somehow reassuring. Lunatics of the dangerous variety did not whistle, she told herself. Charles Manson, for example, it was hard to imagine whistling. He sauntered ahead of her up the corridor, with the swaggering confidence of a staff member rather than a guest. Suddenly she wondered if she had been wrong to think him insane. It came into her head that he might be something to do with the Dutch rock star who had apparently bought this tumble-down place some time ago. He looked, she thought, a bit like a Dutch rock star himself or at the very least a Dutch rock star's associate. Yes, perhaps she had been mistaken about his lunacy. Rock stars, after all, frequently did appear quite disturbed when one saw photographs of them in the newspapers, their associates even more so; indeed, if it came to it, Dutch people generally looked more than a little unstable, if not downright psychotic, not that she was anyone to talk. He stopped at the room two doors before her own and went in. She realized then that she was relieved to be rid of him.

Alone at last in her bedroom, she felt suddenly quite giddy with anticipation. She found herself thinking dreamily for a moment or two about the strange grinning Dutch rock star, and wondering what he was doing right at that very moment down the corridor. Perhaps he was composing a song. Maybe he would be taking drugs; the combination of Dutchness and musical creativity certainly did not give grounds for optimism. And thinking about what might be going on all around her, in the rooms above and below, and in those on either side, was so exciting that soon her head began to swim. She wished the walls were transparent. She knew it was ridiculous, quite irrational, but yet she felt the excitement of being alone now in a new hotel room fizz inside her, like champagne overflowing the rim of a glass.

There was something about being in a hotel room that made her feel young. It was always the same; as soon as she would cross the threshold of a hotel – which she did, somewhere in Ireland, at least once a week, and sometimes twice if her husband was out of town with his new mistress – she would once again experience that familiar, quiet ache of desire as it began to flicker through her nerve endings. She would feel grateful for the sensation then, grateful as any addict, alive once more, restored, reinvented, plugged back in to the force of her self. Alive and kicking. She said the words out loud. She said them out loud to see if they were true.

She went to the window and glanced out. The river was very muddy, full of oily-looking swirls and eddies. Gulls flew at the surface as though attacking it. Here and there, a branch or battered bough sped past madly rotating in the foamy water, the result, she told herself, of the recent and unusually powerful autumnal storms. She sat on the bed and looked around.

The room was small and far too hot. It smelled of dust, stale cigarette smoke, laundered but not thoroughly dried linen. She lay on the bed and peered up at the ceiling. Beneath the thick cream-coloured gloss paint she thought she could make out the ghostly outlines of the original plaster ornamentation, palm, myrtle, willow and citron motifs all seemingly struggling to escape.

She lay very still, her eyes fixed hard on the strange shapes. Half-remembered lines from Keats came into her mind. The 'Ode on a Grecian Urn'. What wild ecstasy. What struggle to escape. She made a mental note to mention this to the sixth-year English class when she saw them next, first thing on Monday morning, her favourite class of the whole week, the upturned, curious faces still raw with weekend kisses and hungry for poetry. Well, as hungry for poetry as they were ever going to get. Peckish, at any rate. What good would poetry do them? She had often faced that question – What good will poetry do us at a job interview, Maureen (she had insisted that her students call her by her first name) or on the boat over to London? – and had argued back that poetry was sustenance for the soul, that poetry was for the moments in every life that conventional language could not encompass. In her heart, though, she knew that they were right, as the young almost always were these days. Was there even one employer in Galway city would want to know what her girls felt about Yeats or Hopkins? (Perhaps her husband, but then he was unusual. Few men, even in Galway city, would choose as their lover a recent former pupil of their wife.) But which ambitious technocrat running an EC-funded factory out in Connemara would want to discuss Patrick Kavanagh? Could you put an interest in Chaucer on your curriculum vitae? She had a sudden sharp image of herself standing in front of her class, a foolish, fond middle-aged woman full of second-hand phrases, rigorously anatomizing the images and similes that young men had mined from the depths of love or fear. Her husband's jowly sneering face loomed up at her then, an image from some recent domestic argument, followed, a moment later, by the grim picture of his pendulous sweating arse between the outspread thighs of a teenage girl to whom she had once taught the definition of pathetic fallacy.

Would she stay in Dublin for the whole weekend? Well, perhaps she would now. It was Thursday evening, after all, she had no class on a Friday. Remaining in Dublin seemed an attractive idea. Look up some of the old crowd. Maybe go to a play or a concert at the National Concert Hall. Walk the length of Grafton Street, perhaps stroll through Saint Stephen's Green if it was sunny tomorrow, look at the piles of yellowed and golden leaves. Perhaps she would come across some more hotels to put on her list. They were building new hotels in Temple Bar all the time now. They were throwing them up faster than the guidebooks could include them. She liked Temple Bar, its small daubed shops, its hysterical giddiness, the cool young people skulking about in their sunglasses whether or not it was sunny. Yes, Temple Bar might prove fruitful, she would go down there with her notebook tomorrow and see what she could find for her list. She thought about Galway, hard Atlantic rain falling on the narrow, labyrinthine streets of the stony old city. It seemed so far away from her now.

In the shower she felt another intense surge of sensual excitement as the warm water sprayed her tired face and splashed down over her breasts. Soap stung her eyes and made her moan gently, which she enjoyed doing so much that she did it again. She thought about the pleading voice of her son on the telephone. Could the family go to France next summer? The noise on the station forecourt had been so loud that it was hard to talk and she had been glad about that; she could not have brought herself to tell him the bitter truth, that for her there might be no next summer. When she had said there was a problem with the train, that the train was delayed because of a tree fallen onto the line, that she would have to stay the night in Dublin, in Finbar's Hotel, just across from the station, her son had said in a hysterically teenage tone, 'What, Ma? What?' and then she had replied, in as casual a voice as she could muster, 'You know, Finbar's, that place the Dutch rock star's after buying? Is it Ricky Van Something? Or Rocky Van Something maybe?' and then her money had run out.

When she got out of the shower she dried herself in a half-hearted way but did not dress. Instead she lay on the bed again, her fingers exploring her body. She touched the soft, small rolls of fat on her abdomen, the nodes in her armpits, the wiry hair of her pubic mound. She thought for a while about what the doctor had told her on that bright afternoon six months ago. She thought about her body and how it was slowly failing her. Another line of poetry came. *My soul is fastened to a dying animal.* Yeats had written those magnificently cold words, near the end of his life. Through the floor she thought she could hear a radio playing. She was sure that it was a song by Oasis, 'Wonderwall', her fifth years were mad about it and she had allowed them to have a special class where they discussed the lyrics, even though she herself was not sure what exactly a wonderwall could be. The wind threw a handful of dust and leaves against the window. Her mind began aimlessly trying to recall the words of the song – and after all, you're my wonderwall; what on earth could that possibly *mean*? – but nothing after this line would come. This annoyed her at first, but then a different song started downstairs, or in some other part of the hotel, and she forgot all about Oasis. She felt dreamy, warm, comfortable as she listened to the new song. Her fingers strayed to her sex. She caressed herself there. Some minutes later, as though emerging, startled, from a kind of trance, she realized that she had been crying.

She sat up and began to get dressed, deciding not to bother with underwear, just pulling on slacks and a top. Suddenly she was bored. She looked at the telephone on the table beside the bed – it was a modern telephone, a gleaming slab of white plastic with a keypad that seemed far too detailed. She told herself that she should really call her son or daughter again to make it clear that she was staying the night here in Dublin. She was relieved that at least there was no need to lie about her whereabouts today. She had told them that she was coming to Dublin for an afternoon's shopping. Well, it was only a half lie. But when she picked up the receiver there was a crossed line and she could hear a man talking. She almost hung up, an unthinking reflex of politeness. But then smiling, enjoying her guilt, feeling her heart thump, she began to listen instead:

'Was down in Cork yesterday on a lead. New shop openin' down there next month but the bossman isn't around so I have to go and find his house. And y'know the way them houses are down in that place, impossible to find. Anyways

I'm starvin' with the hunger by the time I do. I'm so hungry I'd ate a tinker's mickey.'

A second male voice laughed here and said, 'You're fuckin' lovely. Where's your room, by the way?'

'The top floor. Yeah. So anyways, and then, right, what happens, I find the place, this Indian chap comes to the door. Pakistani or some fuckin' thing. Family owns a restaurant down there in Cork. The Montenotte Raj be name, but now he's gettin' into the book trade.'

At this point the second voice cut in again. 'Come on, meet me downstairs, we'll talk about it over dinner. They're nearly finished servin'. I'm on the mobile, down here in the restaurant.'

She replaced the telephone but found herself feeling a little curious about these two men. What were they? Salesmen of some kind, that much was clear. But what were they selling? Had one of them said something about books? Were they book salesmen? They both had strong Dublin accents, yet they seemed to be staying in this hotel. Why would anyone who lived in Dublin need to stay in a Dublin hotel for the night? Well, if it came to it, what reason had she to do this? No reason. No reason at all that she could understand. Had they said that they were going downstairs for their dinner? To the hotel restaurant? Perhaps it would be fun to go down there herself and see if she could pick them out of the crowd.

In the lift, she stared at her reflection again. The odd thing, she felt, was that she did not appear like a woman who was dying. She looked tired admittedly, pale, and a little frayed around the edges; but not like a woman who had less than a year to live. Was it true? How could it be true? She had a sudden sharp metal image of the cancer cells like the little circular munching monsters in the Pacman video game her son had loved so much as a child. How those greedy bleeping scavengers had raced around the screen, remorselessly devouring all in their path. It was difficult to accept and believe that now she too was being consumed. Yet she had seen with her own eyes the dark cloudy shadows on the X-ray screen. She was dying, the doctor had told her. There was no doubt about it. She had maybe ten months. She had actually apologized to him. She was sorry, she'd said, that he'd had to give her the news. It must be very hard for him to give out news like that every day.

In the lobby, a party of savagely tanned Americans had congregated around a noticeboard on which was a poster of the triple spiral carving on the massive stone outside the passage grave at Newgrange. Another smaller group was converging on a stocky handsome man who seemed, from the way they jabbered and poked at him, to be somebody important. Was he a tour guide, someone from a travel company? Outside the wind was gusting so hard that the revolving door was slowly turning as though placed in motion by some invisible God. She smiled to herself as she overheard one of the tourists, a doughy-faced, humourless old man in a turquoise golf jumper, asking the barman, 'Hey there, sir, let me get an Irish coffee without the whiskey.'

The small square restaurant smelled of grease and disinfectant. Staff were moving between the tables, setting them for breakfast. Two middle-aged men, one small and thin with a horsy face, the other as large as a rugby player, were sitting at a circular table in the middle of the room; although they were whispering to each other, she thought she could just barely make out their Dublin vowels and intonations and told herself, yes, these were the men whose telephone conversation she had overheard. They looked so easy with each other, so happy and relaxed, their privacy so quintessentially male, that she felt ashamed of herself for eavesdropping. She glanced around the room. There were poorly done charcoal portraits of famous Irish writers on the walls; she recognized Joyce and Brendan Behan immediately but confused Beckett with Sean O'Casey, only correcting her mistake when she went up close to see if she could make out the artist's signature.

The ancient-looking waitress had a flattish nose with prominent purple phlebitic veins showing through the flesh.

'We're closed,' she said.

'Oh, you could squeeze me in,' said Maureen, with a smile. 'Go on. See if you can.'

The woman sighed and said all right, if she was quick about it, and nodded towards one of the circular tables. She asked if she could have a booth.

'You don't want one of them booths, pet,' the waitress said. 'A table in the middle is nicer.'

'I'd rather a booth,' she said. 'If it's all the same to yourself.'

The waitress gave another plangent sigh and beckoned her towards a booth, making a great show of shaking loose the conically folded serviette and spreading it across her lap. The menu was made of plastic – she noticed, with a small shudder, that it offered 'a bowel of fresh soup'. As she read on, she tried hard not to listen to the two salesmen, but found that once the small horsy-faced fellow raised his voice he was almost impossible to ignore.

'So I'm showin' this Pakistani all the catalogues and givin' him the full SP and he's noddin' away at me, fierce polite chap he is, y'know, it's all please this and please that and whatever you're havin' yerself.'

She opened her copy of *Hello!* magazine but found that she could not concentrate. The horsy-faced salesman telling the story was growing more animated and enthusiastic all the time, waving his hands in the air and bobbing from side to side.

'Anyway, his missus is in the kitchen while all this is goin' on and she's cookin' up this curry. And it smells only gorgeous. And then, says he to me, "Mr Dunne, we'd be delighted if you'd join us for a bite t' ate." And I go, "Ah fuck off, no," not wantin' t' impose, like, although be now I'd ate a nun's arse through a convent gate.'

'Merciful hour, you're lovely,' the large man said. 'Lovely is the only fuckin' word for you.'

Just then the stocky man she had seen in the lobby and thought to be a tour guide came strolling into the restaurant. He caught her eye, smiled, nodded quickly and strangely formally in her direction. The waitress approached him and led him to a table. She wondered why *he* had not been told that the restaurant was closed. She felt a little aggrieved. The horsy-faced salesman leaned in close to his colleague and began to speak in a confidential whisper that she could not hear.

When she turned her head to attract the waitress's attention she noticed with a start that the tour guide seemed to be smiling across at her. He had a kindly red face which a novelist might have described as florid, thick but tidily cut light grey hair, eyebrows that almost met above his long straight nose. He pointed at her.

'She used to run around with Bryan Ferry,' he said. 'Isn't

that right? Bryan Ferry, that guy who used to be in Roxy Music? You remember that group?'

His accent was East Coast American, his voice as soft as a new dishcloth.

'Who?' she asked.

'Jerry Hall,' he said. 'The model.'

'Did she?'

He smiled again. 'I'm sorry. I just saw her there.' He pointed again. 'I mean on the cover of your magazine. And for some reason that came into my mind.'

'The fact she used to go out with Bryan Ferry out of Roxy Music?'

'Yeah.'

'I see.'

'Just as well they didn't get married, isn't it?' he said.

'Why's that?'

'Well, because then she would've been called Jerry Ferry, wouldn't she?' His crimson cheeks crinkled up into a grin.

She couldn't help laughing.

'I suppose that's right,' she said.

'That is right,' he chuckled. 'My kid told me that once. Killer, isn't it?'

'It's a good one right enough.'

Something about his timorous smile was encouraging. He looked, she thought, partly like a small boy, but also like a man who was genuinely comfortable with women.

'Won't you join me this evening?' he asked. 'If you're dining alone?'

'Oh, no thank you,' she said. 'I wouldn't interrupt you.'

'You wouldn't be,' he said. 'As you see, I'm all alone too.'

She thought about his suggestion for a moment. This was certainly not what she had planned. But what harm? It was a public place, after all. What could happen? It was a very long time indeed since she had had dinner with a handsome American possessed of a sense of humour. If she ever had. Before she had quite made up her mind to accept his invitation he had stood up and was pulling out the second chair at his table.

'Please won't you?' he asked again. 'You'd be doing me a real favour. I hate to eat alone.'

He was called Ray Dempsey. When she gave her own name he repeated it several times – 'Maureen Connolly, Maureen Connolly, how lovely.' His handshake was warm and very firm. How inky-black his eyes seemed and how white his small, straight teeth. He was from New York, he told her. Yes, she was absolutely correct, he was a tour guide. He had worked in many countries, Mexico, Argentina, Spain, Peru. He had majored in Spanish at college. But he loved Ireland best of all. Every year for the last ten, he had accompanied a party of holidaymakers to Ireland in the autumn. He always liked to spend time in Dublin – 'I mean, it's a great European city' – but he loved Connemara especially.

'The Becketty nothingness of it,' he said, 'is a line I read in a short story. A story by John Updike, I believe. Whatever. But it sums up Connemara, though, doesn't it?'

'Yes,' she said, startled by the rightness of the phrase. 'Yes, it does.'

'The Becketty nothingness of it,' he repeated, and smiled. 'I love that.'

Her mind was racing during the few minutes that they spent looking at the menu. And yet, at the same time, she felt so immediately comfortable with him. He was so unthreatening. It was something to do with the largeness of his hands, the incipience of his gestures, the slight clumsiness in the way he held himself, always seeming to abandon a movement halfway through. She told the waitress that she wanted plain sole, grilled, and a side salad. The American ordered a large rare steak, with mashed potato, carrots and extra fried onions.

'We're lucky to get fed at all,' she said, when the waitress had gone, 'they told me they were closing.'

'They usually make an allowance for me,' he said. 'One good thing about being a tour guide. Hotels look after you. And I'm glad, because boy, am I hungry tonight? I have an appetite here.'

He beamed at her. 'Tonight is a big feast night actually, for Jews. I'm a Jew.'

'Really?' she said. 'Is that right?'

'Well, kind of. I'm Jew-ish, more than a Jew.'

'So what's the festival?'

'Oh, well, today is the first day of Succoth. The festival of the close of the harvest.'

'Really? And is it on the same day every year?'

'No, no. It begins on the fifteenth day of the Jewish month of Tishri, in the fall. It goes on for eight days if you're reform. Nine if you're orthodox.'

'And what are you?'

'Well, my family wasn't orthodox.'

'Oh,' she smiled. 'Neither was mine.'

He laughed. 'Right. Whose is?'

'But tell me more about your festival. I'd like to know.'

He nodded. 'Well, let's see, the final day of the festival is called Simchat Torah – Rejoicing of the Law. And on that day, the yearly cycle of reading the Torah begins again.' His face took on a mock stern expression and his eyebrows went up and down as he waggled his finger.

'Amid much dancing and singing,' he intoned, and then his face creased up into a laugh again, thin crowlines appearing at the corners of his twinkling eyes. 'Is what the rabbi used to tell us as kids. Like he was ordering us. Judaism is the only religion I know where you're actually ordered to have a good time. On pain of death!'

'Catholicism isn't like that, I can tell you,' she said.

'Yeah, I know,' he grinned. 'My dad was Irish Catholic.'

She was taken aback to hear this, but thought it might be rude to say so. Still, he seemed to pick up on her surprise. His father came from Mayo, he explained, and he had emigrated to New York in the twenties. He had worked for a time on building sites and in bars, and, briefly, as a longshoreman on the Hudson River. He had met a Polish Jewish girl, converted to Judaism and married her. After they had married he had tried to join the police force many times but he had never passed the tests, because he had bad feet. He told the story of his father and his bad feet with charm and confidence, pausing from time to time to ask if he was boring her. She kept saying no, he was not, which was true. His voice was so beautifully gentle. Listening to him talk about even a subject as seemingly uninteresting as his father's bad feet reminded her somehow of being in the warm shower earlier, and having the delicious water pour down over her. She noticed, while he talked, that he had the American habit of adding a superfluous question mark to the end of a sentence. She found this strangely involving, producing a need in her to interject with 'yes' and 'I see' or 'I know what you mean', when usually she would have remained silent in a conversation with a strange man about his father's feet, or, indeed, if it came to it, any of his father's appendages.

When the food came, plates almost fizzing with microwave heat, he continued to talk about his father. 'He had this weird thing about Ireland. This love–hate thing? Most of the time it was, "Oh, Ireland, that awful place, I'd rain bombs down on that priest-ridden dump if I could." But when he was drunk it was different. When he was drunk it was long live the IRA and three cheers for Michael Collins and all that. He used to get these I guess Republican newspapers mailed over from Belfast and read 'em. "I'm a Democrat every damn place in the world, son," that's what he used to say, "but in the North of Ireland I'm a god damn Republican. And you should be too."'

He looked at her. 'But enough,' he said. 'I don't know what's got into me tonight. Boring you to death like this.'

'Oh, no, you weren't, really.'

'You're very kind,' he smiled. 'But tell me something about yourself.'

She thought about this request as she pushed the food around her plate. She truly did. For one moment, she had the most terrible compulsion to be absolutely honest with him, to say, 'Ray, here is something about myself: my name is Maureen Connolly and I am married to Hugh, a damaged, silent man, a county councillor and a supermarket manager who has sex in his Mitsubishi Lancer most nights with a woman younger than our own daughter, a girl really, I taught her, who works in a record shop in Galway city, and I wouldn't really mind any more except that sometimes I actually see her footprints on the glove compartment door, Ray, he can't even be bothered to clean them off. And I am dying, Ray. I am dying. My children do not know that in less than a year I will be dead. I can't bring myself to tell them. I have cancer. There is no hope for me, none at all. I have known for some time. I don't want to die, Ray. I love being alive. I am so afraid. I want to live. But I have cancer. And once a week, when my husband thinks I am having an overnight treatment in the hospital, I drive to Galway station and park my car there and get on the first train. No matter where it's going. I have coffee and a sandwich on the train. I think about things. And when I get to wherever the train is going I stay the night in a hotel. Often it's Dublin. Most of the time it's Dublin. I have a long list of hotels in Dublin, Ray. I stay in hotels because somehow they make me feel alive. They're so full of life, don't you think, Ray? So full of life.'

She looked at him as he peered at her, his bushy eyebrows raised in a question.

'There's nothing much to tell,' she said. 'I've a very uninteresting life compared to yours, I'm sure.'

'Well, what do you do, Maureen? Are you a working lady?'

'I'm afraid so, yes,' she laughed. 'I teach part time. Down in Galway city.'

He nodded. 'Oh, you teach. What? You teach high school or college?'

'I teach fifteen- to eighteen-year-olds. Girls. English literature.'

'Oh, that's great. That's so wonderful. Do you enjoy that, Maureen?'

Nobody had ever asked her this before, as far as she could remember. 'I suppose I do, yes,' she said. 'I mean, the kids are great. They keep you on your toes too these days. They're so aware. They grow up so fast now, I feel sorry for them sometimes.'

He pointed towards the ceiling. 'Through a chink too wide comes in no wonder,' he slowly said.

'Patrick Kavanagh,' she smiled.

'One of my dad's favourites,' he said. 'And mine, I guess.'

'Oh, yes, and mine. I love Kavanagh. That sums it up well, too, doesn't it? Kids now, they get everything so soon, whether they want it or not.'

'Really,' he said. 'I have an eighteen-year-old daughter myself. Trying to keep up with her drives me just about nuts. So I can imagine how challenging that must be for you. You have kids yourself, Maureen?'

She paused for a moment and stared across at the window. 'Yes,' she said, then, 'a boy and a girl.' She paused again before allowing the lie to come. 'They're grown up now. Both married. Living in England.'

The hotel manager stalked up to the table like an executioner and asked if everything was all right. They both nodded and murmured a few words of satisfaction, even though in truth the meal had not been very well cooked. The manager peered down at their plates, then moved away with a bow.

His officiousness amused them; when he had left they allowed themselves a small and secret laugh at his expense. But her companion seemed like a man who could laugh without being cruel or superior, and she liked that about him. After the dinner they talked some more but she found that she could not concentrate. She kept asking herself why she had lied earlier about the ages of her children. Why had she said that they were married? It was a thing she had been doing lately, for no reason at all telling the most ludicrous lies. A waiter came and poured coffee. She noticed and found it oddly moving that her new acquaintance was so polite to the waiter, and said 'please' and 'thank you' and addressed him as 'sir'. When the waiter left, he took a sip of his coffee and looked at her.

'Maureen,' he said, with a nervous expression, 'I have something a little naughty I'd like to ask you now.'

'What?'

'I have a guilty secret. You promise you won't tell?'

'I suppose so, yes.'

He leaned forward.

'Would you mind if I smoked a cigarette?' he said. 'I'll tell you the truth, I have a weakness for a cigarette with my coffee.'

'Not at all,' she laughed. 'Smoke, please.'

He grinned. 'You looked worried there.'

'My God, did I? Well I didn't know what you were going to say.'

Chuckling lightly, he took a packet of Marlboros from his jacket pocket and lit one up.

'Oh, my gosh, I'm terribly sorry, Maureen. Would you like one? Do you smoke?'

Again came the flash of the tiny yellow ravening monsters chewing their way through her leathery ashen lung. She closed her eyes for a second and willed them away.

'Do you know what?' she said. 'I think I will actually, Ray. I haven't in years, but I feel like the one tonight.'

He handed her a cigarette and lit it for her, almost brushing against her knuckles as he curled his long fingers around the flickering flame. She dragged hard on the cigarette, sucked the thick smoke deep into herself. The waitress brought the bill, slapped it down on the table and flounced off.

He put his hand on the bill.

'I must say, I'd be honoured to get the check, Maureen. Could I? Make up for boring you to death about my dad?'

'Oh, no, I couldn't possibly let you do that, thanks. And it wasn't boring at all.'

'Really, I'd like to.'

'No, honestly. I'd rather you didn't. But thanks anyway.'

'Well, then, would you let me buy you a drink, maybe? A nightcap?'

'I don't know,' she said.

'Oh, well, if you've made plans,' he said. 'I understand. But thank you for your company over dinner. I must say it was really pleasant to meet you, Maureen.'

She glanced at her watch and shrugged. Her husband would just be getting in now. She knew his routine better than he did himself. He would come in to the kitchen, go straight to the sink and thoroughly wash his hands, as he always did. For months after he had begun his affair she had wondered why he did this. Then one night he had forgotten to do it and when he had murmuringly stroked her face in his sleep, something he sometimes still did, especially when he was feeling guilty, she had got the faint but unmistakable smell of condom rubber from his fingers. It had broken her heart. She had lain beside him that night and wept like a child. The next day he had brought her home flowers from the shop. That was another tell-tale sign.

'Well, all right, then,' she laughed. 'I could go for a quick one, I suppose.'

He beamed. 'You only live once, huh?'

They left the restaurant and walked across the lobby

towards the public bar. Halfway across he held out his arm and she linked it. Behind the reception desk a radio was playing a song which she thought she recognized from her college days, but she could not think of its name. Years ago her husband had bought the LP for her as a birthday gift. Was it shortly after they had got engaged? Or married? She was not certain. Was it around the time of her first pregnancy? He had brought her to a restaurant on Barna Pier and given it to her over dessert. It struck her as strange that she could remember the record's appearance, all wrapped up in blue and silver paper, but could not recall the name of the song.

She asked the American about it.

'I think that's "You're So Vain" by Carly Simon,' he said.

She squeezed his arm. 'So it is, so it is.'

'As a matter of fact, I think my favourite singer is Carly Simon,' he told her.

'Really? Mine too.'

Maureen Connolly, she said to herself, what an unbelievable liar you are sometimes.

They entered the small smoke-filled bar and moved slowly through the crowd. It was almost completely full – people seemed to be very drunk and someone was attempting to start a singsong – but as if by preordination there were two high stools by the bar and they went and sat on those. When he asked what she wanted, she said she would have a glass of dry white wine. He called for this, and a tonic water and ice for himself.

'Penny for your thoughts,' he said.

'Just Carly Simon,' she told him. 'Brings back a few memories.'

'Me too,' he said. 'Before all this terrible rap stuff, huh?'

'You're not into the rap? The girls in class seem to love it.'

He chuckled again. She really liked the way he chuckled. 'I hear a bit of it, Maureen, you know, with my own kids around the house. But I don't get it. All that MC Hammer drives me nuts. I prefer "You're So Vain". But then I guess Carly's just my era. The Jurassic Era, that's what the kids say to me.'

'Yes. Did you know she was engaged to Bob Marley once, Ray?'

He turned and peered into her eyes. 'Wow, really? No, I didn't know that.'

She felt herself blush a little. 'No, no. It's a joke. Carly Marley, you see.'

'Carly Marley?'

He threw back his head and laughed out loud. They clinked their glasses and smiled.

'You got me,' he said. 'You got me there.'

He drained his glass in one long slug, checked if she wanted more wine and called for another tonic water. 'So don't you like to drink?' she asked.

'Oh, no, no, it isn't that.' He put his finger into his tumbler and stirred the ice cubes around. 'Actually there was a time in my life when I liked it too much. So I can't drink any more. I'm an alcoholic.'

She felt stupid and embarrassed. 'Oh, I'm sorry, Ray,' she said.

'Hey, don't be sorry. It's fine. What are you so sorry about?'

'I'm mortified now, joking you like that. You must think I'm dreadful.'

'Of course I don't.' His eyes stayed on hers for a couple of moments. 'I think you're quite lovely actually. I really do.'

His flirtation unsettled her and she glanced away from him to collect her thoughts. What was the name of that restaurant in Barna? She couldn't recall it now. But after the dinner they had walked the length of the pier and looked out at the Aran Islands for a while. The words 'the end' had been daubed in whitewash onto the broken wall at the end of the pier. They had joked about it together. She remembered the sound of his laughter echoing on the water. Then they had driven into Barna wood and made love in the car.

'I've an uncle an alcoholic,' she said.

'Oh, really?' The American nodded. 'I must look him up in the directory.'

She laughed and slapped his hand.

'I didn't mean it like that,' she said. 'Don't be nasty.'

He offered her another cigarette and she took it. She felt the smoke burn the back of her throat. 'But why did you give up the jar in the end, Ray? Do you know?'

'Well,' he said, 'you remember where you were the moment you heard Kennedy was shot?'

'Of course,' she said.

'I don't.' He smiled, and took a long drag.

'Really?'

'No,' he said. 'I'm kidding.'

'Why then? Really? May I ask?'

He sighed. 'My drinking cost me my first marriage. Rita – that's my first wife – she left me and took our two girls with her. I couldn't blame her. I did some bad things. She was such a wonderful person. Kind-hearted, compassionate. But marriage to a drunk is a full-time job. And I guess she hadn't signed on for that.'

He took out his wallet, opened it, removed a creased Polaroid photograph of his daughters, the taller of the pair wearing an academic gown and mortarboard. 'That's Lisa on the right, and Cathy on the day of her graduation.'

'They're beautiful-looking girls.'

'Yeah,' he said. 'They take after their mom there.'

'Do you ever see her?'

'No, no. She's married again now to a nice fellow. Lives in Oregon. I guess we lost touch over the years.'

He put the photograph back in his wallet and took a sip of his drink.

'And did you ever marry again, Ray?'

'Yes, yes, I did.'

'Well, that's nice for you, isn't it? Doesn't she mind you travelling so much?'

He crushed his cigarette out slowly in the ashtray on the bar. 'She passed away, I'm afraid. Three years ago now. She was killed in an auto accident. By a drunk driver.'

'Oh, Ray, I'm sorry. That's dreadful.'

He shook his head and said nothing.

She touched his arm. 'How truly awful for you.'

'That hurt, yes,' he said. 'That did hurt.' He seemed suddenly lost for words. His eyes ranged around the room and took on a strangely mystified expression, as though he was not sure how he had got there. 'I don't know what else I can tell you about it.'

'No. Of course.'

'I guess life must go on,' he said. Then he stared at his fingernails and shook his head again. 'Well, actually, I don't know that it must. But it does seem to anyway.'

It made her uncomfortable, the sudden darkening of his mood, the downward curl of his mouth. He lit another cigarette and deeply inhaled. He held it between his middle finger and thumb and rolled it to and fro, staring all the time at the glowing red tip. For a few moments she could think of nothing at all to say. She peered around the bar, desperate to find a subject for conversation. 'And are you a religious man, Ray? Would that be a consolation for you?'

He stared into his glass. 'No, Maureen. Not really.'

When he glanced up at her, she saw that he was trying to smile, although now she was horrified to see that there were tears in his dark eyes. 'I hope I'm not offending you, Maureen, but to me religion creates fear where there's nothing to fear' – he paused and took a drag – 'and it gives you hope when, actually, there's nothing to hope for.'

'I never thought of it like that,' she said.

'No. Well anyway.' He pinched the bridge of his nose and suddenly smiled again. 'No politics or religion in the bar, right? Isn't that what people advise?' He brushed the ash from his knees. 'So are you married yourself now, Maureen? May I ask you that?'

'Well,' she said, 'I'm entangled.'

He nodded quickly and diplomatically, as though he had been fully expecting an answer like this. 'One of those complicated situations.'

She pondered his phrase for a moment. 'Well, I suppose so, yes. One of those complicated situations. Would you mind if we didn't talk about it?'

He nodded. 'I've been divorced,' he said. 'I understand the pain of that. The pain of being left, yes. Of course, yes. But there's a pain in leaving too, isn't there? It takes real courage to say goodbye.'

'I suppose it does.' She swallowed some wine and glanced around the bar.

'So can you tell me even a little about this . . . this entanglement of yours?'

'Maybe entanglement is the wrong word,' she said.

'OK,' he said. 'So tell me the right word.'

She gazed into his generous innocent face. He looked quite like her doctor, she thought, the doctor who had given her the news. They could well have been brothers.

'I'm a nun,' she said.

(Good *God*, she thought.)

He chuckled into his glass.

'I am,' she said. 'Really.'

(Holy *Jesus*, woman, what are you *saying* to him?)

'Get out of here.'

'Ray, I'm a nun.'

'Right,' he said. 'And I'm Mother Teresa.'

'Honestly,' she laughed. 'I am.'

He gaped at her blankly for a few moments. Then he pointed at her. 'Ha! Hold on now. I've caught you out.'

'How do you mean?'

'Well you told me earlier you had two kids, Mother Superior. How'd you come by them, huh? Immaculate conception?'

(Don't, Maureen. Stop. *Don't*. That's enough.)

She opened her mouth and decided to let the words come.

'My husband died twelve years ago,' she said. 'Of cancer. Lung cancer. He . . . the day he got the news he came home and told me. I was in the kitchen. At the sink. Washing my hands. And I . . . my hands smelled of rubber, you see. From my gloves. I'd been washing the dishes and my hands smelled of rubber. And I was too shocked to say anything. I just held him for a long time. Close. I told him I loved him. Because if it had been me, I remember thinking, that's what I would have wanted. Just someone to hold me. And to say, "I love you, Maureen. I'll take care of you." But he didn't. I mean, I

didn't. And in the months that came we . . . we got on badly.
We drifted apart. It was as though he thought I was blaming
him for being sick. I couldn't ever understand what it must
have been like for him. I'm sure I must have seemed cold.
He maybe didn't see how much, how desperately I loved
him. Perhaps I couldn't show him. I'm not good at expressing
my emotions. And I must have seemed unfeeling to him,
although of course in my heart I loved him so much that . . .
that if I could have died in his place, then I would have. But
I couldn't, of course. I couldn't. And so then he died.
Without me ever being able to say what I felt. Without us
ever even saying goodbye properly. We never actually talked
about it, although we knew for a year it was going to happen.
It was never said. Nothing was verbalized. And then one day
he died. And my kids were grown up, you see. And so I
entered the convent then.'

His face was white with shock. 'You're a nun,' he said.

She felt hot tears spill down her cheeks. 'That's right.'

'Maureen, I . . . I'm terribly sorry for being so flippant.'

'It's OK.'

'That's terrible for you. Your husband passing away like
that.'

'Yes,' she said. 'He was . . . he was so in love with life. He
really loved being alive. The way some people don't in
Ireland. But he did, Ray. He did. In his last few months I
think he loved it even more. It began to show itself in strange
ways. Most people would find them strange. I . . . For
example, one night every week he was supposed to stay in
the hospital. But without telling anybody, he stopped doing
that. He wouldn't do it. One morning I popped in to visit
him there and found he hadn't been for ages. He'd been
lying to me about where he was.'

'So where was he?'

'I found out that he had been going away. He would drive down to the station in Galway and get on a train. The first train. Anywhere. When I confronted him about it he said he wanted to see the country one last time. Before he died. He'd go to a hotel somewhere, a small hotel usually, and just be by himself. It seemed to give him something he couldn't find at home.'

He offered her a handkerchief and she dried her eyes.

'I'm OK,' she said. 'Really, I'm fine. I just haven't talked about it for ages. I'm fine. Let's just talk about something else now. Can we?'

He looked limp with amazement as he tried to begin a new conversation with her. 'Well, you're a nun now. Isn't that something?'

'Yes. It is.'

'And should I be sitting here in a bar with a nun? Isn't that some kind of sin?'

'Well, I'm fine about it,' she said. 'If you are.'

'I think I need to go to the bathroom now,' he said. 'Would you excuse me, please?'

She watched him walk quickly out the door. The bar seemed to grow more hot. Two burly policemen appeared outside in the lobby, their luminous yellow night-jackets sleek with rain. She felt light-headed with panic. Suddenly she noticed that the salesmen whose conversation she had overheard earlier were at a table close to her, with another man. All three men were clearly drunk. The horsy-faced one seemed to be telling the same interminable story about curry and Cork, or certainly a similar story, and his friend, the man who looked like a rugby player, had a look of almost sculptural boredom on his face.

'I could not fuckin' believe it,' drawled Horse-Face, 'when I woke up the next mornin' *me arse was like the Japanese flag*!'

Why in the name of God and all the saints, she asked herself, did you have to say you were a bloody nun? Of all things. Where did that come from? All right, yes, the man was trying to flirt with you. But all he wanted to know was whether you were married or not before persisting. A nun? Good Jesus. You don't even *like* nuns. Why are you doing this kind of thing? *Why*? Her mind drifted back over some of the more recent of her trips to Dublin. In the Gresham Hotel on O'Connell Street she had found herself telling the night porter that she was separated from her husband, a well-known poet whose name she could not reveal. On the train home to Galway the previous month she had got into an argument about politics with a fanatical young priest in the dining car and told him that she had just obtained a divorce. In Jury's Inn at Christchurch only last week she had told the waitress who had served her breakfast that she was a widow whose husband had been murdered by armed burglars from the inner city. How did *that* happen? Now she was a nun. She amazed herself.

To her great surprise, Ray finally came back from the bathroom. He sat down, drank what was left of his drink in one go and said he thought there had been an incident outside, he had overheard the police in the lobby say something on their radios about suspecting that drugs were being sold in the nightclub downstairs. Just at that moment, as if to confirm what he had said, the manager suddenly appeared in the doorway. At a nod from the manager the staff moved quickly to make a great show of the bar being long closed. They lifted the glasses off the tables in the corner where some sort of office party seemed to be going on, even though most of the drinks were unfinished. Two revellers stood up shouting and began to square up to a barman.

One of the policemen strode in, followed by the manager, who raised his hands in the air and clapped them together. The lights in the bar came on. The conversation quickly faded.

'This bar is closed as of now,' the policeman announced.

A low groan filled the room.

'Is the residents' lounge still open?' someone shouted.

'Only to residents,' the barman replied.

'Is it too late to book a fuckin' room?' the man shouted, and everyone laughed.

'It'd be as well now,' the policeman said, 'if you'd all go on up to bed or the residents' lounge or wherever you're bound for. Because otherwise I'll have to take statements from everyone here.'

Grumbling and complaining, people began to get to their feet and shuffle out, some with glasses or bottles concealed under their coats. She and the American slowly followed. The lobby seemed cold and draughty. He had a tired and washed-out look in his eyes. He stared around himself as though he was trying to think of something to say.

'The licensing laws in this country,' he finally did say.

'Yes,' she said. 'It all makes for a very sudden goodnight.'

He glanced at his watch. 'I guess,' he agreed. 'Unless you feel like a trip to the famous residents' lounge.'

Her heart seemed to hammer against her ribs. Her face felt as though it was on fire.

(Maureen, *don't*. Just leave now. It's late.)

'I don't know,' she said. 'Would you like to come to my room for a while? For a cup of tea or something? I think I saw a kettle up there.'

He pursed his lips and refused to meet her eyes. 'OK, sure,' he said. 'Why not? Maybe we've had enough of bars for one night.'

In the lift they said nothing at all to each other. She thought about what her husband would say if he could see her now. He would be fast asleep at home in their bed, the bed where their two beautiful children had been conceived. There would be a cup of tea on his bedside table. He would have the radio on, as he always did when she was not there. She found it attractive about him that in her absence he could not sleep without the radio playing. Walking down the corridor, she found herself hoping that she had not left her underwear lying on the floor. She need not have worried. The room was as bare and neat as a cell. She filled the kettle and told the American to sit down somewhere. It occurred to her that she could not actually remember the last time she had been in a hotel room with her husband or anyone else. He ambled over to the window and stared out for a while as though something specific and highly unusual had taken his attention, then sat on the sill.

'You know,' he said suddenly, 'I have a close friend who's religious. A Catholic priest.'

'I must look him up in the directory,' she said.

He pointed at her and laughed.

'Good one. But I was just thinking just now, it's a funny thing, but he's actually the one responsible for turning me into an atheist in the end. Indirectly.'

'How?'

'He was involved with this born-again thing in New York. Prayer groups. I don't know. A few years ago, I was having a hard time with my drinking and he persuaded me to come along one night. And that turned me off for good.'

'Why was that?' she said. 'Tell me about it.'

'You don't want to know.'

'I do, Ray. Tell me.'

'Well, let's see.'

She handed him a cup of tea and sat on the bed.

'Tell me,' she repeated. 'Sure amn't I after spilling out my soul to you.'

He gave a soft laugh. 'Well, it's a real hot summer in New York. The water's running short and people are going crazy. Everyone's slithering around in these cycling shorts, looking pink and moist. Like miserable chickens. And this night, me and Liam Gallagher, that's my pal, Father Liam . . .'

'Father Liam Gallagher?'

'Yeah, right. It's a blast isn't it? Anyway, I've decided I'm going to this prayer thing. I mean, what the hell, right? Sometimes you'll try anything. And it's in a hairdresser's salon. Because where they usually have it, the air-conditioner's broken down, so – one of the group, the leader, Stephen his name is, he works in a hair salon where the air-conditioning's OK, so the meeting's relocated to there.'

She laughed into her tea. 'Go on,' she said.

'Well, thankfully, we're the first to arrive. Me and Liam. There's coffee and sodas beforehand, even some cold cuts and sandwiches. It all kicks off with a little tambourine playing and guitar strumming. What I'm saying is, it's harmless enough. But it's when the praying in tongues starts up that I really start to feel, Jesus, I want out. This is no way for a grown man to be spending his time.'

A grown man, she thought to herself. You poor deluded frightened thing.

'What I remember is sitting there thinking about the news. I'd seen the CNN news that afternoon in a bar. Something about the ceasefire in Northern Ireland. That made me think about my dad. He'd died the year before. And something about a satellite that was lost – the newsreader said if it crashed into the earth it would leave a hole the size of Manhattan Island. I remember too, I was thinking about Bosnia. It was so strange to me, I was like, people in Bosnia are blowing each other to pieces, and I'm sitting here half drunk in a hairdresser's salon, not feeling right or normal in any way much talking about. The heat, for a start, it's the kind of heat you can get feelings about. I keep feeling, if I put my feet into a basin of water these clouds of steam are gonna come fizzing out of them. There are middle-aged people all around me, people my age. But they're behaving like beatniks. There's this guy across from me and he's sitting in one of these old-fashioned barber chairs? And he's praying away. But this guy has a head like a racehorse. Seriously. You're laughing now, but you should see this guy. And the woman beside him, she's cosying up to me on the coffee table and she's clearly in need of some kind of medical attention. She's rolling her eyes and going, "Praise you, oh, praise you, Jesus," in this weird voice. You know what I mean?'

'Yes,' she said. 'I do know what you mean, Ray.'

(You don't have a clue what he means, you liar.)

'God sent his only son to die. That's what Stephen informs us at this point. Yeah, right, I'm thinking, but not hair dye. And I don't feel great, Maureen. There's this strange light in the room. Strange sodium light oozing in from the street through the slats in the venetian blinds. And something about this light is making me feel sick. I'm looking at the way it glints on the domes of the hairdryers. And there's this hairdressing smell too? That metallic smell you get with hairspray? That pine-scented shampoo. You know? It doesn't smell like pine, it's like a committee's idea of what pine smells like?'

'I know exactly what you mean,' she said. 'I hate it too.'

(You don't hate it at all, Maureen. You quite like it, actually.)

'Right. So this little woman's sitting beside me, with the Little Richard eyes. And right there beside her, I mean *right* beside her on the coffee table, is this pile of women's magazines? And I can see the words SHATTERING ORGASMS in heart-attack pink on one of the covers, stamped across this picture of some actress in a black bikini. I hope that doesn't offend you, me saying that, but there it is, that's what it says, SHATTERING ORGASMS.'

'It doesn't offend me, Ray.'

'Shattering orgasms. And we're supposed to be praying. And I mean I'm looking at this woman beside me and I'm trying to figure out if she's ever had a shattering orgasm herself, you know? And to tell you the truth, I doubt it. And then I wonder if *I* have. And I don't really think so. Certainly, if I've ever had a shattering orgasm I don't remember it now. But then I'm not so sure I'd want to. An orgasm that's actually shattering, I don't know if I'd want.'

'No, Ray,' she said. 'I don't think I would either.'

(Like hell you wouldn't, Maureen. Like hell.)

'And then Stephen, the group leader, he starts with that praying in tongues. This is a big man I'm talking about here. Likes to eat. But he opens his mouth and lets this noise come out. It's not so much verbal diarrhoea as verbal incontinence. And then the whole lot of these people start doing the same thing. Making this noise, bobbing backwards and forwards. Father Liam, he's warned me about this but now it's happening. Now Stephen is really doing it. The man is howling here.'

She did her best to laugh.

'And the noise, it's like, I dunno, all vowels, wah wah, woh woh, and I'm trying to feel pious but it sounds to me like the chorus of some doo-wop song. He's saying, "Join in, people, if you feel the Spirit moving, move with it." And awopbopaloobop is what comes into my mind. To tell you nothing but the God's truth. Awopbopaloobop alopbam-boom. Stephen's saying, "Go with it" again. And I'm think-ing, tutti frutti, oh fuckin' Rudi. Pardon my language.'

'Go on,' she said. 'I hear worse every day of the week.'

He stood up from the windowsill, went to the chest of drawers and poured some more milk into his cup. When he had finished he lit a cigarette, took a long drag and sat beside her on the edge of the bed.

(Maureen! What are you doing? Don't let him sit there, for *God's* sake.)

'"Raymond Joseph Dempsey, take a long look at yourself," I feel myself say. "And then, when you've really and truly sized yourself up? Take a look at them. The Jesus people." Because I feel like I'm watching them on some kind of screen. Or through some kind of lens. Or through an old window that's maybe steamed up and dirty. And then they start again with the singing. All these people, they're singing hymns. Not proper, old-fashioned hymns, you know. But more like folk songs. "Bridge Over Troubled Waters", for instance. "He Ain't Heavy, He's My Brother". I mean, these are hymns now. "You're So Vain" is gonna be a hymn before these people are finished.'

She lay down flat on the bed, kicked off her shoes and stared at the ghostly fruits on the ceiling. She began to get the feeling that he was inching towards her. He loosened his tie and popped open the top button of his shirt.

(*Maureen! Tell him you want to go to sleep.*)

'They say the Lord moves in mysterious ways. Well, so does Stephen. I'm looking at him lurching around. He hands me a tambourine and smirks. "Bang it for the Lord, brother." I'm not kidding you, that is exactly what he comes out with. "Bang it for the Lord", Maureen. Out in the street a burglar alarm's going off. The sound it makes – ooooOOOO – I'm thinking of a person crying. The sun is setting down now and everything is bronze outside. It looks mysterious, beautiful. Through the blinds I can see these black kids wearing baseball shirts and baseball caps. They're playing soccer, except they're using a tennis ball. Every so often the ball bangs against the window and it makes this loud rattling sound. When that happens, all the kids crack up laughing.'

He flicked his cigarette ash into his cupped hand. She looked at the hand, so delicate and beautiful and yet so masculine. She could see the hair on his knuckles.

'So the tongues seems to have stopped now and there's silence. Stephen stands up.

'"Is there anyone here wants to share, people?" And you know by the way he says it, it isn't a question, it's like a statement. And I don't really want to. But now I see Father Liam nodding at me from across the room. Stephen goes, "I really feel there's one among us wants to share the heaviness of his heart."'

(*Of course, you know he's making all this up, don't you, Maureen? You know he's spinning you a line? Were you born yesterday?*)

'I don't want to stand up. But I feel myself standing up all the same. That's me. I'm what Lisa, my daughter, calls a people pleaser. It was the same in the years I was going to AA. Always the first up on my toes and sloshing the story around. The world is divided into two types of person, Lisa says – that's people pleasers and controllers. She has an issue around controllers. This is how she talks since she started seeing a therapist.'

He stopped speaking and stared at the carpet for a moment. When she looked closely at him she thought that he was trembling. She knew then that he was not making it up.

'Are you OK?' she asked.

'Yeah, yeah. Where was I, Maureen? I'm sorry. I got lost.'

'You'd just stood up to speak. At the prayer meeting.'

'Oh, yeah. Well, I stand up. I say, "My name is Ray Dempsey." And just then the crashing metallic sound of the tennis ball hitting the shutter comes. And to give me time to think I whip around and take off my glasses and look at the window, like that's going to achieve something wonderful. I can see the sun now, deep orange in the sky, which has gone this wonderful shade of purple. Then I turn back and look at these upturned faces all around me. As a one-time drunk I should be used to being the centre of attention, right? But I'm not. For some reason that I don't get, I find myself feeling teary all of a sudden. And I mean, I haven't cried in years.

'I tell them my name again, where I'm from. I tell them I'm forty-nine years old and I work for a travel agent. My wife died recently. My wife died. I loved her. And she died. This God of yours, this loving power, well, he took my wife away from me. I hear these words coming out of my mouth but I still feel disconnected. Like I'm floating maybe, or like I once wrote down these words and learned them by heart.

'I feel my face twisting as I try to swallow down the tears.

Somebody gives me a tissue. I'm really crying now. Stephen comes over and puts his hands on my head. He starts going, "Forgive, Ray, forgive, Ray." And he keeps saying it, over and over. And after a while I can't actually figure out whether he's saying I should forgive somebody, or I should be forgiven. That's all he says. "Forgive, Ray, forgive, Ray." Over and over. Then what he does, he puts his hands on my head again and starts pressing down so hard that it hurts my shoulders. Next thing I know he's going, "Do you feel it, Ray? Do you feel it, Ray? Oh, tell me you can feel it, brother." And I guess this is the point of the story, Maureen. Because funnily enough, I did feel something.'

'What did you feel?' she asked.

Wind whistled outside the window. He stared up at the ceiling and sighed. He was silent for what seemed like a long time. When he began to speak again his voice came steady and calm. 'What I feel, really for the first time in my life, as an absolute, ultimate, certainty – that there's no God, never was, never will be. And that this is OK. That the salon, the bottles full of coloured liquids on the shelf, the barber chair – that this is all there is. The street kids banging their tennis ball on the shutter. Nothing else. These people, yes. Their hopes for a God, yes. But no God. No great being out there. No dark thing. There's this conversation, this moment and that's all. Here and now, for example, there's only this room, there's you and me talking in this room, in this hotel, in this city, where neither of us live. We never met before. Tonight we met and talked. Five minutes either way, it wouldn't have happened. But it did happen. That's the sacred moment. If there's a sacrament, that's it. And wider than that? Very little. The things that happen to us in our lives, yes. Our memories, yes. Our desires, yes. The work artists do. If we have children, then our children. And all those we love. Maybe all those we ever loved. But nothing more. We go around once and then it's over. But that's OK.'

'And no afterlife?' she said.

'No,' he said. 'Not for me. Because to live even once, well, that's miracle enough.'

He stood up slowly and walked to the window. He leaned his face against the windowpane. She looked at his reflection. The mordant call of gulls came in from the river. Grey light had begun to appear in the distant part of the sky. An ambulance sped along the north quays, its blue light flashing and reflecting on the water.

'It's late,' she said.

'Yeah,' he said. 'Yeah, it's late. I'm sorry, Maureen. I don't know why I wanted to tell you all that stuff. I got carried away.' He looked at the clock on her bedside table and pulled a face. 'I better go.'

He turned to look at her. She stepped off the bed and moved in his direction.

'If I've offended you in any way, I'm sorry,' he said. 'It's probably all crap.'

She took another step towards him and kissed the side of his face. He touched her hair.

Before she knew what she was doing she was kissing him hard on the lips. He kissed her back. She slid her tongue into his mouth. She felt him pull away from her.

'I guess this isn't such a great idea,' he said.

'If you wanted to stay here, Ray, that'd be all right.'

'If I wanted to stay here? I am staying here. I'm upstairs.'

'No. I mean stay the night. Here. What's left of it.'

'Let me understand this. If I wanted to stay the night here. In this room?'

'In this bed. With me.'

He laughed. 'You're a nun.'

'Yes.'

'You want me to spend the night with you, and you're a nun?'

'I mean just to sleep with me. To share my bed. I feel very close to you.'

'Hey, listen, I know people say the Catholic Church is changing a lot these days, but, you know, Maureen, this is . . .'

His voice trailed off. She did not return his laugh. He gaped around the room, scratching his head. 'Just to sleep together?' he said.

'I'm not the kind of nun who has sex on a first date.'

'Oh, you're not, huh? Just my luck.'

'Won't you take your clothes off, Ray, and come to my bed.'

'Take my clothes off?'

'Please. As a favour to me.'

'What are you kidding here?'

'Ray, I'm fifty-two years old. Fifty-two. I'll never again see another naked man as long as I live. That's the truth. I'll never be kissed again in my whole life. Ever. Not once. There's nobody wants to kiss me. And that's fine. I've no complaints. That's the life I've chosen. But just this one last time I'd like to see a naked man. Please.'

She watched while he took off his jacket and shoes. Next came his socks and tie. 'You're serious about this?' he asked and she nodded. He undid his shirt and took it off. He opened his trousers, let them fall to the floor. 'This isn't a joke?' She shook her head and told him no. He peeled his underpants down over his thighs and feet. He stood before her naked then, his long thick arms hanging down by his side, and said nothing. On his left shoulder was a faded heart-shaped tattoo. Thin grey hair covered his chest and ran from his navel to his genitals. He had a scar across his right knee. His toenails were too long. Although he was stocky and had a small pot belly, he was nevertheless a little trimmer than her husband. Goosepimples began to form on his skin. He gave a small shudder and patted his stomach a few times.

'I'm sorry you couldn't have found a better specimen,' he softly laughed. 'For the last naked man you're ever going to see.'

'You look gorgeous,' she said. 'Do you think you could undress me now?'

He helped her off with her sweater. She stood up and removed her slacks. Naked they slid together underneath the continental quilt. She turned away from him, he slid his arm around her from behind. She switched off the bedside lamp and they lay very still in the half light for a few minutes. Out in the street an articulated truck trundled past. She felt his small thick penis begin to harden against the back of her thighs.

'Ray,' she said.

'I'm embarrassed here,' he said, gently. 'I'm aroused by you.'

'That's all right,' she said.

'That's not all right. I'm being sexually aroused by a nun here. I'm gonna be in therapy the rest of my damn life.'

'You're going to have an issue around being sexually aroused by nuns,' she said.

'You're damn right I am. That's one of the more expensive issues too, let me tell you.'

She switched the bedside lamp back on and turned to look at him. 'You made me laugh tonight, Ray.'

'You made me laugh too. Really.'

'Can I tell you something? I needed a good laugh more than you did.'

'Why's that?'

She touched his lips. 'It doesn't matter. Something difficult has happened in my life. Something very painful. I don't want to talk about it. But you made me laugh and you moved me. You're a lovely, tender, beautiful man, Mr Ray Dempsey. I hope you know that. Really. I'd run away with you given half the chance.'

'If you could, right?'

'Yes. If I could.'

'Well, why couldn't you?'

'Because there wouldn't be any future to it, Ray. And that's the truth.'

It was when she put her arms around him that he began to weep. She was glad that he did, because from the moment she had met him he had looked and seemed to her like a man who badly needed to cry. He put his hands to his face and shook silently with tears. For a long time hardly any sound at all came from him, just the softest of tremulous sighs. He shivered a little as he cried, and she held his head. She put her arms around his shoulders and kissed his hair.

'It's all right, Ray,' she whispered. 'It's all right. I'm here.'

'I'm sorry, Maureen,' he sobbed. 'I don't know what's wrong with me now.'

She kissed him softly on the side of the mouth and held him in her arms until he fell asleep.

The mournful sound of a vacuum cleaner outside in the

corridor woke her just after half-past eight. The damp sheets were wrapped hard around her thighs. The room was airless and stultifyingly hot. Her mouth felt as though she had swallowed a cake of salt. When she sat up to take a drink of water she saw the note on the pillow.

Gone to Newgrange, back 6pm. Would like very much to see you then? Please? Will put do not disturb sign on the door. Happy succoth. All best, Ray. PS. Thank you for everything.

She took a long, cool shower and then sat naked on the king-sized bed for a while. She found herself pondering the word king-sized. What did it mean, really? A king could be any size, when it came down to it. Richard III, for example, was almost a midget, whereas Henry VIII was six foot tall and could have worn his stomach as a kilt. She smoked two of the three cigarettes left in the pack that she found on the carpet, while she stared down at the river, its whorls and pools blurring in her eyes, and she thought about the meanings of words. She would talk to the sixth-year girls about this on Monday morning. 'The Different Meanings of Words' would be the title for their next essay. Love. God. Ireland. Sex. Goodbye. These were some of the words she would suggest to her girls as being words that had different meanings, depending on how they were used, and when, and by whom, and most of all why.

Downstairs the exhausted-looking night porter was standing like a sentry by the doorway of the restaurant; it was almost as though he had been expecting her. Behind him, the yellow light was shining very brightly, seeming to bathe him in a gorgeous shimmering lacquer, such as an angel might have in a medieval painting, or so it seemed to her. When she went to enter the room he stepped into her path and regarded her disapprovingly. 'You're the lady was late for dinner last night,' he said.

'Yes, I am. I'm sorry.'

He tapped on his watch. 'Well now, you're after leavin' it very late again, missus.'

'I know,' she agreed. 'I slept in.'

He shrugged. 'Breakfast's over at nine. That's the rule. We're short-staffed.'

'I know. But maybe . . .'

He held up his hand. 'I didn't make the rules. The rules is the rules. I was never asked my opinion on them. But there they are.'

'But do you think – do you think just one last time – that you might be able to make an exception for me?'

He stared at her for a few moments, as though what she had said was somehow preposterous.

'Please,' she said. 'I know I'm in the wrong. I do see that.'

He sighed and shook his head. 'Well, I suppose anyone can make a mistake. Come on so. We won't let you starve. But just this once, mind.'

He stepped out of the doorway and beckoned her in with a graceful wave of his white cloth. The small room seemed to sing with clean light. He sat her down in a booth. She thought about her husband getting up, shaving and shower- ing, brushing his teeth, putting on his fresh clothes. She thought about the lemony smell of his aftershave. She pictured him leaving the house and driving into work. He would listen to the beginning of the *Pat Kenny Show* on the radio. He would stop at Lafferty's on the way into town to buy the *Irish Independent*, a packet of cigarettes, two tickets for the Lotto. He could get them in his own supermarket just as easily, she was always telling him, but no, he had always bought them in Lafferty's shop and he always would. He was a creature of habit. It was one of the things that annoyed her about him, but also, and simultaneously, one of the things she loved most. She tried hard to imagine how he would even begin to cope when she was gone. They would have to talk about it soon, the inescapable fact of her going, the absurdity and yet the truth of it, the onset of the final autumn. It would have to be faced. The thought stirred tears in her eyes but she blinked them away. The porter brought her a bowl of cornflakes and a cup of greasy-looking tea.

'That's absolutely all I can do for you,' he said. 'And if it was known I even done that much I'd be sacked.'

'Thank you, that's lovely.'

Five minutes later he brought her a rack of hot, soggy toast, a basket of bread rolls, a little silver dish of marmalade.

'Thank you,' she said. 'You're very kind.'

'Indeed and I'm not.'

'You are. You're a godsend.'

He pantomimed a scoff. 'I've been called a lot of choice things around this place but that's a new one now.'

'Could I ask your name?' she said.

'Simon, pet. Ask for Simon any time.'

'He's a good fellow to be named after.'

'Oh, he is,' he laughed, and threw his eyes to the ceiling. 'Didn't he help the man upstairs carry his cross? My mother was never done telling me that as a lad. But all I carry around here's bloody bags and suitcases.'

She allowed herself a smile.

He glanced furtively over his shoulder towards the door, as though he thought that somebody important might be listening. But nobody was there. The lobby was almost completely empty. The revolving door was slowly turning but everything was quiet now in Finbar's Hotel. He ran his finger around the collar of his shirt. He peered back down at her and winked.

'Just don't be leaving it so late next time, love,' he whispered. 'That was all I meant.'

'No,' she said. 'Next time, I promise I won't.'

He walked away from her and began to set the tables for lunch. She considered going out to the lobby and telephoning her husband in the supermarket, just to say that she had missed him, that they needed to talk, that the time for forgiveness had come and the time for mercy. But it could wait. She would see him tonight when he got home. She would book a table somewhere. Maybe the restaurant on Barna Pier. She lit her last cigarette and watched the wisp of purple smoke rise through the air, knowing, in her heart, that she would never see Dublin again. But that was all right. That was fine. Because somehow she knew that she had at last found the courage to say goodbye.

106

AN OLD FLAME

May would not go into Finbar's Hotel. She stood on the quays with the river at her back and looked up at it; a cube of weeping concrete, the curtains dirty in a streak that showed just how far you could open the windows. She tried to remember the building she had seen over thirty years ago, an ordinary terrace, with a child's picture of flames coming out the top. She remembered its reflection burning on the river behind her and the surprising sound the fire had made, low and straining, like the building had a throat – the crack of rafters and the dull rip of ceilings giving way. There was something so old-fashioned about a fire.

So this is what they had rebuilt – this awful lump of a thing. How modern. Like a wino in a new suit, it aged faster than you could look at it. May had arrived that morning straight from the airport, and when the taxi pulled up to the revolving door, she realized her childhood was not just gone, but stolen from her. They had put up this instead.

A group of schoolgirls walked towards her and May wanted to tell them to leave the country, and never come back. She wanted to tell them about the fire – how when she was their age she had wanted to swoon. Just swoon. How she had stood on this quay and watched the flames, thinking about love that could kill you.

She smiled at one, a big beautiful galoot of a girl, her cheeks whipped into a blush by the wind. 'Blotches', she would call it. May smiled at her – this was Dublin, after all – but the girl just flicked a cigarette butt into the river, her hair tangling across her mouth, and walked on. Everything was wet in this town. There was nothing sexy about it.

May stood at the kerb, afraid she might fall into the river, afraid she might fall into the road – jet lag, this damp wind bashing her full of nothing. She clutched the book to her chest and tried to wish the cold away. Yesterday, just yesterday, she had been in New Mexico, ninety degrees in the shade. Standing in her bedroom, she had looked at the two jumpers she possessed in the world, thick and shapeless, and tried to remember what cold might be, what it could feel like. In the end, she had packed just one. The body is so stupid, she thought. The body has no imagination.

May tried to think hot. She thought of the desert, the sun swelling as it set. She tried to imagine a cup of tea, something warm in the winter. She tried to imagine a kiss and, as she stepped out into a gap in the traffic, her body was scattered with the memory of sex, a dreadful collapsing fire that shot up to her lips and across her breasts.

So much for that theory.

The wind switched off with the sigh of the revolving door. May walked with her sea legs across reception and into the bar. She found a stool and waited for her blood to settle, trying to decide between a hot whiskey and a vodka martini. She tasted each of them in her mind, and when the barman came to take her order she said, 'Do you have those little triangular cocktail glasses? Or olives?'

He looked at her steadily.

'I'll have a hot whiskey,' she said, and laughed at herself as he turned to the kettle. 'Where do you think you are,' she said to herself, 'May Brannock?' – Mary Breathnach as was. Where do you think you are? She was in Dublin. She was back. Her body knew things. Her wallet was full. She had memories now that Ireland could not even guess at. She was someone else, altogether.

*

Seven years ago a highway cop pulled her over to the side of the road and May had leaned forward, gripping the wheel. Why did she not feel safe? It was dark. She disliked his boots. She was twenty miles out of Phoenix, Arizona and the car was already dirty, streaked with the road. But he let her go and she travelled on, a woman at night, no longer young, with the life she had stolen piled in the trunk. It was her own life, but that didn't seem to help.

She had left a man, of course. Lying on the bed, drinking, despising every inch of her as she moved from the wardrobe to the bureau, looking at her with slow eyes that said, *No one will ever fuck you, ever again.* She had packed and left, walking down the hall, shutting the screen door behind her. In the porch she tripped over the rowing machine where he sat before dinner, pulling his way out over the desert, or not.

In front of her, the road clipped along, the white lines flicking under her hood. Behind her the trunk was full of rubbish: clothes, a few paperbacks, toiletries. They made her feel poor. When you are rich, you don't need things.

May pulled into a deserted gas station, opened the door and got out. She was in the middle of nowhere. She was forty years old. She looked at the moon, cold and kind, and tried to think what to do now. She waited for the coyote howl that did not come, the slither of a snake.

May looked at the moon and decided to make money.

What else? She decided she would never be frightened by a highway cop, ever again.

*

May realized she was staring at a man sitting across the bar. Every face she saw in Dublin looked familiar. She looked into people's eyes on the street, as if to say – Yes, it's me. But they turned away, as this man did, back to his tea and biscuits. Tea and biscuits. No wonder he did not recognize her. She had not eaten tea and biscuits in thirty years.

The barman put the hot whiskey on the counter and May reached for it with her American arm, slightly dry, the muscles twisting around each other from the gym. She wore the heavy simple silver they sold in the Arbol de la Vida on Hunter Street. Some of her friends were Mexican, one was a First American. She slept, now and then, with a guy who was trying to get a construction business going, to satisfy his unpleasant wife. He had come to give her an estimate on a new deck.

She did not know what she was doing here.

Six weeks ago her father had died. Her sister waited until after the funeral to call her and when May complained she said, 'You don't come to funerals,' which was true, as far as it went. But how could May explain that when their mother had died she was waiting for Benny to leave his wife, that when the phone rang with the news, she was disappointed it was not him, that she replaced the receiver and went back to waiting, only crying when he called the next day, 'My mother has died, when can I see you? When can you get away?' inventing a life so that she could give it to him.

This time she was older. There was the question of the house, her sister 'not up to it' – some slow disaster in

Birmingham she did not want to know about. She did as much as she could by fax and then finally, reluctantly, caught the plane.

What was it about hotels? The way they mocked you. You can travel as far as you like, they seemed to say, but you always end up in the same place. You always end up middle-aged. You always end up in some dive; the carpets and curtains a wet dream of the future that some fool had thirty years before. May looked at the swirly green of the floor, trying to tell the pattern from the stains. She looked at the other drinkers who had come into the bar, clots of people connected by God knows what goo of circumstances: family or sex or money, or just drink. They looked grey, their faces ready to collapse into their lives.

When the place burnt down May was sixteen, and in love. When the place burnt down she had watched it go, the crackle and force and heat of it. She had stood on the quays with her pelvis aching, thinking that was what love was – a boy you never slept with. A boy that made you feel it was all too hopeless for words. He was there beside her, watching the flames. Kevin, a child like herself, with an Adam's apple like a golf ball in a nervous breakdown. If she met him now, she would not look at him twice. If she slept with him now, they would call her a paedophile.

May called to the barman, smoothly, like a grown-up. He looked back at her, smoothly, like a grown-up. Non-virgin to non-virgin she ordered another hot whiskey. And fingered the zip of her purse lightly with her thick, manicured nails.

The barman turned to the kettle and May looked him over. He was slightly overweight. She could imagine the two lines the fat made on his back as it fell towards his waist. His face in the mirror was very Dublin, all cheekbones, no eyelids; the kind that looked hungry, even while they slept. May looked away. She should not be thinking of men asleep. Especially barmen. Especially short barmen.

He set whiskey down in front of her, with a paper napkin around the glass. The beer mat said *Wrap yourself around a hot Irish*.

'There was a fire here once,' she said.

'Was there?'

His lidless eyes flickered over her and May shifted on her stool. 'You do not know me,' she wanted to say. 'My sister in England takes Valium with her hands still wet from the dishes, but you do not know me.' The barman did not care, he turned back to the bottles and the glasses, checking her in the mirror.

'My father put it out,' she said. 'I mean helped put it out.'

'Is that right?'

'Yes,' she said. 'That's right.'

May wanted to shout at him. 'I do not belong here. I am in the wrong country. I spent the afternoon in the house I grew up in. I went there by taxi, with the keys on my lap, and I couldn't even remember where the damn place was.'

'The streets of Drimnagh,' the nuns used to teach them, 'are laid out in the shape of an ornate Celtic Cross, in honour of the Eucharistic Congress.' She told the taxi-man.

'That's right,' he said, 'all squiggly bits and bollocks.'

'I grew up here,' she said. And still she couldn't figure it out, as they lost their way from roundabout to roundabout. You might as well have grown up in Iran, she decided as she stared out: Ayatollah Khomeini Street, The Street of Boy Martyrs, Chastity Street. There was nothing sentimental about it. Are we at the foot of the cross, are we at the knees, or the nails? The streets were so familiar she couldn't tell one from the next. She looked out the window for a clue. Then she saw a boy pulling his little sister by the arm of her anorak, and the map became helpless, she knew where they were.

'Left and then left again.'

The driver swung the wheel, sang, 'I'll take you home again, Cathleen,' and May remembered to flirt, the way you did in Dublin.

'Oh now,' as if he had said something witty and slightly risqué. She did not give him a tip.

But when he pulled away from the kerb she felt bereft, looking at the house, the windows blank, the gate stuck in the arc it had worn in the concrete. The path was short but May felt like she was walking and walking and would never reach the door.

She put her key in the lock. The hall was smaller but May was ready for that. She shouldered it by, the walls that leant in too far and the ceiling that threatened her head. She reached down to the kitchen door handle and, though the house was hardly hers, went through to the back window to release the smell of her father's life out into the world.

The garden was a mess.

May turned into the room. Until the papers were signed, the house did belong to her, in a way. Then take the lino up, she thought, and paint the walls. Knock through, knock through. Open the sitting room to the kitchen. Let in the light.

An upturned cup on the draining board showed greasy around the handle. May put it on its empty hook, a bunch of china roses lightly swinging. An eggcup, in the shape of a ceramic rabbit. You put the egg between its ears.

In the hall May lifted the receiver of the phone, a heavy

Bakelite black that could get a price back home, for quaintness. To her surprise, the line was not dead. Her father was dead. She listened to the dial tone and felt like the house was leaking away.

May sat down and wept. If she were really American then this would have been the important bit – the grief assaulting her by the phone, sinking down onto the too-shallow stairs to cry for her dead father, so as to be able to say, 'It was myself I was crying for, the little girl who sat on this step and cried when . . .' But she could remember what had hurt her and it didn't matter – a missed dance, a boy who didn't call, a Saturday afternoon when the silence became dreadful and her mother, menopausal, froze by the sink, her hands trembling and her shoulders unnaturally high.

May did not weep for any of this. She wept for the death of a man who had meant everything to her. Not because she had loved him, but just because he had died. Grown-up tears.

The armchair was waiting for her in the sitting room, still holding his shape. He had died in this chair. He had died surrounded by junk: newspapers, an old TV, a cabinet full of wedding china that had terrified them as children because if you broke a cup it could never be replaced, not even by something that cost more. Things sickened her. She would leave it all for the next owners, a young couple, maybe, with no money and a sense of humour.

Then May saw her father's glasses on the mantelpiece. She sank without thinking into the chair he had died in, reached easily to where he had set them. They looked so empty. And May realized she would have to do it – buy the roll of black plastic bags, knock on the neighbours' door, take tea, leave keys, watch her life drain away into their hideous carpet and smile.

Three hours later she was suffocated by the smell of an old man's clothes, filthy from her father's life, the hall a thick mattress of plastic bags, nothing new, not even a towel to wipe her face. She used a wad from the toilet roll that her father had died in the middle of, and thought of the grave.

On top of the wardrobe she had found one thing that gave her pause. It was a ledger, marked *Drimnagh Fire Station, 1962–1969*. Her father was a fireman. And here was a record of his fires.

It was lying beside her now on the bar, an ordinary cover, blue cloth, frayed at the edges. She flicked through the pages. The writing inside was beautiful and awkward, written by men with big hands who had been taught how to loop their l's and curl their r's.

The barman was wiping the counter with slow strokes. She wanted another drink from him. She wanted to show her smile.

'Excuse me,' she said.

He did not answer. May glanced in the mirror and saw herself as he saw her, narrow, brown eyed. She looked forty, not forty-seven, but why should he bother, either way? She tried to remember the face she once had, and it was not just a question of subtracting wrinkles. Her father had not seen her since she was twenty, she hardly even recognized herself any more. May picked up the book and thought, It does not matter. Her father would have known her. He would not have been surprised.

'Can I have the bill?'

She signed the chit and went up the stairs. A fireman's

daughter does not trust lifts. A fireman's daughter runs cigarette butts under the tap and always checks for exit signs.

May walked along the corridor – more swirly green carpet with vanity board above the dado line. She wondered was Kevin in Dublin somewhere, living with wallpaper just like this. Did he sleep in a Dublin bed, with a velour headboard rubbed greasy where he rested his head? She hoped he had got away, but she didn't know if he was the type to leave, or to stay. She didn't know what sort of a person he could be, the boy she had loved at sixteen. She had expected to bump into him in the street, all day, she had expected to be accosted by a middle-aged man who says, 'Is that really you?'

The virgin I knew.

What a laugh. May let herself into the room. Hideous. The whole evening ahead of her. She should look him up in the phone book, say, 'Guess where I am. I'm in a room with lime-green lampshades with their tassels half gone. Where are you?' All hotels are the same.

In Albuquerque she spent a week in the Old Majestic waiting for a man who had gone off to square things with his wife. The wallpaper was purple sort of brocade with a gold trellis stencilled over the flowers. The bedspread was spattered with lilac daisies. The window looked out on a back wall. He had not come back. She had not expected him to. But there was nothing to do in America except follow men. How else could you make sense of it?

She blamed her friend Cassie, who had married the wrong man. It was part of the first adventure in New York, both waitressing and astonished by the tips, excited, even when they were bored, just by being in this town. Cassie had a law degree and a psychotic mother who sent her Irish underwear in the post. May felt let down when she got a job as a legal secretary. What was the point, when they had thrown it all away? When Cassie started to study for her American law exams May took to sleeping with a Lithuanian with very little English, who used to wake himself up, singing in his sleep.

Then something happened. Cassie gave up. She married a client and moved upstate, an ordinary man with firm, sexual lips and a family business decaying all around him. Cassie moved upstate to be with a man whose mother called daily, whose father drank, who had one brother in California and another working in the local junior high. Her mother came to the wedding, looking normal.

New York was still part of Dublin, but Cassie had gone somewhere you never came back from. It suddenly occurred to May she would not be going home.

Cape Cod, San Francisco. After Albuquerque, May decided against love for a while. She moved south and started working in a travel bureau because it was a way of moving and staying put, all at the same time. The guy who hired her was a sad-sounding man, with heavy eyes that had a way of fixing on you as he spoke. May felt he was always checking up on her, always looking over her shoulder. Until one hot day he stood behind her at the water cooler and May realized that he was smelling the sweat on her back. She felt the soft push of breath between her shoulder blades and the steady, soft, absence of breath as he inhaled. He was married. For three weeks she did not look him in the eye and when she did they had abrupt sex in the back room. It was over almost before it began and still May couldn't tell the number of times she came.

'If you're counting, you ain't coming,' said Benny, years later when she reminded him of this, by which time, it had to be said, counting wasn't the problem.

Of course the heating didn't work. It never does in hotels. May wrestled with the hotel radiator and got into bed, dressed as she was. She would shake the cold out of herself and then, when she could face it, take off her clothes and have a shower. In the meantime, she opened the book.

In 1962, there were fires in St Agnes' Park, Knocknarea Avenue, a chip pan in Darley Street, a paraffin stove in Carrow Road. The hut at the end of the football pitch in Eamonn Ceannt Park blazed up in the middle of the afternoon. A surprising number of the fires happened in the morning, which felt wrong, their flames ordinary and transparent in the sun.

Her father always came home as though nothing much had happened, a day at work, a bit of this, a bit of that. He did not talk of exploding cans of paint, of ladders that swung too close, he did not mention scorched lungs, or the feel of sweat running over a burn. Even so May thought of him as a hero, pulling little girls in their nightdresses out of upstairs windows, the ambulance light splashing his face with blue.

Now she looked at his book, it was a list of careless cigarettes and smouldering mattresses: it was a child crying in the next room, or an old woman fallen into a doze. The water damage was worse than the blaze. It was just dirt and inconvenience and a woman saying, 'I was putting his shirt out on the line. I remembered he hadn't a clean shirt, I just washed one out and was hanging it on the line.'

The fires were nothing. It was the fear before the fires, that was what kept people's lives alight.

One night a face appeared at their bedroom window and May asked, 'Does she have a gun? Does she have a gun?' But all that Benny's wife had was a set of car keys and a hand that she pressed to the glass, with two words scrawled on the palm. *Vegetable Oil.* She stayed there long enough for them to read the words and May was shocked to realize they had no significance, that she wasn't going to die, by curse or by bullet – at all.

Benny had covered his genitals from the sight of his wife and walked slowly towards the window saying, 'Sweetheart. Now.' It should have been a lesson to May the way she backed from him and was swallowed by the dark. She should have learned from it. How Sweetheart did not burst into their bedroom in a shower of splinters and blood, did not beat her messy fists against Benny's amiable chest or cry. She had no gun, no knife, she had no intentions at all.

As it was, May stroked him when he got back into bed and pulled his underpants down, sympathizing with a man who was driven to despair by the helplessness of others. A man who needed a second chance, that was all.

Benny lived life like it was a game you could win or lose, and if you thought you were losing, you could clear the board. She had believed that for a while. Now, looking at her father's book, full of small disasters, May did not believe in chances. You lived your life from start to finish, that was all.

She turned the pages. Dargan, Kelly, O'Driscoll, Boyle.

Cause – electrical, unknown, kitchen stove, unknown.

Damage – neg., extensive, gutted, neg.

Time of call – the night was the worst.

They had dinner with other couples. May could not believe that they had dinner with other couples, that she tossed the salad and baked the chicken and sat there, leaning slightly to the left to show off her waist, while Benny talked about love. He liked talking about love, just to show he could use big words.

'I've been in love,' he would say. 'So many times. But—'

'But what?' they would say. Al and Irene, Pete and Liana, or Bill and Soledad.

'But. Let me tell you.' He made them wait.

'Go on.'

'I never thought I'd end up like this, I guess. I never thought that I'd end up a lucky guy.'

He would touch May's cheek then. Or clasp her hand. Or lift his glass to her, while Bill laughed or Al laughed or Soledad started to cry. Those nights with other couples, someone always cried.

When she was small, May worried that her father would have to make choices. He would get to the top of the ladder and there would be two people to save, one to save first, the other to leave. She paused with her father night after night before this couple in the window. Their clothes ripped off their backs, the heat solid behind them. She saved the woman first.

'Do you save the woman first?' she asked. He said, 'It wouldn't really ever come to that,' but she did not believe him and now, nights, she left the woman behind and, as she climbed down the ladder, looked back to see her ignite, her hair blazing round her like a halo as she stood naked and smudged in the melting window frame.

She remembered Benny in the heat, when the air-conditioner failed. They lay in bed with their legs flopped wide and, 'Come on, Sweetheart,' he would say. 'Come on.' If it was too hot for sex she might blow him instead. May thought he preferred it that way, that men did. So, 'OK,' she would say, 'go for it,' and he would have to get on top of her then, his belly slicking forward and back, the drops from his face hitting her cheek. Those nights – the heat was like a thing in the room that she could not focus on. May dared it until she was light-headed, concentrated on the water that spilled out of her body and tried to breathe.

In the far column she saw the word Arson. A house in Rutland Avenue, near enough to where they lived. One fatality. And she remembered the story of a man who had burnt his wife alive. They said he had fought to get in. They had held him back, as he fought to get in. Perhaps he had only meant to burn the house.

May closed the book. It smelt of men's hands. She left it on the pillow beside her, shut her eyes and tried to sleep. She jerked awake now and then – there was a cigarette left burning in the room next door, someone had left a kettle on, boiling to nothing, its plastic oozing and bubbling over the element. The hotel was a box full of matches waiting to be struck. May rolled over in the bed and tried to think of other things. Money. Her father's house was worth a surprising amount of money. Real money, the kind you could count out and put elastic bands around, the kind you could carry in a plastic bag. She calculated the exchange rate, over and over again, but stacks of notes kept catching fire. Water – she would think about water. There was a flood in Glendale Park in 1963. May imagined a family eating their tea up to their knees in water, the father lifting his newspaper high as he turns the page.

But when she looked at his face, it was some other father. It was so hard to see men, when you loved them. Then he walked into the room, sooty-faced, smelling of smoke. May knew that he was dead and she realized that now he was dead she could look at him. From the outside her father looked very thin, and his watery eyes blinked, like he had seen something funny and terrible. So that was what he looked like. She tried to speak. She tried to say, 'So that is what you look like,' but her father turned towards her so slowly and then he smiled.

May jolted awake, overheated, grief-stricken. The tang of her body reached her, from under her clothes. She went still, trying to hold the face that her dream had given her, but it faded away.

May got out of bed, angry at last. She went into the bathroom and tested the water of the shower. What is it that makes men different? That was what she wanted to ask him. What was the terrible thing that made men different? Benny would say something hilarious like, 'It's a dick,' but her father would not even understand the question. Besides, they had never had a conversation, when he was alive.

May put her clean clothes on the shelf by the sink, leaving her shoes wedged into the towel rail. There was no way she was going to walk barefoot on that floor: go naked in a room where strangers had been shagging since the sixties, and half of them liars. The nozzle was clogged with rust, but the water coming out of it was clean. May stepped in under it, closed her eyes against the mould on the tiles, and lifted her face.

Kevin was the fourth boy she had ever kissed. The first guy wore a big floppy white shirt and liked Elton John. When she tried to put it all together, the shirt, the extraordinary tongue, his taste in music, it did not seem to fit. She spent so long thinking about it, that by the time he had taken his tongue out she had forgotten his name.

The next time she was ready for it, but it never came. The guy circled his open mouth round and round, just like you saw in the pictures, but he didn't know what people did inside. May wasn't going to humiliate him by helping him find out.

She went to a pub, where the guys were more sophisticated, and lost her purse when a man tried to force his knee between her legs outside Rice's. He couldn't get very far because her skirt was so tight, but she couldn't run fast either and had to flirt badly with the bus conductor, just to get herself home. She decided then that she would have to fall in love. If only as a kind of protection.

In broad daylight she leant over and kissed her friend Clare's brother's friend Kevin, who nobody else would kiss, because he had red hair. It was a terrible thing, then, to have – carrotty hair, white skin, freckles, it looked like a sort of disease. Kevin's eye's were brown, that was the only relief, and he looked amused all the time, which was nearly the same as looking happy. They went out for a while and May found herself in love. She thought about him all the time.

They went for walks, caught the bus up to the Phoenix Park. They did a lot, but they didn't go the whole way. They were in despair most of the time, a big throb of despair that started low down and would not go away. They would have to have sex, and then what.

Still, every time she saw him her heart thumped and when she walked beside him, she imagined him without looking at him. When she looked at him, she surrounded his head with the blue of the sky, with the grey of the buildings. When she spoke to him, she saw only his eyes. Everything she said amused him, nearly made him happy. It was the nearly she loved.

One day, in broad daylight, they went to the park and

struggled with sex until they were half mad. They stood against the trunk of a tree and May, unhinged, could see the picture they made, their upright, incompetent lives.

It was easier in the dark, but dangerous to stay. They walked home along the quays, not touching or speaking. Kevin had taken up smoking. He inhaled briefly and blew the smoke out all the way. May was sixteen and felt this city was full of lies.

He asked her why she was crying and they had a fight about something else altogether, something Clare had said about a girl that Kevin used to know hanging around, looking at him.

'She dumped me,' he said. 'What are you talking about?' Over his head she saw the glow of a fire. They had turned to look and Kevin, boyish, no longer confused, had caught her hand and started to run towards Finbar's Hotel.

Later it was all much easier, of course. You just slept with people. It was easy.

May turned off the shower and laughed. Of course he would still be here. He might be walking in the streets even now, somewhere close by, or sitting at home with his children doing their homework, thinking about a pint. By the time she had dried herself, she had made up her mind. She could call him, for the hell of it.

May stood in front of the bedside locker and paused. Then she yanked open the drawer with a laugh – not even a Bible. She rang down to room service and got the receptionist. The woman sounded suspicious. What was so funny about a phone book? She offered to look up the number for her, but May said she wanted the book.

'I don't think we can send one up to you.'

May stalled. She had forgotten how to do this, how to make your way around the simple but completely impossible. She said, 'Give me a break.'

'I'm on my own,' said the woman. 'The porter's busy.'

'So?'

'We keep losing them.'

'Listen, a tenner if it's here in three minutes. Every minute after that, subtract a pound.' May put the phone down pleased with herself, and waited half an hour.

When she made her way downstairs, the young receptionist looked at her as though they had never spoken. May wondered if this was what would have happened to her if she had stayed; a badly cut pastel suit bubbling at the lapel, a bright smile, pure hatred for anyone who thought they knew better.

'Do you mind checking it at the desk?' she said. 'We keep losing them.'

'Not at all.'

Kevin Hegarty. She flipped the pages over. A single column of Hegartys, just two with a K. May stared. She took down both numbers, Sallynoggin, Glasnevin. Where could he have ended up? She decided to call them one at a time. She might have chickened out if the receptionist hadn't been a bitch. But she was a fireman's daughter. She was forty-seven.

Back in her room, May started to clear the clothes from the floor, then realized that she was doing it in case he saw her underwear. She smiled at herself, stopped, and picked up the phone.

On the fourth ring a woman picked up. A wife.

'Is Kevin there?'

'Yes? Hello?' said the woman, an old voice. His mother perhaps. May had a picture suddenly of a balding, frightened boy.

'Can I speak to Kevin?' The receiver was let down with a clatter.

'Kiaran,' said the voice, 'I think there's a girl on the phone.'

May cut the connection. That would give them something to think about. She was still smiling when the second number answered, a man this time, who said, 'Hello,' and May was sitting on the stairs again, the Bakelite receiver in both hands, weighty whispers going down the line, *Why didn't you call?*

'Kevin?' she said.

*

The old hotel was spilling black smoke out of the top windows when they arrived. There was a plump glow behind the curtains of a corner bedroom. It looked quite cosy. Then the fabric caught, flared to black and the flames showed naked in the room behind. The windowpane cracked.

May and Kevin stared at the flames. They had been kissing so long, their bodies felt sad. But looking at the fire as it spread, May knew she was glorious. They would kill each other with love, batter each other with love. She was sixteen, she would sleep with this man and die.

A group of men stood around with their drinks in their hands, their faces wild in the light. A woman ran over with the register to a small man in an expensive suit – the owner, drunk. He swayed and checked the pavement at his feet, glancing now and then at the fire. He looked like he was getting ready to sing. There was a tall man beside them, with a long forehead and a narrow smile. It was May's father. He was smoking.

No one seemed to be doing anything.

Her father pulled on his cigarette and looked down at the register. He looked, finally, like himself, thin in a black waterproof jacket that on one shoulder showed the reflection of the flames. He turned the cigarette tip into the cup of his hand, out of respect for the fire.

May turned to Kevin to point him out when there was a commotion around the door; a man, running out with his shirt open and a woman he dragged by the hand. She did not want to come with him. She leaned back as he pulled her and then stumbled out after him into the street. She was not wearing any shoes.

The group of drinking men turned in on itself and May could hear a low laugh. A single man raised his glass and gave a cheer. The woman started to cry as May watched, hitching her skirt, which was open, up and around, to do the zip.

May looked over at her father. He turned back to the register and she could see his mouth curl over a few words to the receptionist. Another window cracked. And then they ran up with a hose.

You can only see your father once. You can only see your father by accident – because you love your father all the time.

*

'Kevin, it's May.'
  'May?'
  'I mean Mary. Mary Breathnach.'
  'Mary?'
  'I'm in town.'

'Mary! You went to America.'

'I'm here, now,' said May, resisting the need to put the phone down. 'So how are you?' she said. 'I thought I'd ring.'

'How are you?' he said. 'I'm fine, you know, trundling along. So tell us?'

'What?'

'Where have you been?'

*

An hour outside Phoenix, she had stopped in a deserted gas station and swung herself into the dark. She was in the middle of nowhere. She didn't know if she had even left a trace. A film of disgust on a man's eyes, a phone call in the middle of the night to a friend in New York who said, 'Come out East,' as if love were just a question of geography.

Maybe, in this country, it was. May stood in America and looked at the moon. She decided to make money. When she tried to think of what else she wanted, nothing came to mind – except this. She would go to New Mexico, further, redder, drier. Who could leave the desert? It was the place where people ended up.

*

'New Mexico, mostly,' she said. 'My father died.'

'Shit,' he said. 'I'm sorry to hear that.'

'How about you?'

'Oh, married, kids. You know. Happy. Yourself?'

'Oh, happy.' They laughed, with friendly irony. His laugh was just the same. May could not believe it. He was seventeen, when she knew him, and did not know that he laughed like a man.

'I'm in Finbar's Hotel,' she said. 'Remember? The one that burnt down.' There was a pause at the other end.

'Hang on. Yeah. Yeah. Jesus Mary. How are you? Fuck. You sound just the same.' They were there again, looking up at the fire, with skin so fresh it could make you cry.

'I'm just great.' They could not hold on to it. May said, 'I have, you know, a travel business, doing really fine.'

'So how long are you here for?' he said. 'When can you drop in on us?'

'I'm gone in the morning.' He did not mean it, but it was nice of him, all the same. 'So what do you do?' she said. 'You know, as if we don't have phones in the US of A.'

'I'm an accountant,' and they laughed again. 'Mary. Jesus. You know that hotel is a kip.'

'I'm looking at it,' she said.

They thought about it then – about having the sex that they never had, in a hotel bedroom they had once seen in flames. She wondered how disappointing it might be. What did it matter if his body was different, if his laugh was just the same?

*

Kevin was laughing at the woman as she fixed her skirt, his face shifting orange and black, his eyes lit up. He looked like he wanted to run right up to the burning building and dance around her. He looked like he wanted to grab a hose, but not to put the fire out. If the hose were full of petrol he would be just as glad, and so would May. Let it burn.

'That's my da over there,' she said, and saw the admiration change on his face.

'Let's get out of here,' he said. A joke. Her father walked

over to the cab of the fire engine and said something to the driver. The ladder started to move.

The woman with no shoes hopped from side to side, trying somehow not to stand on her own two feet. The man with her had run over to the group and taken a glass from another man's hand. He drank hugely and laughed, while the woman watched him from the doorway. She would not move and May's father went up to clear her back. It was hard to hear what they said over the noise of the engine, but the fire made the woman's face wild. She was crying and pointing, like she wanted to run back in and get her shoes. She grabbed at her father's arm and May drew breath, but he shook himself free of her grip.

Then May's father did something strange. He lifted both arms wide and lowered his head. He circled round the woman until his back was to the door, then he walked towards her, forcing her away from the building, step by step. She faced him, confused, tripping backwards and checking over her shoulder as she went. May realized that her father did not want to touch the woman and, as he pushed her back, so did she. Her face started to crumble. Then she stepped in something and, as he kept advancing, she started to scream.

May had never seen a woman scream like that before. There was a cheer from the drinking men and she swung around to scream at them as well. Then she turned and ran down the quays, her white feet tumbling in the dark.

May's father looked after her a moment, pushed his helmet back and May sighed with relief. He had won the battle of the screaming woman. There was no need to blame him. He did not have to lift her up. She was not even on fire.

Two children stood beside them in the dark, a solemn boy

who gripped the hand of a small long-haired girl. May turned to kiss Kevin, she wanted to say, 'Let's go somewhere. Let's go somewhere and do it,' but their mouths were barely touching when the little girl started to wail. She was looking at the burning building, bellowing at it to stop. Stop burning. Stop burning now.

*

Kevin had being saying goodbye ever since he picked up the phone, but she kept him for a while – warming to his three children and whatever happened to Clare (all horse riding these days, and four-wheel drives), Clare's brother (something that wasn't MS, a year in bed, fine now) and finally the friend who used to hang round making eyes at him (not a clue). By the time they were able to put down the phone, May felt ready to chance it.

'Well, I'll be here this evening anyway, how does that suit?'

'Shit, if you stayed another couple of days.'

'Next time,' she said. 'Next time. Anyway. See if you can get into town.'

'I will,' he said. 'I will. Listen, thanks for calling.'

May changed her clothes, one more time. She put on a dress to match her bracelet and dumped the jumper on the bed.

Downstairs, the restaurant was nearly empty, just a lone couple in a booth along the wall and two loud businessmen. She tried to see what was on their plates and then decided not to bother. The whole place smelt of eggs, years and years of eggs. She might be home, but that didn't mean she had to eat like she had never left. Drink was another matter.

The bar was crowded. A group of Americans made her

voice more consciously Irish as she ordered whiskey, but it was an imitation Irish, she knew as soon as it left her mouth. She knew it as soon as she said the word 'double'.

May sat up at the counter, even though she was a woman alone and it was night. What the hell. In twelve hours she would be on the plane, she could sit where she liked. She felt the burn and glow of the drink as it reached her stomach. It was an option. If she had stayed here, she would be drunk all the time.

She realized she was waiting for Kevin – waiting big-time. She was waiting soprano. Kevin was sitting at home with his wife. His wife was saying, 'How many years ago?', jealous – as if there was something about this man she had missed. He was watching the telly, putting out the cat and still May could see him on the journey into town, remembering how he had pulled away from her in the Phoenix Park, coming in his jeans.

He was sitting at home with a garden seed catalogue while she saw him walk in the door, fat, balding and disappointed, or fat, balding and delighted with himself – perhaps even slim. She rearranged herself on the stool so she could check the first expression on his face. He would scan the room and see her. He would put on an look of pleasant surprise.

Over and over she pulled him towards her on the ridiculous elastic of her desire, before he snapped back to Glasnevin and his daughter's geography homework. It was unbearable. It was how she had spent her life. She had loved her father, who was not a pleasant man. Benny had been a bastard and she loved him too. May turned the cliché of her heart over and over in her mind and, suddenly, she did not care.

*

An hour out of Phoenix, she had stopped in the middle of the night, clicked the trunk and got out of the car. It was winter and the night was thin. There was the bare smell of gasoline. No wind. The bonnet of the car gave a tic of relief and May smiled. Benny had loved that sound, he said it always made him want to take a leak. She pressed her hand to her mouth and smelt him still on her fingertips. Then she looked at the grey-black desert hills, and thought, I could just walk. I could just walk and leave it all behind.

May had an picture of herself lying on the empty roadway, waiting, the white line running under her waist. She listened for a while. No cars.

Then she hauled her suitcase out of the trunk, carried it into the middle of the road and set it on the asphalt. The sun would come up on it in the morning, a big blue suitcase, with the road empty for miles. The garage man would walk out into the sun, scratching his belly and yawning. He would see it there and stop. He would think it was a dead body, chopped into bits – and maybe it was. He would walk around it, get a dog to sniff at it. Paperbacks, toiletries, a few clothes.

May shut the trunk and got back into the car. She hit the road.

*

The bar exploded with noise. May dipped her finger into her whiskey and pushed the heavy silver bracelet back up her forearm. She picked up a box of matches from the counter, fold-over green cardboard, with the words FINBAR'S HOTEL.

Fuck Finbar, she thought and struck them one by one. She would catch the plane and go back to the desert. She would sleep with her builder and sympathize with him about his wife – genuinely sympathize. She would take the money from the sale of the house and buy herself a yellow Corvette. She might even fall in love.

In the meantime, May looked around the bar for a man she might sleep with, or not. No one noticed her, except the man who had been in the bar that afternoon, with his tea and biscuits. He looked like a friend already, in this crowd of strangers; as though he understood. May tried not to listen as the men shouted around her. Now that she thought about it, she had never had sex with an Irish man. She wasn't sure they were clean. The place was full of them, at any rate, their faces smudged with drink. There was something so private about it, she did not want to watch.

May's heart rose and burst. She would go back home and fall in love. In the meantime she stood on the crossbar of the stool and lifted herself up, as though scanning the place for a friend. She checked the tops of their heads. Bald, brown, bald-and-blond, curly brown, black, black.

Flaming red.

ROOM
107

PORTRAIT OF A LADY

The city was a vast emptiness. He stood at the window of Finbar's Hotel and looked down at the River Liffey which was mud-brown after days of rain. He closed his eyes and thought about the rooms all around him, empty now in the afternoon, and the long empty corridors of the hotel. He thought of the houses on the long stretches of suburbs going out from the city: Clontarf, Rathmines, Rathgar, the confidence they exuded, the sense of strength and solidity. He thought about the rooms in these houses, empty most of the day and maybe most of the night, and the long back gardens, neat, trimmed, empty too for all of the winter and most of the summer. Defenceless. No one would notice an intruder scaling a wall, flitting across a garden to scale the next wall, a nondescript man checking the house for a sign of life, for alarm systems, and then silently prising a window open, sliding in, carefully crossing a room, opening doors, not making a sound, so alert as to be almost invisible.

Another memory came into his mind then as he walked back from the window: a moment from the Bennetts' jewel robbery. A few minutes after he and four others had taken over the place he had ordered five of the staff, all men, up against a wall with their hands in front of them and one of them had asked if he could use his handkerchief.

He had been alone guarding them with a pistol, waiting for the others to round up the rest of the staff. He had told the guy that if he needed to blow his nose then he'd better use a handkerchief. He had sounded casual, trying to suggest that he was not afraid to answer such a stupid question. But when the guy had taken it out of his pocket all his loose change had come too; coins rattling all over the floor. All five of the men had looked around until he had shouted at them to face the wall quickly if they didn't want any trouble. One coin had kept rolling; he had watched it and had felt bad about shouting. He had then set to picking the coins up, moving around, bending over, getting down on his knees until he had them all. He had walked over and handed them to the guy who'd needed to use his handkerchief, feeling calm again. He would rob jewels, but he'd give a guy back his loose change.

He smiled at the thought of it as he took off his shoes and lay down now on the narrow single bed with the green candlewick bedspread and started to think about the row they'd had with one of the women that night who had refused to be imprisoned in the men's toilet.

'You can shoot me if you like,' she had said, 'but I'm not going in there.'

The men looking at her, Joe O'Brien with his balaclava on, and Sandy and that other fellow, suddenly not knowing what to do, turning to him as though he might give orders that they should indeed shoot her.

'Take her and her friends to the ladies',' he had said quietly.

He turned to look again at the painting on the wall of his hotel room – a reproduction of Rembrandt's *Portrait of an Old Woman* – and wondered whether it was the painting which had reminded him of that story, or if the story reminded him to look at the painting, or if there was no connection. The woman in the painting looked stubborn too, and difficult and troubled, but older than the woman who had refused to go into the men's toilet. That woman was the sort you would see coming back from bingo with a group of her friends on a Sunday night. She did not look like the woman in the painting at all. He wondered what was happening to his mind.

Your mind is like a haunted house. He did not know where the phrase came from, if someone had said it to him, if he had read it somewhere, or if it was a line from a song. No, he thought, it could not be a line from a song. He had stolen these paintings from a house that looked haunted. It had seemed like a good idea at the time, but it no longer seemed so. He had stolen the Rembrandt whose reproduction he was looking at now, plus a Gainsborough and two Guardis and a painting by a Dutchman whose name he could not pronounce. The robbery made headlines for days in the papers. He remembered laughing out loud when he read about a gang of international art robbers who had come to Ireland. The robbery had been linked with others which had taken place in recent years on the European mainland.

Three of these paintings were now buried in the Dublin mountains; no one would ever find them. Two of them were in the attic of Joe O'Brien's neighbour's house in Crumlin. Between them, they were worth ten million pounds or more. The Rembrandt alone was worth five million. He looked at the reproduction on the wall and couldn't see the point. Most of it was done in some dark colour, black he supposed it was, but it looked like nothing, and then the woman appeared as though she needed cheering up, like some sour old nun.

Five million. And if he tore it up or burned it, it would be worth fuck all. He shook his head and smiled.

He had been told about Landsborough House and how much the paintings were worth and how easy the job would be. He had spent a long time thinking about alarm systems and even had an alarm system installed in his own house so that he could think more precisely about how they worked. Then one day it had come to him: what would happen if you cut an alarm system in the middle of the night? The alarm would still go off. But what would happen then? No one would repair the system, especially if they thought that the ringing was a false alarm. All you had to do was withdraw when the alarm went off, and wait, then an hour later when the fuss had died down you could return. He had driven to Landsborough House one Sunday afternoon. It was only a year since it had been open to the public and the signposting was still clear. He had needed to check out the alarm system and to look at the paintings and get a feel for the place. He had known that most visitors on a Sunday afternoon would be family groups, but he hadn't brought his family with him, he didn't think that they would enjoy a trip to a big house or tramping around looking at paintings. He liked getting away on his own in any case, never telling them where he was going or when he would be back. He often noticed men on a Sunday driving an entire family out of the city. He wondered what that felt like. He would hate it.

The house had been all shadows and echoes. Only a section – a wing, he supposed the word was – was open to the public. He had presumed that the owners lived in the rest of the house, and smiled to himself at the thought that as soon as he could make proper plans they were in for a shock. They were old, he thought, and if they were in the way then it would be easy to tie them up. At the end of a corridor there had been an enormous gallery, and this was where the paintings were hung. He had the names of the most valuable ones written down, and he was surprised at how small they were; if there was no one looking, he thought, he would be able to take one of them and put it under his jacket. He imagined that there was an alarm behind the painting and a guard somewhere. He looked at the wiring system, it seemed simple. He walked back down the corridor into the small shop where he bought postcards – on a later visit he would buy posters – of the paintings he planned to steal.

He had relished the idea that no one – no one at all, not the guard or the other visitors or the woman who had taken his money and had wrapped the cards for him – had noticed him, or would ever remember him.

This was why he had come to like Finbar's Hotel. It, too, was the sort of place no one noticed. It was not especially modern, or especially opulent or especially decrepit and his own presence there seemed to go unnoticed. Simon the porter knew who he was, and watched him in the same way as a reptile in a zoo observes a visitor, and the manager, Johnny Farrell, knew too, and made clear that any wishes he had would be instantly fulfilled, including his wish to look like a maintenance man as he made his way through the hotel, his wish to sign the register under a false name, his wish to pay in cash in advance and his wish never to be there for breakfast in the morning. He made his reservation by calling in personally the day before his visit; he was always given this room, 107, at the end of the corridor. Sometimes he came here when he wanted to meet someone; other times he came here to think, to work out a plan over a few hours in a place which was neutral and where he could not be disturbed.

He lay on the bed of Room 107 and looked at the painting again. Just one hour earlier he had parked his van in the car park at the back of Finbar's Hotel. He had left one framed reproduction of the Rembrandt wrapped in brown paper in the boot, and taken the other framed reproduction, also wrapped in brown paper, up to his room. He had taken down the view of the Lakes of Killarney from the wall opposite the bed, opened the wrapping of the Rembrandt and hung that up instead. If he had been asked which of the paintings was worth five million, he would certainly, he thought, have said the Lakes of Killarney.

The cops knew he had the paintings. A few weeks after the robbery he had read an article in the *Irish Independent* in which his name had been 'linked' to the international art robbers. Thus, if they were following him, they now had a glorious opportunity to repossess the Rembrandt. They could snatch the one in the van or the one hanging on the wall. And it would take them several hours to realize that all they had were reproductions. The problem was that there was just him; there was no international art gang. The problem also was that he had three men with him on the job and each one thought that he was going to get half a million pounds in cash. All of them had plans for the money and kept asking him about it. He had no clear idea how to make these paintings into cash.

He waited. Later that evening, at eight o'clock, two Dutchmen, pretending to be financial journalists, were going to book into a room on the next corridor. They had made contact with him through a man called Mousey Furlong, who used to be a scrap dealer with a horse and cart, and now sold heroin on the North Side. He shook his head when he thought about Mousey Furlong. He hated the heroin business, it was too risky, there were too many people in on each deal, and he hated seeing kids strung out on the streets, skinny, pale-faced kids with huge eyes. Heroin turned the world upside down, it meant that men like Mousey Furlong had contact with Dutchmen, and this, he thought, was an unnatural state of affairs.

The Dutchmen were interested in the Rembrandt, Mousey said, but would need to verify it – Mousey said the word 'verify' as though he had a freshly boiled egg in his mouth – before they could talk about money, but they had the money, they said, available to them in cash. They could come up with the money within a short time of seeing it, they said. They could talk about the rest of the paintings later. He supposed that they had to be careful too; if they had the money with them, it would be easy to tie them up and steal it and leave the reproduction on the bed for them to take home to Holland. He had left the Rembrandt buried in the mountains and planned to show them a Guardi and the Gainsborough first to prove he had the paintings.

A robbery was so easy. You stole money and it was instantly yours; you kept it somewhere safe. Or you stole jewellery or electrical goods or cigarettes in bulk and you knew how to offload them, there were people you could trust, a whole world out there which knew how to organize such an operation. But these paintings were different. This involved trusting people you did not know. What if these two Dutchmen were cops? The best thing to do was to wait, then to move cautiously and wait again. He stood up from the bed and went to the window. He half expected to notice a figure watching him from the quays, but there was nobody.

He believed that the cops did not know he was here; if they had seen him coming upstairs with the painting they would have followed him and arrested him and snatched the painting. They were hungry for success. They were, he thought, useless.

He still had several hours to wait in Finbar's. He went back to the bed and lay down. He stared at the ceiling and thought about nothing. He slept well at night and was never tired at this time of the day, but he felt tired now, and lay on his side and slowly faded into sleep. When he woke he was nervous and uneasy; it was the loss of concentration and control which disturbed him and made him sit up and look at his watch. He had only been asleep for half an hour, but then he realized that he had dreamed again about Lanfad, and he wondered if he would ever stop dreaming about it. It was twenty-five years since he had left it.

He had dreamt that he was back there again, being brought in for the first time, between two guards, arriving, being shown along corridors. But it was not him as a thirteen-year-old boy, it was him now, after all the years of doing what he liked, being married, waking in the morning to the sound of children, watching television in the evening, robbing, making deals. And what disturbed him was the feeling in the dream that he was happy to be locked up, to have order in his life, to keep rules, to be watched all of the time, not to have to think too much. As he was led through those corridors in the dream he had felt resigned to it, almost pleased.

He had felt like this for much of the time when he served his first and only sentence, in Mountjoy Jail, eight years ago. He had missed his wife and their first child and missed making plans and going where he liked, but he did not mind being locked up every night, having all that time to himself. Most of the time he had his own cell, and did nothing much during the day. He hated the food, but he paid no attention to it, and he hated the screws, and he made sure that when his wife came on visits once a week he gave nothing away, no emotion, no sense of how lonely and isolated he some-times was. Instead they spoke about plans for when he would get out, and she gave him news about neighbours and families, and he tried to laugh or at least smile, and he was fine after a few hours when he was alone again. He had relaxed and taken things easy during his time in jail.

But the first days in Lanfad were not like that at all. Maybe it was because he was thirteen or fourteen and it was in the midlands, miles away from Dublin. He was stunned by the place, by how cold it was and unfriendly and how he would have to stay there for three or four years. He had felt nothing. He never cried and when he felt sad he learned to think about nothing for a while, to pretend that he was nowhere and he discovered that he could do this anywhere, and it was how he dealt with his years at Lanfad.

In the three and a half years he was there he was only beaten once and that was when the entire dormitory was taken out one by one and beaten on the hands with a strap. The rest of the time he was left alone; he kept the rules when he knew there was a good danger of being caught. He knew that it was easy to slip out on a summer's night as long as you waited until everything was quiet and you chose the right companion and you didn't go too far. He knew how to raid the kitchen and how often you could do it. As he thought about it now, lying on the bed, he realized that he had liked being alone, standing apart from the others, never the one caught standing on the desk when the brother came in or shouting in the dormitory or fighting.

On his first night there or maybe his second, he was not sure, there was a fight on the dormitory. He heard it all starting, and then something like, 'Say that again and I'll burst you,' followed by cries of encouragement all around. So that there had to be a fight. There was too much energy in the dormitory for something not to happen. It was all dark, but you could make out shapes and movements. And he could hear the gasping and the pushing back of beds and then the shouting from all around. He did not move; soon, it would become his style not to move, but then he had not developed a style. He was too uncertain to move. He watched it from the bed. When the light was turned on and one of the older brothers, Brother Walsh, arrived he did not have to scramble back to his bed like the rest of them, but still he felt afraid as the brother moved around the dormitory. There was now an absolute silence and a sense of fear which was new to him. Brother Walsh did not speak. He moved around the beds looking at each boy. When the brother looked at him he did not know what to do. He met his gaze and then looked away and then back again. Eventually, the brother spoke.

'Who started it? Stand out who started it.'

No one replied. No one stood out.

'I'll pick two boys and they'll tell me who started it, and it'll be worse for you now if you don't own up and stand out.'

The accent was strange to him. He had listened to the brother's voice, but pretended it was not happening. If he was picked on he would not know what to say. He did not know anyone's name. He wondered how all of the rest of them had learned each other's names. It seemed impossible. As he thought about this he looked up and saw that two boys were now standing beside their beds, their eyes cast down. One of them had the top of his pyjamas torn.

'Right,' Brother Walsh said. 'The two of you will come with me.'

The brother went back to the door and turned the lights out, leaving pure silence behind. No one even whispered. He had lain there and listened. The first sounds were faint, but soon he heard a shout and a cry and then the unmistakable sound of strap again skin, and then silence and then a howl of pain. He wondered where it was happening; he thought it must be in the corridor outside the dormitory or the stairwell. Then the beating became regular with constant crying out and yelping. And soon the sound of voices shouting 'No!' over and over.

Everyone in the dormitory lay there and listened, no one moved or spoke. It did not stop. Finally, when the two boys tried to make their way back to their beds in the darkness, the silence became even more intense. They lay in bed crying and sobbing while the other boys listened. He had wished he knew what their names were and wondered if he would know them in the morning and if they would look different because they had been beaten.

In the months which followed it seemed to him unbelievable that the boys around him would forget what happened that night. Other fights would break out in the dark dormitory and boys would shout and get out of bed and leave themselves wide open when the lights came on and Brother Walsh or some other brother, or sometimes two brothers together, suddenly switched on the light and stood there watching as everyone scampered back to bed. And each time the main culprits would be made to own up and taken outside and punished.

Slowly, the brothers noticed him, realized that he stood apart from the others and gradually they began to trust him. But he never trusted them, or let any one of them become friendly with him. He learned how to think nothing, feel nothing. In all his time there he never had a friend, never let anyone come close to him. A few times he stopped fights, or took the side of someone who was being bullied, or let a boy depend on him for a while. But it was always clear that this meant nothing to him, that he would be ready always to walk away.

The brothers had allowed him to work out on the bog and he loved that, the silence, the slow work, the long stretch of flatness to the horizon. And walking home tired at the end of the day. Then in his last year they allowed him to work in the furnace and it was when he was working there – it must have been the winter of his last year – that he realized something which he had not known before.

There were no walls around Lanfad, but it was made clear that anyone moving beyond certain points would be punished. In the spring each year as the evenings became longer boys would try and escape but they would always be caught and brought back. Once, in his first year, two boys were punished with the whole school watching, but that did not deter others who wanted to escape as well. If anything, it egged them on. He found it hard to believe that people would escape without a plan, a definite way of getting to Dublin, and maybe to England.

That last winter two boys older than him had had enough. They were in trouble almost every day and seemed afraid of nothing. He remembered them because he had spoken to them once about escaping, what he would do and where he would go. He had become interested in the conversation because they seemed to know where to get bicycles, and he knew that this was the only way to escape, to start cycling at maybe one in the morning and find enough money to go straight to the boat. He had added, without thinking, that before he left he would like to stab one or two of the brothers, or give them a good kicking, and he had said this in the same distant, deliberate way he said everything. He noticed the two boys looking at him uneasily, and he realized that he had said too much. He stood up abruptly and walked away, then he realized he should not have done that either. He was sorry he had spoken to them at all.

In the end, the two boys escaped without bicycles and without a plan and they were brought back. He heard about it as he was bringing a bucket of turf up to the brothers' restaurant. Brother Lawrence stopped him and told him. He nodded and went on. At supper he noticed that the two boys who had escaped were still not there. He supposed that they were being kept somewhere. He went down to the furnace.

It was later, close to lights-out time, when he was crossing the path to get more turf that he heard a sound. He knew what it was, it was the sound of someone being hit and crying. He could not make out where it was coming from, but then he realized that it was in the games room. He saw the lights on, but the window was too high for him to see in. He went back to the furnace to fetch a stool; he put it down under the window. When he looked in he saw that the two boys who had tried to escape were tied face down to an old table with their trousers around their ankles and they were being beaten across the arse by Brother Fogarty with a cane and then with a strap. Brother Walsh was standing beside the table with his two hands holding down the one being beaten. And then suddenly he noticed something else. There was an old light-box at the back of the games room. He had noticed it before; it had been used to store junk. Now there were two brothers standing in it, and the door was open. He could see them clearly from the window – Brother Lawrence and Brother Murphy – and he realized that the two other brothers must have been aware of their presence, but probably could not see what they were doing.

They were both masturbating. They had their eyes fixed on the scene in front of them – the boys being punished, crying out each time they were hit with the strap or the cane. He could not remember how long he watched them for, but it stayed in his mind as though he had taken a photograph of it. Before this he had hated when boys around him were punished, he had hated the silence and the fear. But he had almost believed that the punishments were necessary, part of a natural system in which the brothers were in charge. Now he knew that there was something else involved, something which he could not understand, which he could not bring himself to think about. The image had stayed in his head: the two brothers in the light-box did not look like men in charge, they looked more like dogs panting. He had already known he was able to protect himself from certain feelings which made him uncomfortable; now he had something new to resist.

That brought him back to the problem of the paintings. He sat on the side of the bed in the hotel room and scratched his head. He walked over to the window and looked out at the river again. He experienced that same feeling now as he had then – that something beyond him was beckoning and he wanted to leave his mind blank, to feel nothing except resistance. He felt afraid. He knew that if he had done the robbery alone he would dump the paintings, or leave them here along the corridors of Finbar's Hotel, replacing the sea views and the prints of horses they had on the walls. When he had left Lanfad, he brought with him the feeling that behind everything lay something else, a hidden motive perhaps, or something unimaginably dark, that the person you saw was merely a layer, and there were always other layers, secret layers which you could chance upon or which would become apparent if you looked closely enough.

Somewhere in this city or in some other city there was someone who knew how to offload these paintings, get the money, divide it up. He wondered if he thought about it enough would he know? Every time he considered it he came to a dead end. But there had to be a way. He wondered if he could go to the others who took part in the robbery – and they were so proud of themselves that night, everything had gone perfectly – and explain the problem. But he had never explained anything to anyone before. Word would get around. And, also, if he couldn't work this out, then they certainly couldn't. They were only good at doing what they were told.

He stared out of the hotel window blankly, and then he focused for a moment on the quayside. There was nobody watching, unless they had planted somebody in the hotel. But maybe the cops knew they did not need to watch him, that he would make mistakes himself. But that wasn't the way their mind worked, he thought. When he saw a cop or a barrister or a judge, he saw a brother in Lanfad, somebody loving their authority, using it, displaying their power in a way which he knew had hidden and shameful elements and sources. He went over to the sink and turned on the cold tap and splashed his face with water. He stretched and took one more look at the painting and smiled. At least it was a painting of a woman.

He still had an hour to wait. He took his key and went downstairs. He walked by the reception desk, enjoying the idea that the receptionist there looked through him as he passed. If someone should ask her a few minutes later, she would not be able to describe him, she would remember nothing about him. He went into the bar and sat by the window; eventually he went up to the counter and ordered tea. The young man behind the bar asked him if he wanted biscuits. He nodded and said that he did.

He felt sad as the afternoon faded; he hated this feeling and tried to think about the paintings again. Maybe it was all simpler than he imagined. These Dutchmen would come, he would take them to see the paintings, they would agree to pay him, he would drive them to where they had the money. And then? Why not just take the money from them and forget about the paintings? But they must have thought of that too. Maybe they would threaten him and make clear that if he broke any agreement they would have him shot. He was not afraid of them. Tea and biscuits came. He sighed as he paid, then poured the tea and put in sugar. He felt sad again, and always when he was like this things came back to him which he regretted. He tried to think about something else again, but he couldn't. There were only a few people in the world whom he trusted, loved perhaps – although love was not the word – and wanted to protect. There was his daughter Lorraine, she was four now. She loved talking and knew what she wanted. Everything about her was perfect and he looked forward to coming home and having her there.

He liked when she was asleep upstairs. He wanted her to be happy and secure. He did not feel like this about his other children.

He had felt the same about Frank, who was his youngest brother, and had hated it when Frank started robbing. Frank was no good at it. He panicked easily. The minute Frank was arrested he talked; the cops took advantage of him. He hated it when Frank was in jail. He had never gone to see him, but waited until he was released when he gave him money and tried to talk to him about going to England or starting a business. He did not know that Frank was already addicted then, and would spend the money on heroin in a few weeks before starting to rob again.

It was just a few months after he had been released that Frank broke into the basement of one of those houses on Palmerston Road. He was innocent, there were things he never knew. One golden rule was that people who own a house are much more afraid of you than you are of them. If they find you in the house, there is no need to go near them. Run. Get out. But don't approach them.

Frank must have been surprised when the owner of the flat returned. He must have found the kitchen knife on the table and stabbed him out of fear. Frank – he saw him now as soft-faced with a weak smile and his heart went out to him – left fingerprints everywhere and the man bled to death. Frank was found guilty of murder, and somebody in the prison or a visitor, maybe even one of the family on a visit, gave him enough heroin to do him for a week. He must have taken it all in one go, or most of it anyway, because he was found dead with a needle beside him. The cops wanted the family to come and identify the body, but none of them would go near the cops.

He sat there thinking about his brother who was under the ground, who no longer needed protection. Now, it seemed inevitable, something which could not be avoided. But at the time it had not been like that, it all could have been avoided, every moment of it.

If he could get rid of these paintings he would be OK, he thought. He could go back to normal. Maybe he should take a risk with these Dutchmen, try and get the money from them and give them the paintings and have nothing more to do with it. But, he thought, he mustn't do that. He must be cautious. He sipped his tea and looked at the bar. A woman came in and sat at the bar; he watched her asking for something and the barman shaking his head before she asked for something else. She had an American accent, but she did not look like an American. He caught her eye for a moment and glanced away as quickly as he could. When he looked up again, she was staring at him. He looked around in case she was staring at something else, but, no, it was him. When her drink came she concentrated on the barman. One of the reasons he came to Finbar's Hotel was that no one paid him any attention. It wasn't possible, he thought, that she was a cop. But then he thought about it from the cops' point of view and it made sense to send in a woman dressed as an American. He supposed they thought that no one would notice her; they should have told her, he thought, not to stare at people. When he looked up she was staring at him again. He couldn't believe it. He wondered what he should do now. He waited for a few moments and then checked her out again. This time she had her head buried in some sort of old ledger. He thought of going up behind her and shouting: 'Boo!' Maybe she was just an innocent American who stared at people. But there was something about her face and her hair that was wrong. She was just the sort of woman who would join the cops. She had that vacant, hungry, half-hunted look you often found on cops. He thought that he would be better to go back to his room and wait there. He walked out into the lobby and took the lift to the first floor.

Some time later there were footsteps along the corridor. They stopped just before his door. He knew they were a woman's. He opened his door just enough to catch sight of the back of the woman from the bar as she opened the door into the room next to his. He sat on his bed and thought about her some more.

Finally, a long time later, the phone rang and he told the Dutch voice at the other end to come to his room. In his mind he went over everything from the police point of view. They needed the paintings more than they needed anything else. They wouldn't do anything until they were sure they had the paintings. If this is a sting, he thought, they will need a bugging device. Maybe that was what she had been doing before going down to keep an eye on him in the bar.

He opened his door and watched a middle-aged man struggle with his key outside a room at the far end of the corridor. The man looked at him as if for help and then disappeared into his room. He did not think that he could be working for the cops, he looked too frightened, but maybe that was just a ruse he was playing. When the man had closed his door the two Dutchmen came into the corridor. One of them carried a briefcase.

As they approached he put his fingers to his lips. He had already written out *This is a fake* on a piece of paper. When they came into the room he closed the door and pointed to the reproduction, then handed them the piece of paper. Both of them were blond; one was skinny and wore glasses. He wrote *Stay here* on another piece of paper and put his finger to his lips. He left them in the room and locked the door behind him. That will give them something to think about, he said to himself as he walked down the corridor, pausing at the end to see if the woman's door would open.

He went downstairs and sat in the bar again. He thought that he would leave them there for twenty minutes, let them cool off. Maybe they would enjoy looking at the painting. He had a lemonade and then walked out to the lobby and sat down on a sofa from where he could see everyone coming and going. There was a fellow wearing a Temple Bar T-shirt talking to the porter and he looked so obviously not a cop that he probably was one. But that in itself was too obvious, he thought. He must be careful. He had now seen three people whom he imagined were cops, but it was still possible that none of them was a cop, or all of them, or just two or only one of them. If he didn't stop thinking about it, he would go mad.

He went out onto the quays and then around to the back of the hotel. He stood in the car park. There was no one around. He decided to go back upstairs and take the two Dutchmen out of their misery. But as he walked along the corridor it struck him that he should break into their room. On his keyring he kept a piece of wire that usually did the trick on these simple locks with the help of someone's credit card that was long out of date. He looked around him: there was no sound, no one approaching. He turned and went up the stairs to the second floor. Still no one was around. This was what corridors were usually like, he thought, empty, undisturbed, silently waiting for a lone intruder. Within a few seconds he had the door open. There was a suitcase and a holdall on one of the beds. He closed the door quietly and moved across the room to unzip the suitcase. There was nothing inside. The holdall was also completely empty. He checked under the mattress and in the wardrobe and in the bedside lockers, but there was nothing to be found. He did not know what this meant, if it was good or bad, or to be expected. He opened the door and checked for sounds. He crept out into the corridor and down towards his own room. As he walked along the corridor he saw the American woman come out of Room 106. He paid no attention to her, but he wondered why she was coming out of her room just now. As he got to the door of his room and looked behind, she had disappeared. He had never known so many odd people in the hotel.

When he opened the door of his room he saw that the Dutchmen had been sitting on the bed. They stood up. They looked like two men who wished they were elsewhere.

Where is the money? he wrote on a piece of paper.

Not far, one of them wrote.

I need to see it, he wrote.

We need to see the painting, the Dutchman wrote.

He looked at this note for a while, wondering how he should respond. He needed them to feel that if they messed with him they would be in danger, but he supposed they knew this already. Their last reply was, he thought, very cheeky. He wondered if he should not just tell them to get to hell out of here, but then it struck him that they seemed businesslike and professional. He wondered once more if this was a good sign or a bad sign. Suddenly, he felt confident. If he had found money in their room, or passports, or valuables, he would have known that they were amateurs. He wondered what they thought about him. He must act as though he knew what he was doing.

He motioned them to follow him down to his van. In the corridor he stopped when he heard voices and then made the Dutchmen stand behind him. He stood and watched and wondered what to do. This was really out of order, he thought. He knew the man who stood outside the open door of Room 104 with the manager, he had known him for years, but hadn't seen him for a long time. How odd that he should appear just now! One of the reasons he came to Finbar's was to get away from scumbags like this guy. His name was Alfie FitzSimons, he was a real scumbag, he thought. He was arguing with the manager.

He knew that FitzSimons could not be working for the cops. He was the sort of guy who would rob his granny and get caught; no one would touch him. Drugs as well. He looked at him carefully, trying to make clear that he had the measure of him. Dublin was full of guys like that, he thought, as FitzSimons scuttled away along the corridor. He motioned the Dutchmen to follow him. He thought FitzSimons had gone to London; he was sure Alfie FitzSimons had been told to go to London and stay there. He made a note to talk to Joe O'Brien about him. There were too many people in the hotel, yet it was possible they were all harmless, and he was just being too careful, too paranoid.

They went to the car park; he drove the van first to the North Circular Road and then down through Prussia Street to the quays. He crossed the river again and made his way to Crumlin. No one in the van spoke. He hoped that they did not know what part of the city they were in.

He drove down a side street and then a lane, turning into a garage whose door had been left open. He got out of the van and pulled down the sliding door of the garage. They were now in darkness. He wondered how the Dutchmen felt. When he found a light he signalled to them to stay in the car. He went out of a door into a small yard and tapped on the kitchen window. He saw three or four children around a table and a woman at a sink with a man standing beside her who turned when he heard the tap. It was Joe O'Brien. Suddenly, the children stood up and took their plates and cups and moved into the front room. The woman gathered up her things and left as well.

Joe O'Brien opened the door and walked out into the yard without speaking. They crossed the yard to the garage and watched the Dutchmen through a small, dirty window. Both men were sitting motionless in the car.

He nodded to Joe O'Brien who went into the garage and told them to follow him. It was the first time anyone had spoken. They went into the lane and through a door to the yard of the neighbouring house. There was an old man at the kitchen table reading the *Evening Herald* who stood up to let them in when Joe tapped at the window. He did not speak either, but went back to reading his paper. They closed the door and walked past him and went upstairs into the back bedroom.

He did not know whether the Dutchmen looked uncomfortable all the time, or whether they looked uncomfortable just now. They peered around the upstairs bedroom as though it were outer space. He was going to ask them if they had never seen a bedroom before. Joe had put a ladder against the small opening in the ceiling which led to the attic and come down with two paintings – the Gainsborough and one of the Guardis. The two Dutchmen looked intensely at the paintings. No one spoke.

Where is the Rembrandt? one of them wrote.

Pay for these two. If there are no hitches, we get you the Rembrandt tomorrow, he wrote.

We're here for the Rembrandt, the Dutchman wrote.

Are you deaf? he wrote. Both Dutchmen looked up at him, their expressions hurt and puzzled.

The money? he wrote.

Not far, the Dutchman wrote.

You said that before, he wrote. *Where?*

Another hotel, the Dutchman wrote. And then: *We need to see the Rembrandt.*

He examined them both carefully. They did not look afraid.

Bring half the money back to Finbar's Hotel, he wrote. *You can have these paintings. At the same time tomorrow, if there are no hitches, you can have the others.*

We'll think about it. The one with the glasses took the pen this time.

Fuck thinking about it, he wrote. *Go back to Finbar's Hotel and wait.*

This time the other one wrote, and the one with the glasses looked on. *If we have not come back by midnight, the deal is off. We came here to see the Rembrandt. There is no Rembrandt. We have to get instructions.*

Suddenly, he realized that these two men were serious about the rules they had established. He had agreed to show them the Rembrandt and now he broken the rules. But he could not adjust his tactics. He could not weaken. He realized that he was in danger of losing the deal. He was aware that Joe O'Brien was watching him. Maybe they should grab one guy and tie him up and tell the other guy to go and get the money or they would kill his companion. But this would not help him to sell the paintings. It would also mean that the cops could become involved. He hesitated. All three of them watched him as he stood there.

This man here, he wrote, pointing to Joe, *will accompany you*.

No, one of them wrote. *He can drive us into the city. That's all. When can we see the Rembrandt?*

They both looked at him calmly and it was that calmness which disturbed him, held him back, made him think, and then made it impossible for him to think.

I've already told you, he wrote. They both nodded. They looked like men whose skin was too soft to shave. He could not work out whether they were very stupid or very intelligent. There was nothing more to say. He had the paintings, but they had all the power because they had the money. He knew that there was nothing he could do except go back to Finbar's Hotel and wait.

I'll be there until midnight, he wrote as though he was the one who had first mentioned midnight. He realized that he had no way of contacting them except through Mousey Furlong, who was unlikely to know what hotel they were staying in. He took the pen again and the piece of paper.

If you come to the hotel before midnight, you can see the Rembrandt, he wrote.

In the hotel? one of them wrote.

Close by, he wrote.

OK, the Dutchman wrote. *We'll have to get instructions*.

There was nothing more he could say. He would have to go to the mountains now and dig up the other paintings. He nodded to Joe and they left the room. The old man, still reading the newspaper as they passed through the kitchen, did not look up. Joe took the two Dutchmen to his own house; his car was outside his front door. They walked away without speaking.

Joe O'Brien was the only man he had worked with who would always do exactly what he was told, who would never ask questions, never turn up late nor express doubts. He would do anything. He also knew about wiring, the inside of cars, locks, explosives. When he had wanted to blow Kevin McMahon the barrister into kingdom come, Joe O'Brien had been the only man he approached and told about it. He had watched McMahon strut and prance around the court for the prosecution when Frank was up on charges for the first time, and then when Frank was up for murder McMahon became very personal in the court about Frank's entire family. He had seemed not to be just doing his job, but to relish it. It was then that he decided he was going to get McMahon. It would have been easy to shoot him, or have him beaten up, or burn his house down, but what he had wanted to do to McMahon was blow him sky high when he was in his car. It happened in the North all the time; the aftermath always looked good on television. It would give the rest of the legal profession something to think about. Even now, driving towards Wicklow, he smiled when he thought about it. How careless these people were! McMahon had left his car in front in the driveway of his house. There were certain hours of the night in Dublin – say, between three and four – when you could do anything, when there was dead silence. It had only taken Joe O'Brien fifteen minutes to put the device under the car.

'It'll blow up the minute he starts the ignition,' Joe had said as they walked back towards Ranelagh. Joe never asked why McMahon was going to be blown up. He wondered if Joe O'Brien was like that at home. If his wife asked him to do the washing-up, or stay in babysitting, or let her stick her finger up his arse, would he just say yes and get on with it?

He laughed to himself as he slowed at a set of traffic lights. In the end the bomb had not gone off when McMahon started the car, but about fifteen minutes later on a busy roundabout. It hadn't killed McMahon either, just blown his legs off.

He remembered meeting Joe O'Brien a few days later and not mentioning the car or McMahon for a while, and then saying that the whole affair gave the word 'legless' a whole new meaning. O'Brien had just grinned for a moment, but said nothing.

He drove on towards the mountains, stopping regularly to see if he was being followed. It was a quarter to ten so, if he worked fast, he thought, he could be back to the hotel by eleven thirty. Once he got off the main road there was no traffic. When he finally stopped the van and turned the ignition off there was absolute silence. He would be able to work in peace.

He kept a shovel under the back seat. He knew where he was, everything was carefully marked. As long as he was alive these paintings could be easily brought back to the city. Joe O'Brien and one of the others knew the area where they were buried but not the exact spot. You walked up a small clearing until the ground to your left began to slope away. You counted twelve trees and then turned right and counted six more, and just beyond that there was a clear space overhung by trees.

The ground was soft, but the digging was not easy. He stopped all the time and listened for sounds, but he heard only stillness and the wind in the trees. Soon, he was out of breath from digging. But he enjoyed working like this when he did not have to think or let anything else bother him. He had to dig gently when the spade hit the frames of the paintings. It was hard work before he could pull them out. They were protected by masses of plastic sheeting. He laid them on the ground and filled in the hole, then left the shovel down and walked back to the car. He wanted to check that there was no one around.

It struck him for a moment that he would be happy if everything was dark and empty like this, if there was no one at all in the world, just this stillness and almost perfect silence, and if it would go on for ever like that. He stood and listened, relishing the idea that in this space around him just now there were no thoughts or feelings or plans for the future.

He then walked up to fetch the shovel and the paintings. There was nothing he could do except find somewhere safe to leave them and go back to Finbar's Hotel and wait. This idea that he had no power now, that he was under the control of these two Dutchmen, made him feel that he was worth nothing, that he might as well crash his car into the ditch, or give himself up, or spend years in jail, or kill someone. In that instant he was not afraid of anything. He felt an extraordinary surge of energy and concentration as he drove back into the city.

He thought of leaving the paintings in the van in the car park of the hotel. If the cops did not come for them the first time they would hardly come now. But he had started thinking again and gradually, as he came from Rathfarnam into Terenure, he became cautious and frustrated. He drove to his sister-in-law's house in Clanbrassil Street and told her when she came to the door to open the gate into her back yard. She smiled at him.

'I was just going out,' she said, 'but the kids are here.'

'Could you open the gate?' he repeated.

'You're in a hurry tonight,' she said.

He looked up and down the street to check that there was no one observing him, then drove the van around to the back of the house, took the paintings and left them in her small outhouse.

'Make sure these are safe,' he said.

'I'll guard them with my life,' she said. 'You know me.'

'I thought you said you were going to the pub.'

'I am.'

When he looked into her kitchen he wished that he lived here with her rather than in his own house. She smiled at him again, but he turned away.

He drove the van back to the hotel. It was twenty past eleven. He wondered why they bothered having a car park in Finbar's Hotel since no car ever parked in it and anyone could steal a car from it as there was no gate or nightwatchman. He left the van in the corner away from the entrance and walked around to the main entrance. He could hear the blare of disco music from the basement. He would sit here in the lobby for a while, then go to his room and wait. Through the doorway as he sat there he could see an office party going on in the bar. Then he spotted the American woman at the counter sitting on her own. Once more, she caught his eye and held his gaze. He looked away and back again, but she was staring now at something else. Maybe she was just an innocent American, but he wondered why she was looking at him. It would be easy to check who she was by going up to her room and looking through her belongings. If her suitcases were empty, like the Dutchmen's suitcases, then he would know that she was a cop. And he would have to do something about her. There had been too many funny people around the hotel all day, he thought, not just the American woman but Alfie FitzSimons.

It had never been like that before. He was sure now that something was going to happen, but he could not think what it was. He was suddenly glad this hotel was closing.

He took the stairs to the first floor and moved quietly along the corridor. He always found that if you concentrated hard enough at times like this, people would disappear, no one would disturb you. It was easy to open the door of her room, these locks were shameful they were so easy. He closed it behind him and turned on the light. She had a bag all right, but when he looked inside he saw that there was hardly anything in it – just underwear and an old hairbrush and some toilet things. Could she have come all the way from America with just this luggage? he wondered. And then he saw the book, a sort of ledger, old-fashioned. It was on the bed. He picked it up without looking at it too closely and moved across the room with it under his arm. He turned off the light and stood for a moment listening before he opened the door. He went to his own room and left the ledger down.

He drew the curtains in his room and thought for a minute before walking out into the corridor again and closing the door behind him. He felt that someone had been here on the corridor a moment ago. He needed to check the Dutchmen's room. He thought that maybe he should wait for them there in the darkness. It would really frighten them if they came back and found him crouching in their room, but if they did not come back he would feel like a fool. It was now twenty to twelve.

He looked around him when he switched on the light.

The suitcase and holdall were still lying as he had left them. No one had been here. As he went down to his own room he thought about it from the Dutchmen's point of view, and he knew that they would keep him waiting, that they would not turn up now. Maybe the next time they would send other people. The price had not been agreed, and they would need to do that. As he went down to his own room and thought about it, he felt better. They had made contact with him; they knew he was the guy to do business with. Soon, they would be in touch again. He was one step closer to getting rid of the paintings. He thought that he should go now, clear out of here.

As he opened the door to his room he remembered the ledger. He would take that and the reproduction painting down to his van when things quietened in Finbar's Hotel. He sat on the bed and stared at the ledger. It said *Drimnagh Fire Station 1962–1969*. He opened the ledger and looked at the old writing. *Damage – neg., extensive, gutted, neg.* He looked through the names: *St Agnes' Park, Knocknarea Avenue, Darley Street, Carrow Road*. Who was this woman? Where did she get this? Why did she have this and nothing else much in her room? He wished that things were simpler, that he could prove that she was a cop, or a spy for the cops, or an American on her holidays. She was none of these things. She was some sort of fire-maniac or someone from Drimnagh with an American accent who stared at men in bars. He wished that she had not stared at him. Nearly an hour passed as he flicked slowly through the pages of the ledger.

Suddenly he heard footsteps and voices in the corridors. Even before the knock came to his door he knew it was the cops, he knew there were three of them and they were in uniform. He also knew that they could prove nothing. He opened the door and fixed his eye blankly on them. He was right, there were three of them. He stepped back as if indifferent as to whether they entered the room or not, as if this had nothing to do with him. But he was careful not to look cheeky or difficult. All three of them came into the room. Immediately he noticed the youngest one looking at the Rembrandt reproduction. He was prepared for anything.

But he was not prepared for the American voice that screamed from outside in the corridor: 'It was him! I saw him leave the room with my ledger! Get it back from him!' The woman from Room 106 appeared. They all turned and looked at her. He knew that she could not have seen him take the ledger from her room.

'Do you have a ledger belonging to this lady?' one of the guards asked him in a country accent.

'She gave it to me earlier on,' he said. He looked at them coldly. He realized that they did not know who he was.

'Give it back to me!' the woman screamed. 'I saw you taking it.'

'Ah, you give me a pain,' he said to her as though he knew her well, and handed her the ledger as though it was something private between them. 'Why did you give it to me if you didn't want me to keep it?' he added. He knew the rule with the guards: things must be either very simple or very complicated. This, he knew, would sound complicated. And the woman had been drinking. But he was still not sure. She took the ledger from him. He noticed that the youngest guard had taken off his cap, his head was bald and he was still staring at the Rembrandt.

He concentrated. He said nothing. He knew that if he kept his mind clear, they would leave the room, laughing at the American woman and her ledger as they went down the stairs, and forget about him. They would be unable to describe him within five minutes; if he kept his nerve he would make no impression on them. But the bald guard continued staring at the painting and the two colleagues were shifting uneasily. If they looked around enough, he thought, they would realize that he had no luggage. They still hadn't asked him for his name.

'If you go down to the lounge,' he said to the American woman, 'I'll follow you down in a few minutes. I know you're upset.'

He spoke to her as though she was his wife, or his sister-in-law.

'Don't talk to me,' the American woman said. 'I don't know you. I don't want to have a drink with you. You broke into my fucking room.'

As soon as she said 'fucking' the three guards turned and looked at her.

'Come on now,' the oldest of them said. 'There's no need for that.'

'You are a fucking thief,' she said.

'Ah, now,' the oldest guard said.

At this moment the guard who had been looking at the painting put on his cap and took a few steps towards the door. The American woman turned and left the room and walked down the corridor away from them. She was muttering something.

'I'll follow her down in a minute,' he said to the guards.

'Right so,' the oldest one said. 'We'll leave it up to you. She was upset down below about the ledger.' The guard spoke as though he was confiding something important.

'She has it now,' he said. 'But I'll go down to her in a minute and she'll be fine.'

'Right so,' the guard said.

All three of them hesitated. At this moment they did not know his name, or his relationship to the woman, or what he was doing in the hotel. They were embarrassed as they stood in the corridor. He still knew that he had to leave his mind blank, think nothing, have no expression on his face, except a look that was subdued, but not too subdued. Now that there was silence, he knew he had to fill the silence.

'Ah, she'll be all right in the morning.' He sighed.

'Right so,' the oldest guard said again. He nodded and the three of them walked slowly down the corridor.

He closed the door and went to the window. At these moments he felt he could kill someone. He clenched his fists. The next time he might not be able to do it, he thought. It was hard. He stood with his head against the wall and closed his eyes.

He lay down on the bed and listened to his heart thumping. He went to the window again and stood there with his fists clenched and his eyes wide open. He watched the cop car driving away. He decided to get out now, before one of them had second thoughts and came back for him. He would leave the reproduction Rembrandt for the next guest to enjoy. He took his key and turned off the light and went down the corridor.

In the lobby he saw Simon with a tray in his hand. He looked so thin, like he was dying on his feet.

'Are you all right, sir?' Simon asked him. 'Is there anything I can do for you?' There was no one else in the lobby.

'You know the American woman in the next room to me,' he said. 'Would you buy her a drink out of this?' He handed Simon the key of his room and a twenty-pound note.

'Are you off, sir?' Simon asked, but it was clear that he did not expect an answer. 'Have a nice night, sir.'

Simon walked out to unlock the front door for him and held it open, standing out a moment in the night air. Nearby the night club entrance was quiet, too late for anyone to enter and too early for them to leave.

'What will you do when the hotel closes?' he asked Simon. He knew that he should not be standing here, that he should quickly get into his van and go home. Simon clearly had not expected the question. He thought for a moment.

'I don't know, sir.'

'I'm sure you'll find something,' he said. He wanted to walk away, but he did not feel that he could. Or he wanted to touch the man, say something to him that would help. He did not know what he wanted.

'It's kind of you to say that, sir.' Simon turned away then, with the tray still in his hand and went back into the hotel.

There was a sound of a police siren, or an ambulance siren, crossing the river at the bridge. As he walked away from Finbar's Hotel for the last time he turned and looked at it, but he knew it had nothing to do with him.